"Words ha____ ____ ____'t they?" Soph____

"Sometimes the____ ____ they should stay put. And you aren't the first to accuse me of being garrulous." She smiled ruefully, and he could breathe again.

"Nor will I be the last, I suspect," he said with a forced chuckle.

Then she laughed gaily and relief flooded through him. "Do you know what I think? I have had quite enough of this Miss Montgomery and Mr. Lockwood business. You are my only friend in all of Estes Valley, and I would like you to call me Sophie." She paused. "And might I call you Tate?"

His first thought was that this informality moved them into an intimacy he wasn't sure he was willing to undertake, but his second thought trumped the first. "I would welcome that," he said.

"All right then, Tate. Take me home."

He knew she meant her cabin, of course. Yet, for an instant, her words shook every nerve in his body. "Home…yes."

After twenty-five years as a high school English teacher and independent-school administrator, **Laura Abbot** turned to writing the kinds of stories she'd always loved to read. She sold her first book to Harlequin Superromance, followed by fourteen more. Her other professional credentials include serving as an educational consultant and speaker, and as a licensed lay preacher. But her greatest pride is her children and eleven grandchildren. Laura enjoys corresponding with readers; please write her at LauraAbbot@msn.com.

Books by Laura Abbot

Love Inspired Historical

Into the Wilderness
The Gift of a Child
A Family Found

Visit the Author Profile page at Harlequin.com for more titles

LAURA ABBOT

A Family Found

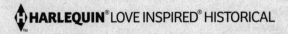
HARLEQUIN® LOVE INSPIRED® HISTORICAL

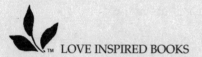

LOVE INSPIRED BOOKS

Recycling programs
for this product may
not exist in your area.

ISBN-13: 978-0-373-28313-2

A Family Found

Copyright © 2015 by Laura A. Shoffner

www.Harlequin.com

Printed in U.S.A.

I will lift up mine eyes unto the hills,
from whence cometh my help.
My help cometh from the Lord,
which made heaven and earth.
—*Psalms* 121:1–2

In grateful appreciation for the wisdom, encouragement and friendship with which my fellow authors have blessed me through the years, especially my "cyber-friends" and the Ozarks, Oklahoma City, Kansas City and Tucson RWA chapters. You have made a difference in my life.

Chapter One

Denver, Colorado
Early May, 1879

"You're absolutely sure you want to do this, Sophie?" Effie Hurlburt, never one to mince words, watched her houseguest pack. "The Estes Park area is barely settled. It's not too late to change your mind."

Sophie Montgomery finished folding a flannel petticoat and then turned to Effie, her eyes dancing. "Run from a challenge? You've come to know me over the past weeks. Do I seem faint of heart?"

Laughing, Effie threw up her hands. "Stubborn. Strong. Independent. That's you. I should've known better than to question your determination." The older woman took Sophie's hand in hers. "Regardless of what you encounter, please know you're always welcome here."

"That's a comfort. You and the major have given me a much-needed sanctuary, but it's time I made my own destiny."

"Very well, my dear. Mr. Lockwood will be here at five for dinner. You two will need an early start for

your trip into the mountains tomorrow." She turned in
the doorway and once more looked appraisingly at Sophie. "You will be in my prayers."

After Effie left, Sophie sat on the edge of the bed,
her mind racing. Effie wasn't the only skeptic. Sophie's
entire family had, in one way or another, questioned
her judgment. Although it had been difficult for them,
they had accepted her decision to leave Kansas and re-
locate to Colorado. What neither they nor the Hurlburts
could understand, though, was why she would resolve
to spend six months living alone in the mountains.

Sophie stepped to the window and drew the lace curtain aside. There they were—the glorious peaks rising
majestically from the plains, their snowcapped summits
sparkling in the afternoon sun. They were beautiful
from afar, but what she had been unable to convey to
others was their compelling call, as if they were summoning her back to life. No longer content merely looking at them, she wanted—no, needed—to be *in* them.
Everyone had been too polite to call her crazy, but she
knew that's what they thought. To be charitable, those
who loved her also feared for her safety. That was one
worry she didn't have. Realistically she knew she would
encounter harsh weather conditions, wild animals and
the lack of creature comforts. She'd heard the stories,
read the travelogues, seen the drawings. But the beauty
and freedom awaiting her made up for any deprivations.
She was a rancher's daughter, accustomed to hard days
driving cattle and haying, and a fair shot if she did say
so herself. If Englishwoman Isabella Bird could trek
through the Rockies alone in 1873 and write a book
about her adventures, Sophie Montgomery could like-
wise flourish there.

She went to the closet and removed the last of the

garments she was taking to the mountains—a plain green dress, a knitted scarf and a shapeless felt hat like the ones her brothers wore. Tonight, in celebration of her upcoming adventure, she would wear a fine gown of ice-blue satin. It would be the last time in many months. *Please, God, let this be a beginning. I've had enough of endings.*

Tate Lockwood folded the document and stowed it in his inside coat pocket. Done. The money he got from selling his stock in the Central City mine coupled with his recent inheritance from his parents' estate had made him a wealthy man, so he could speculate in the silver fields opening up at Leadville and on the western slope of the Rockies. Leaving his Denver lawyer's office, he turned down Broadway and strode toward his hotel. He took satisfaction from how far he'd come since the grueling days of getting his hands grubby in mining operations to now, when his livelihood resulted from investing and reaping profits. There was much he missed about the culture of a mining camp—the competition, the rapid changes of fortune, the streets bustling with all manner of men—but it was no place to rear two young boys. It had been a good decision to build a house in Estes Park, where they could grow in the peace and quiet of the high mountain air and learn to hunt and fish. He smiled to himself, recalling little Toby's tussle last summer with the rainbow trout he'd finally landed.

Of course, his wife had left him little choice when she'd abandoned them four years ago. His jaw worked as he fought the rage that could still take hold of him when he recalled Ramona's perfidy. He'd worked his fingers to the bone to raise the money for his young family to come from Philadelphia to join him in Central City. He'd built her a magnificent two-story house on the hillside and furnished it with items imported from the East. He had promised Ramona splendor and ease, and he had succeeded in providing it. But apparently he had misjudged her and miscalculated what it took to please her. From the moment she set foot in Colorado, she had made it known daily that she had never bargained for steep, unpaved sidewalks, a view of shanties in the distance or a husband more often in smelly work clothes than a suit. Nor had she found any joy in motherhood. A crying baby was a source of headaches and a tumbling toddler, a nuisance beyond bearing. Only rarely could Tate remember how he'd ever fallen under the spell of whatever charms she'd initially seemed to possess. Looking back, he admitted he mistook frivolousness for fun, flirtation for adoration and self-indulgence for beauty. More fool he. Never again would he fall under the spell of a female.

Dodging a buggy careering down the street, he groaned. Females. Why in the world had he burdened himself with escorting an idiot woman up to the park tomorrow? If he didn't think so highly of Robert Hurlburt, his mother's cousin, he would never have agreed to such folly. No doubt Miss Montgomery had read the recently published *A Lady's Life in the Rocky Mountains* and figured she could replicate Isabella Bird's adventures. Not likely. He certainly hoped the major didn't expect him to play nursemaid. Once he deposited her at the cabin she'd rented, she was on her own. He hoped she had made arrangement for adequate provisions, but he seriously doubted she had. Folks up in the park were good enough about sharing, but had little tolerance for those who looked upon a trip there as a lark.

Well, he'd take her measure tonight at the dinner party. Fortunately it wasn't required that he like her.

No matter the occasion, the dinner clothes that had been like a second skin in the East had come to feel suffocating to Tate. He adjusted his collar and cravat before knocking on the Hurlburts' door. He hadn't long to wait. Effervescent Effie flung open the door and embraced him in a cloud of lavender fragrance. "Tate Lockwood! Dear boy, it is a treat to have you here once again."

"The pleasure is mine, Effie. As always I will enjoy your company and that of Robert, and your fine meal will help fortify me for the trip home."

"Ever the flatterer." She took him by the arm. "I'm eager for you to meet our friend Sophie." She led him into the parlor, where Robert stood by the fireplace, one arm on the mantel, talking to a small woman with a nimbus of red-orange curls perched on a straight-backed chair. "Tate Lockwood, may I present Sophie Montgomery."

He made his way across the room and picked up her small hand. "Miss Montgomery."

Her hazel-green eyes sparkled. "It's lovely to meet you. I am so appreciative of your offer to escort me to Estes Park."

My offer? Little did she know it was only as a favor to Robert that he was undertaking such a mission. He turned and shook hands with Robert. "A pleasure to see you again, sir. What word of our family?"

The major's recitation kept Tate from dwelling on the woman sitting across the room. He had expected a hatchet-faced, sturdily built female, not a tiny one with lustrous hair, twinkling eyes and a dusting of freckles, wearing a becoming and stylish gown. She wouldn't last a week in the high country.

After the news of the relatives had been shared and thinking it might be ill-mannered of him to ignore this Miss Montgomery, of whom Robert and Effie were obviously quite fond, he addressed her directly. "Have you known Effie and Robert for some years?"

"I had never met them until earlier this spring, but I have long heard wonderful stories about them. My brother Caleb was stationed at Fort Larned, Kansas, then under the major's command. It was there he met the post surgeon's daughter Lily Kellogg. If I'm not mistaken, our Effie was a bit of a matchmaker." Sophie smiled at Effie. "Am I right?"

Effie nodded vigorously. "Those two. Born for each other, they were, but blind as bats about it. It would be fair to say I gave them a bit of a nudge."

"And it worked!" Sophie was alight with pleasure. "Lily is now my dear sister-in-law."

"That's not all," the major interjected. "After Caleb mustered out and married Lily, they settled in Cottonwood Falls, Kansas, and Lily's father and sister moved there, too, and even without Effie's assistance, another match was struck."

"A perfect match," Sophie added. "Lily's sister Rose and my brother Seth, neither of whom ever thought they would marry, found each other."

Effie leaned forward, eager to add to the conversation. "Here's the great part. They were brought together when a little half-breed boy was abandoned in Rose's barn. While Rose and Seth were falling in love with the boy, they ended up falling for each other at the same time."

"That's quite a story." Tate didn't know what else

to say. Apparently some people were lucky in love. He wasn't one of them.

Effie stood. "You and Sophie have a big day tomorrow, so let's adjourn to the dining room."

The four of them sat around a circular table laden with a beef roast, mashed potatoes, gravy, stewed tomatoes and yeast rolls. "You haven't lost your touch," Tate said after the first bite. "Delicious."

"My serving girl helped. She'd never cooked a day in her life when she came to me, but she's learning."

Sophie patted Effie's hand. "She has an excellent teacher."

"Do you cook?" Tate asked.

"Almost all my life. My mother died in childbirth with me, so as soon as I could reach the stove, I was cooking for my brothers, Seth and Caleb, and my father."

"I'm sorry about the circumstances, but I'm sure your family appreciated your culinary efforts. However, cooking in the mountains is a different matter."

"I'm sure I shall manage." She looked straight at him. "Yes, I know it takes longer for water to boil at high altitudes and for cakes to bake. To the extent that I could, Mr. Lockwood, I have tried to prepare myself."

He doubted anything could prepare her for what she'd encounter. "That's all one can do, I suppose." He cleared his throat. "I presume you are acquainted with Miss Bird's mountain adventures?"

"Yes. I hope to prove as intrepid as she. Although I'm sure some of the challenges I encounter will surprise me, I have confidence I can deal with whatever befalls me."

How can the woman be so impossibly naive? "I wish you well."

"As do we all," Robert said. "I admit when Sophie first proposed this adventure, I was skeptical. I've seen frontiers, and they can be most inhospitable, especially to women. But this gal?" He looked fondly at the young woman. "She's fearless. In our short acquaintance, I've seen her outride many men I know. I'm an old cavalryman, and I know horses. So does she." He shook his head emphatically. "If any woman can make it in the mountains, Sophie has my vote."

Tate glanced at Sophie, noting the blush coloring her cheeks. She couldn't weigh much over a hundred pounds. How would she face down a bear? "Time will tell," he mumbled, aware he sounded churlish.

"So it will," she replied merrily. "I can't wait for tomorrow."

"Is this your first trip beyond Kansas?" he asked, scooping up a roll and buttering it. In the pause before she answered, he glanced up. For some reason, her smile had faded and a sudden melancholy clouded her expression.

"No, I, uh, I spent 1876 and 1877 in New England studying history and classics at an academy for women." Hesitating for a moment, she went on. "I was at a point in my life where I needed…a change."

When she didn't elaborate, he noticed both Robert and Effie were busying themselves with their meals. Well, he might be a man of the mountains, but he hadn't forgotten all social graces. He'd stumbled into awkward territory and the only way out was to change the subject. "I'm a Pennsylvanian and even attended university there. I hadn't been much of anywhere until I came to Colorado. I believed all the newspaper accounts about making a fortune in the West."

"And did you?" she asked in a neutral tone.

"As a matter of fact I did."

Robert beamed. "Our boy here has not only done well for himself, he has made quite a name in the mining and banking communities."

"Congratulations," she murmured, bent over her meal. Then she looked up. "It's the land of opportunity. That's what I'm seeking."

He couldn't imagine Estes Park would offer her that. "What kind of opportunity?" he asked merely to keep the conversation alive.

He wasn't prepared for her candor. "The opportunity to find myself. To learn who I am all by myself. To discover what I'm meant to do now."

In the *now* he heard a mournfulness that caught him off guard. Maybe she wasn't quite the flibbertigibbet he'd judged at first. Her last word suggested a history. A burdensome one. His question had led them far beyond dinner-party conventions. "It's a good place to do that," he finally said.

Effie came to the rescue. "I would like to pack up some of the remaining food for your journey."

"That would be welcome," Tate said.

"When should I be ready in the morning?"

"I will be here at six. Have your horse packed and saddled, and we'll be off soon after to go to the livery to pick up the wagons loaded with our supplies and summer provisions. Prepare yourself, Miss Montgomery. It is a long, uncomfortable trip."

She lifted her head in a way that suggested defiance. "I can handle it, sir."

From that point on, Effie dominated the conversation with tales of the military wives she'd met, some suited to the life and others woefully unprepared.

When Tate rose to leave later in the evening, the

others followed him out onto the front porch. A breeze cooled the air. Overhead a canopy of stars twinkled in the ether. "Come back soon, son. Bring the boys," the major said, patting him on the back.

"The boys?" Sophie asked.

"Tate has two young sons. Charming little fellows," Effie explained.

"I should like to meet them." Sophie approached him and held out her hand. "Good night, Mr. Lockwood. Until tomorrow."

He stood there, momentarily stunned into silence. She only came up to his shoulder, but her eyes held his in an unflinching gaze. Her hand was warm. He pulled away, hoping his abruptness wasn't discourteous. "Until tomorrow," he echoed, then thanked the Hurlburts and went to the barn to mount his horse, all the while thinking, *Never was there an unlikelier mountain adventurer.*

Sophie turned to reenter the house, momentarily flustered by Mr. Tate Lockwood, whose tall, muscular body had towered over hers and whose dark brown eyes seemed to drink her in. Yet *acerbic* was the only word that came to mind to describe his personality. Although he hadn't come right out and said it, it was obvious he thought her upcoming stay in the mountains was the height of folly. It was as if he deliberately withheld his superior knowledge of the place, hoping she would learn the hard way the arrogance of her expectations. Well, she'd show him—and all the other doubters.

"Did you enjoy Mr. Lockwood?" Effie hovered at her elbow.

"I'm not sure *enjoy* is the best word."

"What is, do you think?"

"He was *interesting* maybe, or…" Sophie floundered.

"A bit brittle perhaps?"

"Certainly self-contained." Sophie frowned. "He doesn't want to take me."

Effie sighed. "I suppose not. But he's right, dear, it's a harsh environment."

"I think that may be exactly what I need."

Behind them Robert locked the door. "I'm off to read, ladies. Good night. Sophie, I'll see you in the morning."

Effie put an arm around her shoulders. "Would you have time for another cup of tea?"

"I would welcome one."

In the kitchen, Effie bustled with the kettle, her back turned to where Sophie sat at the table. "The past still weighs you down, then?"

"I doubt it shall ever leave me, but I am determined to quit living in the limbo of my regrets."

"Is Estes Park the answer?" Effie set the cups down and took a seat.

"I know it sounds ridiculous, but I truly think it may be. I need a new place. One where my lungs fill with fresh air and my eyes are dazzled…"

"Are you running away or running toward, I wonder."

Sophie watched the steam rise from her tea. Outside a dog barked. "In truth, a bit of both." She took a warming sip. "I love my family, but I couldn't stay in Cottonwood Falls, as much as the Flint Hills are my heart's home. To watch Caleb and Lily together, so happy and fulfilled by little Mattie and Harmony. To live in the same house with Rose and Seth, the dearest souls on earth, and envy their luck with Alf and little Andy was stifling. All the time knowing what I'd had and lost, never to regain. I caught myself becoming resentful, self-pitying and, worse, angry with God."

"I'm so sorry, dear."

"Then whenever I saw that beautiful new court-house, where every single stone had passed through my Charlie's hands, I…I…" She swiped at her eyes, then laughed derisively. "Well, you see, then. Something had to change. I have to change." Clearing her throat, she went on. "I've always enjoyed reading travel arti-cles and books, and descriptions of the Rocky Moun-tains captivated me. Then one day, sitting in church, I heard these words as if for the first time, 'I will lift up mine eyes unto the hills, from whence cometh my help.' And I knew. I had to come here. Thanks to dear Caleb, I have been led to you and the major and your loving hospitality."

Effie cupped her drink in both hands. "I know some of your story from Caleb, but you've never spoken of your Charlie."

Sophie wondered if she was able to bare her soul. After a moment of thought it became clear to her that doing so was an essential part of this journey upon which she was embarking.

She fortified herself with a gulp of tea before begin-ning. "My Charlie. He *was* mine. I was his. He came out of the blue, as if God-sent. Who would suppose a master stonemason from New England would come to tiny Cottonwood Falls? It defies belief. Yet there he was, supervising the building of our new courthouse. I had always heard about Yankee reserve, but Charlie was outgoing and fun and had never met a stranger. He was steady and had a deep side to him, a sensitive side, you might say. Although I tried at first to hide it, it was love at first sight. For both of us, I think." She managed a sad smile. "Believe me, it wasn't easy courting under the eyes of two brothers, a father and a host of workmen. Buggy rides, picnics by the river… Oh, Effie, what good times we had." She paused, remembering Charlie's piercing black eyes, his ruddy complexion, his tender kisses.

"Go on," said Effie kindly.

"One of the best days of my life was the Courthouse Ball celebrating the completion of the building. It is a splendid structure, the limestone quarried locally, with beautiful woodwork and a clock tower—far more elegant than you would expect in our little town. At the ball, my Charlie stepped onto the platform and told the world that I had agreed to marry him. He looked so handsome, so proud…" How could she tell the next part—the part that had gutted her?

"I'll understand if you prefer not to go on, dear." Effie's eyes were filled with compassion.

"No. I've started. It's important for me to finish." Sophie shoved her cup to the center of the table, squared her shoulders and continued. "We were to be married after Charlie finished a job at one of the colleges some miles away. During that time, we were able to see each other occasionally. It was fun planning a wedding and talking about our future. Then shortly before the wedding, he received an attractive offer to go to Chicago and oversee a huge project. I could have gone with him. However, fearing he would have little time to devote to me there, we decided to postpone the wedding, save some money and then settle permanently someplace." She shook her head. "So that's what we did."

"But…?"

Caleb had undoubtedly told the Hurlburts about her past. She could stop now. It would be all right. To do so, though, would diminish the power of the love they'd shared. "It was the autumn of 1875. I was gathering pumpkins under a bright October sky. The Flint Hills spread out before me like a giant jigsaw puzzle. In the distance I could see Charlie's clock tower. Lost in my memories of him, I looked up and saw a sudden cloud obscuring the sun. A cold blast swept over me, and I shivered. Later, I remembered that moment, remembered that hint of premonition." Swallowing, she forced herself to finish. "Two days later the telegram came. My Charlie... A scaffold high on the building had broken. My beloved plunged to his death."

Effie gasped in sympathy. "Oh, my poor dear. How devastated you must have been."

"Still am," she whispered. "I loved him so." A long minute passed. "So you see why I had to leave the one place where I saw my Charlie at every turn, where I encountered the richly deserved happiness of those I love, a happiness of which I am deprived. I was making myself sick brooding about what might have been. That's why I'm going to the mountains, Effie." She paused momentarily, remembering the Devanes' gift of the money Charlie had saved to set up housekeeping— money that was funding her stay in Colorado. "There I hope to find myself and make peace with the God who claimed my love too soon."

Effie gripped Sophie's hands in hers. "Sophie, child, you are doing what you must. I will be praying in the days ahead that you find the solace you seek and the peace God has in store for you. Indeed. Lift your eyes to the hills. Your help *will* come from the Lord."

"Thank you."

Effie rose. "And now, off to bed with you or you'll fall asleep on your horse tomorrow."

Sophie embraced Effie and retired to the guest room. As she hung up her lovely blue satin gown, she ran her fingers over the soft fabric, knowing that it would be many months before she again had need of such a frock, if ever. One chapter of her life was closing and a new one was opening. Thanks to Effie, she felt lighter, less burdened. A good way to begin her new adventure. She slipped between the sheets, said a prayer for the repose of Charlie's soul as she always did and fell into a peaceful sleep.

Chapter Two

Dressed in riding bloomers concealed under a full overskirt, Sophie waited with Effie in the early-morning light while the major led her recently purchased gray gelding from the barn. "You know your horseflesh," he said, stroking the animal's neck. "Ranger here should have the stamina and agility for mountain trails."

"I agree. Besides—" she grinned "—he's handsome, as well." Turning to Effie, she let herself sink into the older woman's warm embrace. "Thank you for everything, most of all for your encouragement. It's been a difficult few years, but now I feel ready for whatever comes."

"Keep in touch, my dear. We'll be eager to hear of your adventures." Effie held her at arm's length. "But don't be foolhardy."

"I'll try to behave myself."

Robert handed her the reins and stood by while she mounted. "If you have half the good sense your brother Caleb showed with the cavalry, you'll be fine. Godspeed, dear girl."

Tate Lockwood rode over from the stock tank where he'd been watering his horse. "All set?"

Sophie blinked twice. This mountain man—dressed

in worn breeches, scuffed boots, a chamois shirt and a leather, sheepskin-lined coat—bore no resemblance to the gentrified man of the evening before. In fact, last night, she'd questioned whether such a sophisticated gentleman was capable of handling the rigors of the high country. "I'm ready."

His look begged the question "Are you really?" "Adequate clothing, full canteen?"

How irritating to be treated like the greenest of greenhorns. "Yes, sir," she said, barely controlling her indignation.

"Robert, Effie, I'll see that she arrives safely."

"We have no doubt of that," Effie said with a smile. "Now, off with you."

Lockwood wheeled his horse and trotted toward the road. Sophie followed, her heart beating wildly. It had been many months since she had been this excited about life. What lay ahead, she did not know, but anything was better than the paralysis that had enveloped her since Charlie's death. She faced the mountains, their purple-gray shadows slowly dissolving into a brilliant orange as the sun crested the horizon and bathed them in light. A new dawn. Appropriately symbolic, she mused.

Tate Lockwood said not one word until they arrived at the livery stable. Three men were piling sacks of flour and sugar on top of boxes in the two wagons and strapping them down. Tate dismounted and gestured to them. "Miss Montgomery, meet my hands Curly, Sam and Pancho. They'll be our traveling companions."

Was there a hint of mockery in his tone? Well, never mind. "I'm pleased to make your acquaintance." Dismounting, she walked to the first wagon to satisfy herself that her belongings and provisions had been loaded and secured.

"Everything meeting your specifications?" Lockwood loomed over her, the brim of his hat pulled low.

"Quite."

"Tonight we'll stay at a hotel in Longmont, but once we start on the trail, there's no turning back."

"I certainly hope not."

With a grudging "Good," he conferred with the men, who climbed into the wagon seats. "Saddle up, miss," the one named Sam called to her. She noticed that all four men were armed with both rifles and pistols.

They had covered a few miles, Lockwood in the lead and her trailing along behind him ahead of the wagons when, without looking at her, he said, "It's a rocky and demanding climb to the park."

"So I've heard."

"I doubt anything you've read or been told will have prepared you adequately. Robert tells me you have rented a cabin in Estes Valley sight unseen. I assure you it will lack the amenities to which you're accustomed."

While she fumed under his patronizing attitude, they rode for a time in silence until he spoke again. "The mountains are no place for a lone woman such as yourself."

There was no holding back. "I beg to differ. As I hope you will come to recognize, I am not just any woman. Nor am I bothered by being solitary or lacking creature comforts."

By way of acknowledgment, Tate merely grunted. Except for pointing out landmarks, he said little until they arrived at the hotel in the late afternoon. "I'll see to the horses and wagons," he said after she dismounted. "Get a good night's sleep. You'll need it."

When Sophie inspected her lodging, she quickly realized amenities were, indeed, being left behind. Saddle sore, she ate a bowl of bland stew, noting that there was only one other woman in the company gathered in the public room. Too weary to be sociable, she retired early and, despite her excitement over what the morrow would bring, fell into a deep sleep.

Tate Lockwood greeted her in the dawn with curt advice. "Bundle up."

Sophie buttoned her heavy coat, wrapped a woolen scarf around her neck and clapped her weathered felt hat on her head. Before long, they left the flat land and began climbing. She reveled in the piney smell and fresh air. As the canyon narrowed and the trail bordered the river, she watched in wonder as the cascading water from the high peaks, laden with ice and snow runoff, splashed across rocks, creating a thrilling music. At each turn of the trail, a new pleasure awaited—the raucous cry of a mountain jay or the sight of a graceful doe bounding across their path.

When the sun was high overhead, they reached a spot where huge boulders bordered the river. Lockwood signaled a halt. Sophie was glad to dismount, remove her coat and stretch her limbs. The hands lounged on the ground to eat lunch. She settled on a flat rock beneath a spruce tree and pulled out the bit of roast and potato from the dinner at the Hurlburts'. Lockwood hunkered a few feet away, his dark brown eyes intent on her. "Bearing up?"

"I assure you, Mr. Lockwood, that I am managing quite well and that if I require assistance from you or the others, I will not hesitate to ask."

"Hmm." He stood and unfolded the oilskin holding his food. "From this point, the ascent is demanding, treacherous in places, especially this early in the season."

Was he trying to scare her? "I shall follow your expert lead."

He bit into a piece of meat, chewing thoughtfully, but saying nothing. Sophie found him intriguing—a man comfortable in different worlds, yet guarded, as if he avoided intimacy and rarely exposed his inner thoughts. He was handsome in a chiseled sort of way, and she could see how some women might find him attractive. She wondered about his wife and sons. Perhaps his wife would provide her with some female companionship during her stay in the mountains. From her reading, she understood that there were few women there and that she, as a single woman on her own, would be an oddity. She looked forward to meeting the woman who had overcome Tate Lockwood's reserve.

"Usually we can make this trip in one day, but ice will slow us from this point on. Best get going if we're to make the valley by nightfall." He refolded the oilskin and put it in his pocket, then took off his hat and ran his fingers through his wavy brown hair. "'Course, if we encounter delays, the ground will be your bed."

"That will be a comfort after the long ride."

She thought she heard him snort as he walked away. As if she hadn't slept under the stars on every cattle drive she'd ever been on. The prudent course of action under the circumstances was to keep her mouth shut, difficult as it was to do, and show the man she was equal to any hardship. One thing was certain: she was not a conventional woman, whatever that might be.

Much as he'd hoped to make it home from Longmont in one day, Tate wasn't surprised when that didn't happen. At several points they had been forced to push the wagons over icy spots, and once, they'd even had to hitch two teams together to haul each wagon around points where avalanche debris had blocked the trail. It had been a grueling day, but to his surprise and relief, Sophie Montgomery had been more help than burden.

Easing his aching muscles, Tate lounged by the fire idly watching sparks ascend into the night air and fade into the darkness. Curly, Sam and Pancho were rolled up in their blankets beneath one of the wagons. Miss Montgomery had carefully prepared a bed of pine boughs under an overhanging rock ledge and had lain down and covered herself with her bedroll blanket. Despite the campfire, the evening was cold. Earlier, he'd noticed her pulling her coat tighter and often reaching her gloved hands toward the warmth of the flames. If she thought it was cold now, wait until she reached her cabin at 7,500 feet above sea level. She probably had no idea they would be lucky to reach Estes Park before another spring snow blanketed the mountains. He hoped to deliver and store the provisions before that happened. Over the winter and early spring, snows had kept him and his men from getting to Denver, although he had been able to work in one quick trip down the canyon to Lyons.

Crossing his legs, he picked up his tin cup and took a welcome sip of hot coffee. He hoped Marcus and Toby would like the books he'd picked out for them in Denver. Very soon he should hear from the Ohio tutor he'd engaged for his sons. There was no school in Estes Park. His boys loved the place, but he himself was no great shakes as a teacher. He didn't want them to grow up without an education, yet it wouldn't do to send them off, even if he knew of a suitable place for them. They'd had enough of change and loss in their young lives.

Leaving their home was not an option. This prospective tutor, a recent graduate of Oberlin College, had solid academic credentials and claimed to crave a mountain adventure. However, thumbing through the mail he'd picked up in Denver, Tate had seen no correspondence from the young man, despite the fact he was scheduled to arrive at the end of May.

Throwing the remainder of his coffee into the fire, he got to his feet, knowing from the position of the moon that he needed to get to sleep. The haul from here to the park would demand grit. He turned to study the small form huddled beneath the blanket, shaking his head. She might be dressed in drab, utilitarian clothes, but there was no hiding her femininity. He wondered what had prompted this young woman to undertake not only this trek, but a prolonged solo stay in the mountains. Did she, too, have demons chasing her? Well, it was none of his business.

Before he settled under the second wagon, he wrestled with himself. Miss Montgomery, being so small, might be cold, despite her blanket. By morning the temperatures would be below freezing. It wouldn't do for her strength to be compromised. He eyed the buffalo robe enclosing his bedroll. He untied the leather thongs and spread out the robe. He had a blanket and his coat was plenty warm. He scooped up the robe and started toward the woman's resting place. Then he stopped, arguing with himself. She wanted to be independent, didn't she? Why should he concern himself with her comfort? Yet he knew the toll such frigid nights could take on a person. Before other arguments occurred to him, he carried the buffalo robe to where she lay nestled on the pine boughs. Kneeling beside her, he gently spread it over her, struck once again by how small and vulnerable she seemed, especially for one so fiercely determined to make her way in inhospitable country.

Back under the wagon, wrapped in his own bedding, he chastised himself. He could not assume responsibility for Miss Montgomery after this trip ended. He had enough to worry about managing his ranching and mining affairs and, of course, caring for his boys. That having been decided, he rolled over on his side, freed from concern. Until just before he drifted off. Until he was honest with himself. Tate Lockwood would never turn his back on a woman in need.

Sophie awoke with a jolt, trying to work out in her mind why she was so cozy, covered in a heavy layer of warmth. Then, smelling coffee, her mind focused. The trail. She was on the trail. Sitting up, she noted it was still dark, but flames illuminated the immediate vicinity. Tate Lockwood and the others sat around the fire. Carefully she stood up, leaning back to unkink her spine.

"Breakfast," Tate said, pointing to the cast-iron skillet. The others looked up, studying her.

"I'm starving," she said, advancing toward them. Sam handed her a cup of coffee, and Pancho folded a piece of ham in a flapjack and brought it to her. Finding a stone, she sat down, aware only now of a faint lightening in the eastern sky. Yet here in the canyon darkness lingered. The chill morning air, though invigorating, made her long once again to be cocooned under the blankets. No one spoke while they ate, and she certainly wasn't going to intrude upon their silence to ask how much farther they had to travel or what time they might arrive at the valley. She trembled with excitement—at last the day had come! The prospect of locating her cabin and exploring new possibilities elated her.

"Can't delay," Lockwood said, rising to his feet. "Let's pack up and move out."

Sophie gobbled the last bite of her flapjack, washed it down with a swig of hot coffee and moved to her sleeping place to gather her things. Once there, she stopped in her tracks. No wonder she'd been so warm. Atop her makeshift bed lay a thick buffalo robe, certainly not hers. She turned around to see who might have provided her with such comfort. Holding up the robe, she caught Mr. Lockwood's eye. He shrugged, then turned away. She didn't know whether to be irked by his presumption that she didn't have adequate blankets or pleased that he had a protective side. She smiled to herself. Maybe his bark was worse than his bite. No matter, she had slept well. Then she remembered. A man had come to her, covered her with warmth and then lingered by her side. At the time she'd thought she was dreaming of Charlie.

She folded the robe and walked over to return it. "Thank you, Mr. Lockwood. I slept very well."

"Courtesy of the West, miss." He took the robe and nodded. "Didn't figure you'd counted on quite how cold it can be up here."

She bit back the retort on her lips. Despite all her planning, he was right—she'd underestimated the temperatures. "I trust my other preparations will be more effective."

"You'd best hope so. It's a long ways between houses in the valley. You'll be fending for yourself."

She understood both the rebuke and warning in his words. "I will, of course, do everything I can not to be bothersome to others. That having been said, may I count on your friendship and goodwill?"

He looked at her, as if assessing her mettle. "Friendship and goodwill? No gentleman would turn his back on a woman in distress."

Hardly the heartiest of endorsements. She voiced what he had left unsaid. "Nevertheless, I'm sure it is your hope I will not pose such inconveniences for you."

"I have my own concerns, Miss Montgomery. They must come first."

"Understood."

Once on the trail, the rugged terrain again took a toll on the horses. Often she had to dismount and lead Ranger around barriers. The higher they went, the more she gloried in the various trees along the way, especially the beautiful spruce. And she thought no Parisian perfume could surpass the fragrance of the pines. It was as if inch by inch, foot by foot, mile by mile, she was being exposed to a wonderland of sights and sensations. Even though her lungs ached and her muscles protested, she pushed on, eager to arrive at her destination.

At one point when the trail leveled out a bit, Lockwood rode alongside her. "Has anyone told you about the travelers and tourists?"

"I know that in summertime the population of the valley grows. Hikers, fishermen, mountain climbers, those who seek the altitude for health reasons."

"Yes, and although there is a hotel or two, they don't all stay there. Care to venture a guess about where else they find lodging?"

"In private homes?"

"Exactly. Most travelers are harmless, but some might enjoy, er, finding shelter with a lone woman."

"Are you trying to frighten me, Mr. Lockwood?"

He looked over at her, eyebrows raised in question. "Am I succeeding?"

She stared forward, resolute. "I'm by no means defenseless, sir. I have brought along weapons, primarily for hunting, but if necessary, I can hold my own against someone threatening my life." She glanced over at him, reading skepticism in his expression. "I am an accomplished and accurate markswoman." Then with gleeful malice, she added, "Would you care to test that boast?"

"No, ma'am. But then, I'm not the type of man to be in such a position." An edge came into his voice. "I'm simply trying to educate you."

"Protect me, more like," she snapped before he shook his head sadly and trotted off. Great! She'd done it again—assaulted his pride in the effort to prove her independence. Yet deep down, if she was honest with herself, she knew she would undoubtedly need Tate Lockwood in some future capacity. Where else would she have to turn? It was ticklish business when he so clearly wanted nothing more than to deposit her at her cabin and be rid of her.

If he lived to be a hundred, Tate knew he would never forget the look on Sophie Montgomery's face when they came up out of the canyon and reached the point where the entire Estes Valley spread out in front of them, rimmed by the timeless snowcapped peaks. Her gasp was audible, and her cheeks flushed with excitement. He turned in his saddle to study her more carefully as she took in the spectacle before her. It was as if he were in communion with her, experiencing the splendor of the mountains for the first time. For long moments she didn't speak, and the silence of the space below them seemed almost sacred. That is, if he believed anything at all could be sacred.

Finally, with eyes awash with emotion, she looked

at him. "I had no idea," she whispered breathlessly. "The beauty and scope are beyond description. Books and illustrations can't begin to do this scenery justice."

He took off his hat and scanned the horizon. "It's impressive, all right. No place on earth is quite like it."

"Which is Longs Peak?"

He pointed toward the southwest. "There."

"The front of it looks as if some giant hand took a meat cleaver and sliced the mountain in two."

"That's the famous east face. The drop from the top of it into the lake below is hundreds of feet."

She fixed her gaze on the famous peak. "I'm going to climb it one day."

Was there no stopping this woman? For all her slight size, she made up for it in sheer nerve. "I wouldn't count on it."

"*You* wouldn't, Mr. Lockwood, but I *do* count on it. It's merely a matter of time."

"Hardly any women have been successful."

"May I remind you once again that I am not 'any woman'? Ask my brothers if you don't believe me."

Once more, he took in the majesty of the peaks, the miles and miles of high meadow, with streams etching silver ribbons across the surface, and felt the tug of home. "Begging your pardon, but I can't dawdle here gawking all day."

"Just one more moment, please. It will never again be the first time I take in this scene."

He had to give her that—at least she recognized the power and uniqueness in the place. He wondered if Estes Park would grip her the same way it had him. As they rode on, no words passed between them, yet he had the disturbing sense that Sophie Montgomery had gotten under his skin as no woman had in a great long time. Against his better judgment, he found himself admiring her determination while at the same time finding her maddeningly independent, even reckless. The contrast to Ramona couldn't have been more startling.

Finally she broke the silence. "I shall look forward to meeting your wife and children, Mr. Lockwood."

"I have no wife. Only my two boys."

She turned to him, eyes wide with pity, and her face reddened with embarrassment. "I'm sorry…I…uh, had no idea. Effie didn't mention… Oh dear, please accept my condolences."

"The Hurlburts, always discreet, probably didn't regard it as their place to convey my personal information." In that moment, he had an irrational urge to shock her. Bitterness churned in the back of his throat as he said, "My wife, excuse me, my *former* wife, saw fit not only to abandon me but our two children, as well."

He had succeeded. Bald shock registered on her face. "Dear me, I fear I have stumbled into your private concerns."

"You would find out sooner or later. She returned to the East. We are divorced."

"But…the boys?"

"She prefers to have nothing to do with them. Frankly, that makes it easier for all three of us." Easier emotionally, he thought to himself, but difficult in the day-to-day reality.

"I'm sorry. I don't know quite what to say."

"That must be a first for you." He watched her face crumple and swore at himself for his insensitivity. "Now I'm the one to offer an apology. That was uncalled for. I would take the remark back if I could, Miss Montgomery."

"Words have a life of their own, don't they? Sometimes they just slip out when they should stay put. And you aren't the first to accuse me of garrulousness." She smiled ruefully, and he could breathe again.

"Nor will I be the last, I suspect," he said with a forced chuckle.

Then she laughed gaily and relief flooded through him. "Do you know what I think? I have had quite enough of this Miss Montgomery and Mr. Lockwood business. You are my only friend in all of Estes Valley, and I would like you to call me Sophie." She paused. "And might I call you Tate?"

His first thought was that this informality moved them into an intimacy he wasn't sure he was willing to undertake, but his second thought trumped the first. "I would welcome that," he said.

"All right, then, *Tate*. Take me home."

He knew she meant her cabin, of course. Yet, for an instant, her words shook every nerve in his body. "Home…yes." He raised an arm and pointed along the northern fringe of the valley. "Your cabin is over there, not too far from my ranch. We'll stop at your place first."

He wished he could cover the intervening miles in a flash. He needed to put distance between himself and this woman…this Sophie.

Sophie couldn't let Tate see her disappointment. *Furnished cabin?* In the real estate flyer she'd been sent, that must have been a euphemism for one-room shack. Never in all her days had she seen such a structure, standing upright only through some act of God, shingles missing, chinks in the walls and dirt and animal droppings in abundance. She stood on the front porch taking in the mountain view. "At least this vista is lovely," she said, shading her eyes against the sun dropping slowly behind the peaks.

"You can't spend your life on the porch," Tate muttered. "Would you like me to send one of my ranch hands over in the morning to help you muck out?"

She gathered her courage. "In the provisions they just unloaded, I have the necessary equipment. I would be much obliged if you could help me gather wood and get a fire started. Beyond that I have some tinned food that will keep me until I can get to baking, so you will be able to take your leave soon and get home to your sons."

She could never admit to him how overwhelming the tasks before her seemed. The place was almost uninhabitable. She had never imagined she would have to start from scratch to turn this place into a home. Somehow she had pictured a snug cabin with perhaps a smattering of dust, but already equipped with a good bed and a sturdy stove, needing only a few touches and some elbow grease to make it hers. Now, with the sun disappearing behind the peaks, the sudden drop in temperature made a fire an even more immediate necessity.

Tate stood beside her on the porch, dwarfing her. "I'll send the boys on home with the wagons while I help you with the fire."

He left her, gave orders to his men and disappeared behind the lean-to that made do for a barn, where she had stabled Ranger.

She gathered some kindling, then went inside and busied herself swiping at cobwebs and sweeping ashes out of the woodstove. She vowed she would not cry, especially not in front of the man who called into question her every move. This task was similar to moving to Kansas and establishing their ranch. Her father had often reminded her and her brothers, *Patience. One step at a time, one day at a time.* She sniffled once, briefly indulging her self-pity. Then she returned to her labors, figuring that for this day, one stove and one bed would be reasonable steps. She could do this. She tried not to look at the bed, sagging nearly to the floor, the filthy mattress having served as home to who knew what.

She heard Tate's heavy footsteps, followed by a loud thump. She opened the door. "Hidden treasure," he said ironically, pointing at the logs he'd gathered. "A wood pile behind the barn. I'll fetch some more."

"I'll come with you." She hurried along behind him, grinning wryly at his use of the word *barn* to describe the ramshackle outbuilding.

Together they made four trips and stacked up a considerable amount of wood. "At least I won't worry about you freezing to death," Tate said when they were finished.

"I don't want you worrying about me at all."

"All right. I won't."

Why did that easy promise disappoint her? After all, she'd asked for it. "Fine."

"There's also a privy over by that grove of aspen."

She was unable to make eye contact. "Useful information."

"One last thing. Let me prime the pump that carries the water from the pond over yonder."

She slumped. She'd been so busy bemoaning the state of her dwelling that she hadn't even thought about water. So much for her foresight and self-sufficiency. Was her bravado merely a disguise for incompetence?

Satisfied that the pump worked, Tate stood in the door, preparing to leave. "Anything else?"

"Not that I can think of." She looked into his eyes, reading concern. "I will be fine. I am grateful for the help." She chuckled sardonically. "Perhaps I don't know quite as much as I thought I did."

"Or were sold a bill of goods by some unscrupulous agent."

"No use crying over spilled milk. I'll just make the best of what is, I confess, a disillusioning end to such a beautiful day."

"Where is your rifle?"

She nodded to a corner. "Over there."

"Load it and keep it with you."

"That's comforting," she said.

"That's reality." He put on his hat and they moved onto the porch. "So now, while it may not be quite what you pictured, you're home, Sophie. Do be wary."

"Good evening, Tate. Once again, thank you for bringing me here."

He glanced around. "That's either irony or supreme gratitude."

"Gratitude," she murmured. "Now get along with you."

Then he was off. She stood on the porch hugging herself for warmth, waiting until the last hoofbeats died away. She was alone in a way she had never been alone. The valley was still and the mountains loomed like sentinels. Tate's absence swept over her, leaving her breathless. This was what she had wanted, wasn't it? Solitude? Peace? God had given her this place to heal, and no matter what, she would honor His gift. Here she would, at last, begin a new life. Not one in which she ever forgot her beloved Charlie, but one of which she hoped he would approve…and one he would bless.

Turning to go inside, she looked up at the sky and gasped in wonder. Never had she seen such a canopy of stars. In that moment, a peace came over her as if God was delivering her from her personal wilderness.

Inside, as she threw the mattress aside and made herself a bed of pine needles and straw, she knew she would sleep like a baby. Tate was right. She was home.

Chapter Three

Wrapping a blanket around her shoulders the next morning, Sophie moved quickly to build up the fire and get water boiling. No friendly elves had appeared in the night to clean the place and dawn did nothing to improve the cabin, but a deep sleep and the satisfaction of arriving at her destination had restored her optimism. She thought of her father, whose life as a widower with three small children couldn't have been easy. *Start in a corner and work your way out,* he always said when faced with a daunting situation. That was exactly what she would do. While she waited for the kettle to heat, she filled a pail with cold water from the pump, added some baking soda and began scrubbing the layers of dust from the crude cupboard shelves and scarred pine table. Later she would go over the surfaces with boiling water. Other chores could wait, but if she was to eat, the kitchen had to be attacked first.

When the sun crested the ridge, Sophie donned her coat, slipped a knife in her pocket and went to the barn. Ranger whinnied in recognition and nosed her shoulder. "Good morning, fella." She caressed his neck. "Ready to eat?" She cut open the bag of oats, poured a generous amount into the feed bucket and pumped water into a trough, grateful that some previous owner had had the foresight to put a pump here as well as in the cabin. She surveyed the building and small fenced corral. It would do for now.

The morning passed swiftly, and by noon she felt reasonably satisfied about her progress. Bread dough was rising, and the food sacks and tins had all been stowed away. She eyed the sturdy broom in the corner. This afternoon she'd sweep and scrub the floor before beginning repairs on the dilapidated furniture. Somehow, she vowed, she'd make the place not only habitable, but homey.

She carried a mug of fresh coffee out onto the porch, taking a moment to soak in the glorious view. No matter the state of her cabin, she knew this panorama of meadow and mountain would nourish her soul. In the quiet she heard the trickle of the nearby stream that fed into the pond. She looked heavenward. "Charlie, do you see me? Even though this isn't where we imagined being, for the first time since you left this earth, I sense you all around me."

The sun warmed her as she reflected on the people who had brought her to this time and place. Her family, of course. The dear Hurlburts. Even Tate Lockwood. Beneath his all-business exterior, she sensed an innate kindness he seemed to prefer not to expose. His warnings to her suggested a protective nature, as did his act of supplying the buffalo robe. In some ways, he reminded her of her father—both of them men rearing young children alone.

Later, on hands and knees scrubbing the rough pine floor, she admitted it was going to take more than this one day to put the furniture to rights and refurbish the cabin. The windows needed cleaning, the dresser drawers had to be scoured and set out in the sun to eliminate the musty odor clinging to them and that didn't begin to take into consideration whitewashing, filling chinks and inspecting the roof for leaks. She sat back on her heels, dried her hands on her apron and let out a deep sigh. "Work your way out," she muttered to herself, unable in her weariness to begin to picture what "out" might look like.

Dusk came early, and with it, the drop in temperatures that had Sophie restoking the stove. After a supper of bread, sardines and applesauce, she huddled at the table and read from the book of Acts by lantern light. For the first time in her life, she could relate to the early disciples who set off for strange lands to spread the Gospel. She, too, was in a "foreign" land, dependent on herself and the kindness of strangers.

Bundled in several layers of clothing, she lay down on her pine-bough bed, reminding herself that she needed to take the thin mattress outdoors tomorrow, beat it and air it and then determine if it was usable. As she planned her chores, she heard horses neighing outside, followed by heavy footsteps on the porch. "Anybody here?" a gravelly voice roared, followed by a loud knock and the insistent barking of a dog. "Hush, Sarge."

Everything Tate had told her about mountain travelers flashed through her mind as she vaulted to her feet and seized the rifle that in her busyness she had forgotten to load, despite his advice. She crept to the door, holding the gun in front of her. "Who's there?" Her voice sounded small.

"Lady, lemme in. I could use a cup of coffee." A man laughed uproariously. "I'm Grizzly, and I won't hurt you."

Sophie's heart beat like a trip-hammer while she considered her options. The man could break down the door with one stroke of his arm. What was the code of the mountains? Was this Grizzly person just a passing traveler or was he one of the few who would prey upon a woman living alone?

"You waitin' fer kingdom come?"

"Just a minute," Sophie yelled, before edging her way to the cubbyhole where she'd left her ammunition. Quickly chambering a shell, she uttered a silent prayer and opened the door. If a man's appearance could be designed to intimidate, his had been. Well over six feet tall and clad in a fur hat and long coat, the stranger, with matted hair and a gray beard that frizzed in all directions, studied her. Beside him, a huge wolflike dog sat, eyeing her with interest. With a gulp, she noted that the animal's tail was not wagging. "Once again, sir, who are you and what are you doing here?"

"Bein' neighborly. You're new to the valley." He doffed his fur cap. "I'm Terence P. Griswold at your service, but everybody hereabouts calls me Grizzly. And this here—" he nodded at the dog "—is my pardner, Sarge. Say hello, fella."

To her amazement the dog lifted his paw for her to shake. Still cradling the rifle, she bent over. "Sarge, nice to meet you."

When she stood back up, she noted a glint of humor in the man's bright blue eyes. "You that gal of Lockwood's?"

She bristled. "I would hardly put it that way. Mr. Lockwood was kind enough to escort me here from Denver."

"Wouldn't have minded that chore myself." He peered over her shoulder. "You gonna invite us in or what?" He edged closer. "Oh, and, honey, you don't need that there gun. I'm about as harmless as they come."

It was the moment of truth—to trust or not to trust. She lowered the rifle. "Let me get you some coffee."

He signaled the dog to wait on the porch and followed her inside.

She put more wood on the fire and set the water to boil. "Would you care for some bread and applesauce? I'm afraid that's all I can offer as I am newly arrived here."

"Wouldn't object to those vittles." He set his hat aside and unbuttoned his coat. Sophie preferred to focus on the aroma of the coffee. The man was ripe. "You prob'ly was scared when I knocked."

"I'm frightened of very little, but your arrival was a bit alarming."

"Know how to handle that gun?"

"Yes, and I'm relieved I didn't have to prove it to you."

He laughed again, and she found the sound pleasant and relaxing. "You're a smart gal to be cautious. I always say, 'Shoot first and ask questions later.'"

Sophie handed him a plate of food, poured two mugs of coffee and offered him sugar. "No cream, yet." She sat down across from him.

"Do you need a cow up here? I know where you might could get one. Or if you're planning to gallivant at all, I reckon you could buy milk and such from a neighbor."

"I'm obliged for that information."

"You probably need a lotta hints I can give you. Don't reckon Lockwood was a fount of information. He doesn't take too kindly to women."

"I welcome any help. I'm not naive enough to think I don't have a lot to learn or that I won't make mistakes."

"What's yer name, by the way? Can't be real friends till I know that."

"I'm Sophie Montgomery."

"Sophie?" He closed his eyes as if deep in thought. "Wisdom, right?" He opened his eyes and grinned at her. "In Greek. Good for you. You're gonna need it."

Sophie grinned. A mountain man who knew Greek? That would teach her to judge solely by appearance. "At least I'm not Pandora."

He threw back his head and roared. "We don't need no one opening a bag of ills up here." After wiping his eyes and taking a big gulp of coffee, he leaned across the table. "Here's the bargain. You let ole Sarge and me sleep in your barn, and over breakfast, I'll tell you how it is in these parts."

Sophie grasped the man's hand. "You may be the best thing that's happened to me lately. You, sir, have a deal!"

After Grizzly finished eating, she handed him a pan of bread scraps for Sarge. From the porch she watched as the two made their way to the barn. She couldn't help smiling. Her adventure had begun in earnest.

The second day after he arrived home, Tate sat at his desk, poring over his account books. Granted, the start-up costs for the silver mining operation he was helping to back near Leadville were significant, but based on engineering reports, he was satisfied the ultimate profits would justify his investment. Although he missed the rough-and-tumble adventure of being on site, Estes Park was a far better place to raise his boys. He glanced around, satisfied with the craftsmanship of his new two-story home overlooking the valley and ranges beyond. A fire burned in the fireplace mounted on a hearth of native stone, and the rich oak paneling imported from the East made this a room any Eastern financier would fancy. From the mounted elk heads to the cowhide rug on the pegged floor, his office was a man's room—and his escape. Aside from the debacle with Ramona, he had never regretted leaving the ease of life in Philadelphia to carve out a position for himself in Colorado by dint of hard work. To become his own man. His surroundings bore testimony to his success.

Bertie Wilson, his housekeeper, and his sons knew not to interrupt him when he retired to this sanctuary. Only here could he immerse himself in business and lay aside the guilt and remorse that so often hounded him, along with the relentless questions. Could he be parent enough for his sons? What kind of men would they become? How could he have so drastically misjudged Ramona? Worst of all, how much of his sons' motherless condition was his own fault? He'd racked his brain to seize on what he could have done differently. Was he incapable of reading the feminine mind? He had thought he was doing the right thing by leaving her and the boys in Philadelphia when he came west to make his fortune. All along, he'd thought his descriptive letters would adequately prepare his wife for Central City. He'd assumed building her a dream house there would serve as a reward for their long separation and prove to her that he could provide all the amenities to which she was accustomed.

He slammed the ledger book closed and leaned back in his chair, hands behind his head. It hadn't taken long for love to die, if, in fact, he'd ever truly known that state. Maybe Ramona's ardor had cooled during their time apart, or maybe they'd both changed from the besotted youngsters they'd been when they'd married. She hated Colorado and, by extension, him. Her resentment and self-indulgent tirades left her little energy for mothering, and the boys had suffered. No matter what he did, he'd been unable to satisfy his wife or make her happy. As much as he'd been blindsided by her departure, he had also experienced overwhelming relief. Fine for him, but poor Marcus and Toby. They were the innocent victims of her fragile mental state and his blindness.

No doubt about it. He had little understanding of women. Take Sophie Montgomery, for instance. She was attractive enough, with her fiery curls, trim body and hazel-green eyes. In that blue gown she had fooled him into believing she was more at home at balls and salons than astride a horse. She was obviously an intelligent woman with a gift for repartee, but illusions about her true nature vanished when he saw her in her riding clothes, bloomers visible beneath her skirt. Independent and saucy, she seemed to care not a whit about defying convention. Women like his ex-wife and other women of her station would most assuredly disapprove of Sophie's behavior. What foolishness for this lone female to come up to Estes Park on her own, thinking… thinking *what*? Why, he reckoned she wouldn't last a month in the valley. Disgusted with himself for allowing such disturbing questions to unsettle him, he stood and went into the great room, where eleven-year-old Marcus and eight-year-old Toby sat on the floor in front of the massive river rock fireplace, playing with tin soldiers. Toby jumped to his feet and flung himself at his father. "Papa! You were busy so long."

Tate ruffled his son's brown curls. "I had lots of work to catch up on."

Carefully studying the make-believe battlefield, Marcus moved one soldier into place before finally looking up, his expression guarded. "Bertie told us not to bother you. So we didn't."

Tate cringed at the censure in the boy's voice. More than Toby did, Marcus seemed to mind his absences. Even the games and books he'd brought from Denver hadn't impressed his older son. Maybe after a week away, he should've postponed his office work, but too much was at stake to delay. "I'm finished for today. How about a hike up to the ridge to watch the sunset?"

"Hooray!" Toby shouted, running for his coat hanging from a peg by the door.

Marcus rose slowly. "It's too cold."

"Bundle up, then," Tate answered quickly in the attempt to overcome his older son's reluctance. "We can hunt for animal tracks." Marcus's interest in nature was sophisticated for one so young. He already had an extensive scrapbook collection of plants and leaves.

The boy shrugged indifferently, then ambled to fetch his coat. Tate sighed. On top of everything else, his sons were very different. What pleased or excited one failed to move the other. Marcus was introspective and didn't settle for easy answers, whereas Toby was an enthusiastic, open little fellow for whom the world was his playground.

Outside, Toby ran ahead on the trail while Marcus stuck his hands in his pockets and followed slowly, his eyes scanning the ground. Tate brought up the rear, wondering what his boys were thinking, especially Marcus, who had been old enough for his mother's departure to disappoint and damage him. Ever since, he'd kept more to himself, within himself, and seemed less trusting. Tate felt helpless to improve the situation, especially when he sensed the boy harbored some resentment of him, as well.

"Look, Papa!" Toby skipped toward him, holding a gigantic pinecone. "See? Is this the biggest so far?"

Tate examined the treasure. "Could be. Let's take it home to add to our collection."

"You carry it," Toby said, thrusting the cone into Tate's hands before racing off again in pursuit of a new adventure.

"Pinaecae," Marcus mumbled as he continued up the trail.

Watching his sons' backs, Tate paused to shake his head. The tutor couldn't come soon enough. Marcus needed direction for his inquiring, thoughtful mind, and Toby needed academic discipline. It was all Tate could do to get him to settle down long enough to encourage his reading and map skills. No matter how hard Tate tried to steer their studies, there simply weren't enough hours in the day.

From the top of the ridge, Toby stood silhouetted by the setting sun. "It's time, Papa. Hurry or you'll miss it!"

A sunset wasn't all he was missing, Tate thought to himself as he trudged along. He was proud of his sons and thankful for his financial success, but the life he'd envisioned for himself as a young man had included a loving intact family. He wasn't sure now if such a life would ever be his.

Each evening in the week following Grizzly's overnight visit, Sophie had fallen into bed exhausted. With the tools she had brought, supplemented by the few she found in the barn, she had repaired furniture, installed locks, straightened the barn door and reinforced the corral fencing. Her next project was preparing the ground for her garden. There was no end of work to be done, but that wasn't what was bothering her. To her surprise, she had not counted on how the lack of company would affect her. After Charlie's death, she had longed for solitude and peace, but after living on the ranch amid the two bustling Montgomery families, she missed the listening ears and pleasant conversations. Now she found that she was talking to herself or Ranger and wondered if she sounded daft. Friday night she consulted a map of the valley, determined to make her first exploration of the territory and in the process locate the store Grizzly had mentioned as a source of milk and other limited supplies. Satisfied with her plan, she went to bed early, determined to set out shortly after daybreak.

She rose with the sun, but after answering the early knock on the door, became aware her plans had undergone a change. "Mornin', miss," a short, plump man with a fringed jacket and Western hat greeted her when she opened the door. "I'm Jackson Tyler, and me and the missus, along with our son and his wife, are here to help." He turned toward the yard, where Sophie saw the others waiting in a wagon. "Soon the Harper clan'll be along, too. I imagine you have walls to chink, a roof to mend and a garden to dig. My wife, Martha, thinks maybe she could help with some fixin' up inside to make the place homier."

Sophie reached out to shake the man's hand. "I'm Sophie Montgomery, and I don't want to inconvenience you, but I'd be much obliged for your assistance." She marveled once again at the neighborliness good people exhibited, both in the Kansas Flint Hills and now here. "I imagine Mr. Lockwood must've told you about me."

Looking puzzled, Tyler stroked his bearded chin. "No, ma'am. Don't know nothing about Lockwood. It was Grizzly. He stopped by our place after meeting you and allowed as how you might need a hand. Said you were a determined little woman, but he thought things might go smoother if some of us pitched in."

"Please invite the womenfolk in. Maybe you men could start on the chinking. The wind whistles right through this place. I'll put on a big pot of salt pork and beans for a midday meal."

Mr. Tyler ushered in his wife and a young woman. "This here's my sweetheart Martha and Dolly, my purty daughter-in-law. My son John and I'll be outside if you need anything."

Dolly was tall and slight, but Martha was as plump as her husband. With her dark hair coiled in a bun and her brown eyes snapping, the older woman looked the picture of health. "Sophie, our friend Grizzly couldn't stop talking about you. He doesn't know whether to think you're brave or foolish comin' here on your own." She grinned at her daughter-in-law, then turned again to Sophie. "But Dolly and I know. We think you're mighty brave and are gonna prove any naysayer wrong. One thing about the frontier—it may be rough and tough, but it won't put a good woman down."

Dolly's flushed face glowed. "What you're doing is something special." She glanced around the room. "Now, then, set us to some chores."

Martha put an arm around Sophie's waist. "Before we start, we brought you somethin' we think you need. Grizzly said you didn't have one. C'mon. It's out in the wagon."

Sophie threw a shawl around her shoulders and followed the women. Dolly went to the wagon bed, leaned over and freed a wriggling mass of black-and-white fur. "Woman on her own needs company," she said. The dog leaped from the wagon and ran in excited circles before coming to stand beside Sophie, as if the animal had known the identity of its mistress all along.

"She's not much of a watchdog yet, but her shepherding instincts will protect you some," Martha said. "We reckon she's about a year old."

Sophie was dumbstruck, not only with her lack of foresight in procuring a watchdog, but at the generosity and kindness of this family. She knelt on the ground beside the dog, scratching her behind the ears. "You are a beauty," she whispered. "I'm sure we will be great friends."

In answer, the dog's tail beat a tattoo on the firm ground.

"Beauty." Dolly looked speculative. "That has a nice ring to it."

Sophie laughed. "It's perfect. No ugly beasts for me, only this Beauty."

The dog nuzzled her hand as if in agreement.

"I brought along some scraps for you to feed her," Martha said.

Did these people think of everything? "Come in and give me suggestions for the cabin, and then I'll set the beans on the stove." Sophie was glad that she'd set beans to soak last night. After circling the interior of the cabin several times, Beauty plopped down in front of the fire and dozed. To Sophie, she looked as if she had always belonged there. The dog would serve as a welcome companion.

The women worked all morning altering, mending and washing curtains and bedding. Dolly had brought along some bright blue paint. She suggested painting the frames on the windows and the door to liven up the place. After the men had thoroughly chinked one wall,

Martha and Sophie were able to hang a Montgomery family photograph, a sampler Caleb's wife, Lily, had stitched for her and a small, colorful quilt made by her sister-in-law Rose. "Thank you," Sophie breathed. "Having these things from home around me is a blessing."

"We hope you will soon regard Estes Park as your home," Dolly said quietly, looking at Sophie with affection.

Just before lunch, Beauty leaped up, ran to the door and began barking. Dolly grinned. "See? She's useful already."

"It's the Harpers," Martha said, turning to Sophie. "Harriet and Joe are a wonderful young couple, and I know you'll enjoy Joe's sister Belle. They operate the community store."

Before Sophie knew it, all the chinks and the roof had been attended to, and everyone pitched in to prepare the soil for her garden. Later after the two families had disappeared into the twilight, Sophie reflected that rarely had she encountered such genuine helpfulness or met such enjoyable people. Particularly Belle. The moment she'd clapped eyes on the young woman, Sophie felt as if they'd always been friends. Belle was tall, with a ruddy, raw-boned face, a magnificent crop of black curls and dark eyes that sparked delight. Her first words to Sophie had been, "You're my kind of gal, Sophie. All guts and nerve."

"Thank you for that vote of confidence," Sophie had said with a smile.

"You just wait. We're going to have so much fun." She turned to face the mountains. "See that one there?" She pointed to Longs Peak.

"Yes, you and I are going to climb it," Sophie said before Belle could complete her speech.

"Girl, you took the words right out of my mouth." She gave Sophie an assessing look. "You're little, but full of grit. We'll show those men what determined women can achieve. I've been waiting for a hiking partner. I'm glad God sent you to me."

Sophie laughed. "I told Mr. Lockwood when I first clapped eyes on that peak that I would climb it. I don't think he thought I was serious. But I am. I'll enjoy doing it with you."

Before the group finished their chores, Martha invited Sophie to ride over the next morning to their home for services. "We don't have a real church or permanent pastor, but we all gather at our place when there's a circuit rider. Tomorrow a reverend is coming from Lyons to preach."

Figuring that would be a good start to familiarizing herself with the territory, Sophie got directions and agreed to come. She didn't know quite how she felt about church. Ever since Charlie's death, she'd had a tenuous relationship with God, but perhaps He had sent these kind people to her. Regardless of where they came from or why, they were a gift. As was Beauty, who lay beside her providing warmth and companionship.

It was a cool spring Sunday as she rode to church, and Sophie reveled in the scenery. Back in Kansas, she had continued attending services with her family in the hope that one day she would understand God's purpose in taking Charlie from her. She continued to go through the motions of worship and daily Bible reading, but with no real expectation of receiving answers. So far, none had come, nor were they likely to come here. Yet her deeply ingrained faith made it impossible to turn her back on God.

It had been a joy to awaken this morning in a home with a solid roof and walls and with personalized touches all around her. Her eyes had been immediately drawn to Lily's sampler, embroidered with flowers encircling the message from Proverbs.

Trust in the Lord with all thine heart;
and lean not unto thine own understanding.
In all thy ways acknowledge Him,
and He shall direct thy paths.

Sophie appreciated the advice, yet it was difficult to follow, given the loss of Charlie and her own rebellious, questioning streak.

As much as she missed her brothers, she missed Lily and Rose more. Her sisters-in-law related to the pain of her loss in ways neither Caleb nor Seth could. Sophie suspected Lily had intended the sampler message as a daily reminder to her.

Riding beside the water that flowed along the valley floor, she noticed an impressive home set halfway up a hill across the river and enclosed by at least a mile of rail fence. Small spruce trees lined the road leading to the house. The few other dwellings she passed on her way to the Tylers' were less impressive and often seemed to be the result of add-ons to an original cabin. A few appeared to serve as primitive lodging for summer visitors. The Tyler and Harper homes were situated along the river and, with their outbuildings, composed the nearest thing to a settlement in the area. A crude wooden sign at the Harpers' read General Store and Post Office. About a quarter of a mile beyond was a large two-story home with a porch on three sides. From the horses and wagons gathered in the yard, she assumed she'd arrived at the site of the service.

Inside, she was effusively greeted by Martha, who ushered her to a bench. "Reverend Justus is about ready to begin."

Sophie settled back, studying the congregation. In addition to the Tylers and Harpers, there seemed to be three or four other families. Small children sat on the floor or on their parents' laps, and the room was warm with crowded bodies. Several eyed her curiously, but the minister began speaking before she could introduce herself. Rather more didactic and long-winded than she would've liked, the rangy preacher had a weathered face and deep voice. He declaimed for nearly an hour on Moses and the Ten Commandments. Sandwiched between two amply built women, Sophie was pinned in her spot. Finally the crowd stood and sang lustily, no doubt as relieved as she with being delivered from the sermon. A meal followed where she was introduced to other area residents.

Belle took her aside and, despite the cool temperature, the two settled on the front porch with their plates. "Isn't this better than being jammed into that stuffy place?"

"We can always go in if we get cold." Sophie took a bite of the cabbage and ham someone had provided. "This is a nice reward," she said, licking her fingers.

"You mean for listening to Reverend Justus drone on?" Belle studied her, as if assessing whether her remark had shocked Sophie.

Sophie giggled. "He was rather full of himself, wasn't he?"

Belle grinned in response. "Whoever heard of A-ron?

I nearly laughed aloud every time he came to the name Aaron."

"It's a relief to know that with you, I can occasionally be irreverent—in the nicest sense, of course."

"I was certain I'd like you the minute I set eyes on you." Belle pointed at Sophie with her fork. "Here's my question. I know we still have the chance of a late snow or two, but how soon will you be ready to go hiking?"

Sophie shivered, not from the cold, but from delight. "Whenever you say."

"If we begin with easy treks, the weather shouldn't be a problem. We can't start too soon to get ourselves ready for the big one."

"Longs Peak," Sophie said, awed by the mere idea of standing on the summit.

"Longs Peak," Belle echoed, holding out her hand to seal the deal.

After making her farewells, Sophie set out for home under a sunny sky. As Ranger trotted along, she counted her blessings. Joe Harper had assured her his store could provide her with milk and eggs, as well as other food and goods.

Lost in plans for the coming days, Sophie failed to see the two boys until she was right beside them. They stood on a wooden bridge throwing rocks into the icy, rushing river. One was thin and dark-haired, while the younger one was rosy-cheeked and chubbier. She deliberated whether she should stop. What if either of them slipped? She drew to a halt and dismounted. Yelling over the noise of the water, she approached them. "Are you two all right?"

The older one shrugged with indifference and threw another rock. The younger one turned toward her eagerly. "We're seeing which of us can throw the farthest. Who are you?"

"I'm Sophie Montgomery. I just moved here from Kansas."

"Where's Kansas?" the talkative one asked.

"The next state east, dummy," his brother said.

"Perhaps you'll study Kansas in your geography lesson," Sophie suggested.

"Lessons? We don't have lessons, except when Papa helps us," the older one said with a frown. "And that's not often enough for me."

"Who is your papa?"

The little one gestured toward the handsome house on the hill. "Tate Lockwood," he said. "I'm Toby."

Sophie extended her hand. "Glad to meet you, sir." She faced the other boy. "And you?"

"Marcus," he said, turning away to study the distant mountains.

"I know your father. He escorted me here from Denver."

Toby looked at her with interest. "Where do you live?"

"A mile or so beyond here in an old cabin."

"Can I come visit?" Toby asked. His brother rolled his eyes.

"Certainly. In fact, I'd enjoy it if you both came. I have a new dog I'd like for you to meet."

"I'll ask Papa." Toby wriggled with delight.

"He won't let us," Marcus said.

"Why ever not?" *Did Tate keep these boys under lock and key?*

"He's too busy to bring us."

Sophie pondered her next move. Her invitation had been rashly extended. On second thought, she had no business insinuating herself into the lives of Tate Lockwood's sons. Yet each in his own way seemed starved for attention. Tate might be more amenable if she visited the boys' home. "Tell you what. If it's nice weather on Wednesday, why don't I bring Beauty and come see you. Be sure to tell your father. If it's inconvenient, maybe he could get word to me."

"He won't care," Marcus said in a tone that broke Sophie's heart. "He'll probably be glad to get us out of the way so he can work."

So that's the way it is. Sophie laid a hand on Marcus's shoulder. "Busy fathers don't have much time to play. But I do. I'll plan to come just after lunch."

"Whenever."

"Yippee!"

After suggesting the boys continue their game on dry land and satisfying herself that they would do so, Sophie headed toward her cabin. Maybe it was missing her nieces and nephews, or the sadness in Tate Lockwood's eyes he tried so desperately to conceal when he spoke of his motherless sons, or her own need for company, but she found herself looking forward to Wednesday. At the very least, these boys were hungry for approval and affection, something it was perhaps in her power to provide.

Her thoughts turned to their father. What would it do to a man to be spurned by his wife? To have full responsibility for two children? It was little wonder he had been reluctant to make any promises concerning their new friendship. One woman had wrecked his family and crushed his heart. Why should he welcome another in any capacity? She groaned. She'd promised those needy children a visit without considering Tate's possible reaction. Would he regard her visit as kindness or interference? Only time would tell.

Chapter Four

The following day Sophie awakened to fresh snow blanketing the ground. Fortunately, by Wednesday the road had thawed enough for her to set out to visit Marcus and Toby. Ranger kept up a steady pace with Beauty following happily behind, although she frequently darted into the trees in search of adventure. This was Sophie's first experience of the spectacle of a linen-white valley stretching as far as the eye could see, surmounted by mountains piercing the vivid blue sky with their icy fingers. It was as if she were riding through a crystal fairyland.

It was only when she crossed the river and started up the road to Tate's home that her nerves began to jangle. He might perceive her visit to the boys as not only presumptuous, but unwelcome. Too late for second thoughts. She reached the hitching post, slid to the ground and tethered Ranger. Beauty followed her onto the porch and sat obediently until, after a deep breath, Sophie knocked. Hardly had she lifted her fist than the door swung open. Toby, atremble with excitement, stood beside a plump, pleasant-looking woman of indeterminate age. "You came!" he cried.

Sophie smiled. "We did. And here is Beauty as promised." Toby leaned over and began talking softly to the dog. Sophie turned to the woman. "I'm Sophie Montgomery. I hope the boys told you I was coming."

The woman reached for Sophie's coat. "Indeed, they did. I'm Bertie Wilson, Mr. Lockwood's housekeeper. Toby has been watching out the window for you."

Sophie scanned the room, searching for Marcus. "The boys expressed interest in my new dog."

Both women turned to observe Toby, who had led Beauty to the hearth and now sat on the floor beside her, one arm draped around the dog's neck. "That friendship didn't take long to develop," Bertie whispered.

"I'm not surprised. Toby seems to be an outgoing little boy."

"A treasure, that one," Bertie agreed. "Now, Marcus...there's another story."

"Where is he?"

"Reading in his room. He's one to stick to himself. Let me hang up your coat and then I'll call him. I have some cookies and tea prepared for your visit."

While she waited for Marcus, Sophie studied the room. A magnificent mountain sheep head was mounted over the stone fireplace. The furniture looked hand-hewn from local trees, and colorful woven cushions covered the settee and armchairs. A long, low table of polished wood sat in front of the settee. On top was a wicker basket of oversize pinecones, a stack of newspapers and a checkerboard. Off in an alcove was a library table and a tall bookcase filled with books and curious artifacts, among them a large geode, a polished piece of petrified wood and a bird's nest. Not wanting to interrupt Toby's bonding with Beauty, she moved to the bookcase and studied the titles on the spines: *Gulliver's Travels*, *The*

Complete Works of William Shakespeare, several volumes of Pliny's *Natural History*, Darwin's *The Origin of Species, Robinson Crusoe* and—

"The boys told me to expect you."

Sophie wheeled around to face Tate Lockwood, who stood in the doorway holding a ledger book, his face revealing nothing about his reaction to her presence. "I hope this is not an intrusion," she said.

"It's no bother for the boys."

Sophie cringed. What was unsaid hung in the air—*but it is for me.* "I promised them they could meet Beauty—" she nodded toward the dog "—and it seemed easier for me to come here than for them to come to me."

Before he could answer, Toby bounded over to his father, Beauty close behind wagging her tail enthusiastically. "Papa, see? Isn't she a great dog?"

Tate eyed Sophie briefly before kneeling in front of his son. "Yes, Toby. She looks as if she has some shepherd in her."

"Shepherds help drive sheep," Toby explained, as if he were a canine authority. "Maybe we could get a dog, right, Papa?"

Sophie watched Tate's shoulders slump as if the same thought going through her mind had just occurred to him. *Why didn't the boys already have a dog?*

"We'll see."

"See what?" Marcus had entered the room and stood observing the scene.

Toby clapped his little hands. "Marcus, wanna get a dog?"

"I didn't say yes," Tate mumbled as he rose to his feet.

"But you will!" There was no denying Toby. "We could call him Buster."

"That's a dumb name," Marcus said, maintaining his distance.

Sophie, sensing tension, turned to the boy. "What's a better name?"

"Well," the boy drawled, inching closer and eyeing Beauty, "something more original like...Seaman, Meriwether Lewis's dog who explored the Missouri, or Bacchus, the Greek god of fun, or—"

"Nobody said there would be a dog to name," Tate interjected.

"But nobody said there wouldn't be," Sophie argued before she could censor herself.

Once more Tate eyed her expressionlessly. "True."

Thankfully, at that moment Bertie Wilson entered the room with a large tray. Toby ran toward the dining table at the other end of the room near the kitchen where she was laying out the food, but Marcus couldn't move. Beauty had wrapped herself around his legs and was looking up at him adoringly. Slowly Marcus sank to his knees so the dog could lick his face. "You're tickling," the boy said and then giggled. It was one of the most welcome sounds Sophie had ever heard. She reckoned this was a boy for whom giggles were few and far between.

The sweet hot tea and spicy homemade ginger cookies were welcome after her cold ride. "You have a lovely home, Tate."

"We like it."

"Papa built it and Marcus and me got to pick our bedrooms."

"I especially like the bookcase. You have quite a collection here."

Marcus turned to her with a curious expression. "Do you like to read?"

"Indeed I do."

"Good," the boy said before filling his mouth with another cookie.

"You are welcome to borrow some volumes," Tate offered.

"Thank you. I may well do that once I get more settled."

Sophie turned the topic to her upcoming hike with Belle Harper, but throughout the rest of their conversation, she had the uncomfortable feeling that Tate was sizing her up.

"Can you play with us?" Toby asked, interrupting the adult conversation.

Sophie smiled. "I suppose I could."

"C'mon, then." He fetched her coat and dragged it over to her. "Outside. I like tag. And Beauty can play, too."

"It's nearly time for us to go home, but a bit of outdoor exercise will do us good." Surprisingly, without a word Marcus, too, put on his coat and followed them outside. Sophie paused in the door and looked back. "Tate?"

"Not today."

The sun was high in the afternoon sky and the air, crisp and fragrant. It was difficult to play tag with only three people plus Beauty, so Sophie introduced them to Follow the Leader. Then just before she left, she asked if they'd ever made snow angels. Their blank stares said it all. Throwing discretion to the winds, she lay down atop the snow and moved her arms and legs. When she stood up, she turned to the boys. "Now, then, what does that look like?"

"An angel," they said in unison.

"Your turn."

Sophie stood over them, reveling in their delight. "I'm making huge wings," Marcus said, while Toby giggled with the effort of moving his arms and legs simultaneously. Then they stood up and began pelting one another with snowballs, between fits of laughter.

Sensing a presence behind her, Sophie turned to face the house. Before a curtain slipped back into place, she had a glimpse of Tate. He'd been watching them. She wondered what had prevented him from joining them. Or didn't he ever play? No use wasting time thinking about such things. The man was a mystery.

Tate couldn't believe his eyes. Marcus was nearly cavorting, Beauty trailed Toby's every step and Sophie Montgomery, why, she might as well have been a child herself. She joined the boys' play with abandon, her cheeks pink from the cold, her red-gold hair escaping her stocking cap and her laughter audible even through the pane of glass. Now accompanied by Beauty and the boys, she approached her horse. He couldn't hear what she was saying to his sons as she bent close to them, one arm around Toby and the other around Marcus. Marcus, who rarely let anyone touch him. Whatever she'd said, each nodded seriously in reply.

Tate turned back to his desk. Why hadn't he joined them? Was he too good for Follow the Leader, or had he feared making a fool of himself in front of the maddening Sophie? Sophie, who in less than two hours had captivated his boys.

He'd barely sat down to pore over his papers when Toby burst into the room without knocking. The rebuke for the intrusion died on Tate's lips when he saw how animated his son was.

"Papa, Papa. Marcus and I discussed. He told me to ask you."

"Ask me what?" Over Toby's head, Tate spotted Marcus lurking outside the door.

"'Bout the dog," Toby said, approaching him and laying a small hand on his knee. "If we had a dog, we'd be real 'sponsible. We'd feed it and give it water and take it for walks and—"

Before Toby could gather more steam, Tate interjected. "Animals require a great deal of care. Not just for a day or a week. Always."

"Always," Toby intoned, his blue eyes, so like his mother's, fixed on him. "We promise."

"Marcus?"

The boy slunk into the room, not daring to look at him. The concern that so often occupied Tate's thoughts returned in force. Was his own son afraid of him? Indifferent to him? Angry? Clearing his throat and knowing there was no argument to be made, Tate said, "Both of you are committed to caring for a dog?"

"Yes!" shouted Toby, while Marcus nodded.

"Well, then, I think what we should do—" he paused, prolonging the suspense "—is ask around the valley whether anyone knows of available pups."

Toby clambered into Tate's lap and captured his face between his hands. "Really?"

"Yes, really."

Marcus took a step forward. "Thank you, sir," he mumbled before leaving the room.

"I don't care what Marcus says. Buster is a good name."

Tate groaned. Solving one problem had created another. He knew there was only one solution. Two dogs. But if that would please Toby and somehow bring a smile to his older son's face, no price was too high to pay. Perhaps allowing them pets would in a small way compensate for the frequency of his business trips. "Buster, huh? We'll see. Now run along like a good boy. Papa has work to do."

The boy slid to the floor. "Beauty is a good dog. Betcha mine will be, too. I'm glad Miss Sophie came to visit."

Tate started to say, "I am, too," but was he really? "It was good of her."

"We had lotsa fun," Toby said as he skipped out the door. "Maybe she'll come again."

He should've thought of getting the boys dogs when they first moved to Estes Park. Ramona preferred cats and wouldn't have let a dog anywhere near her. Was he so out of touch with his own childhood that he couldn't remember how much he'd loved his short-haired mongrel, Buck? How he could tell Buck his worries and secrets and feel relief from the understanding canine eyes studying him solemnly. Growing up, Buck was his steadfast companion in a home too elegant for romping, where his distant, self-involved parents paraded their son before their friends as if he were a prize show animal. Buck and books—his two forms of salvation.

Vowing to procure the dogs soon, he studied the map of the valley on his desk. The Englishman Lord Dunraven had set his agent the task of buying up the entire valley for a private hunting preserve and recreational site. Some of the settlers, overwhelmed by the struggle to make ends meet or weary of mountain living, had succumbed to the lure of easy money. Others, like Tate, had resisted Dunraven's attempt to turn the valley into a rich man's playground and had refused to sell. As they were able, Tate and his like-minded friends had bought up additional available land, both as a buffer against Dunraven's encroachment and as an investment. Beyond any economic advantage, this was a natural paradise that ought to be accessible to all, not restricted to the narrow pleasures of the indulgent few. Tate fumed just thinking about how close the residents had come to losing their piece of heaven. Fortunately, Dunraven seemed to have lost interest in the project, but not before he'd built a grand hotel to appeal to wealthy, adventurous Easterners and fellow Englishmen.

Tate had recently located another parcel of available land. Looking at the map, he considered its access to water and decided to explore it prior to making a bid. It lay a short distance beyond Sophie's cabin. He'd heard about the help his neighbors had given her and thought it only decent, in light of his connection to the Hurlburts, to stop by to check on her after examining the acreage.

Oh, right. Blame it on duty. He stepped to the window. There in the fading sun, three angels lay in the snow, one slightly, but only slightly, bigger than the other two. Sophie's angel. Sophie, who laughed pure melody and brought his sons to life. Sophie, whose mere presence scared him for reasons he was unwilling to address.

By Friday afternoon most of the snow had melted and an unseasonably warm wind soughed through the pine branches. Sophie took the occasion to move two old rockers she'd found in the barn to the front porch. After regluing a couple of joints and sanding the chairs, she was now in the process of painting them white. She wore her brown wool breeches, a long, plaid flannel shirt and a sheepskin vest. She'd tied back her hair with an old bandanna kerchief. She saw no point in prettify-

ing herself every day. Except for Grizzly and the Tyler-
Harper work crew, she might as well be on the dark side
of the moon, and dresses were not the most practical
garb for the hard work of getting settled in her place.

While Beauty lounged on the porch steps, Sophie
daubed paint and sang "Amazing Grace" as she worked.
After finishing with the first chair, she sat back on her
heels and wiped her brow. There was something satisfying about seeing results from her efforts. With that
thought, though, came a sadder one, prompted by the
hymn she'd been singing. Without Charlie, she, too,
needed to be found and restored through grace. Although the sharp, physical pang of grief hit her less
often than it once had, there were times when Charlie
seemed so present with her that she felt as if she could
reach out and touch him. Like now. Sophie dabbed at
the tears forming in her eyes. She gazed at the mountains, vibrant in the afternoon sun. *Charlie, dear, are
you someplace that is as wonderful for you as this is
for me? I hope so.*

She shook her head, knowing that following Charlie
into the maze of her emotions was not helpful. He was
gone. Not that she would ever forget him, but it was time
to move on, time to be thankful she had once known
love and to carve a new identity for herself here. Now.
She picked up the paintbrush and bent to her task with
renewed vigor. So intent was she on her work that she
failed to hear the hoofbeats until horse and rider were
nearly to her yard. Looking up, she was surprised to see
Tate Lockwood dismounting and then mortified that he
would find her in her tomboy getup. There was nothing to do but stand up and extend her hand. "Tate." He
stood in front of her, his face impassive. "Forgive my
appearance. I was not expecting visitors."

He held her hand while she squirmed under his slow examination. For a moment, she thought he might be about to laugh. But he didn't. "I thought I'd stop by to see your progress on the cabin. Nice chairs," he said, turning to survey her handiwork.

"I expect to spend a great amount of time out here this summer, that is, when I'm not in the mountains. Belle Harper and I have grand adventures planned."

He studied her closely. "Not…"

"Yes, Longs Peak, our ultimate ambition."

"I know you're not short on determination, but that's a feat rarely performed even by the hardiest of men."

"Granted." She set down the paintbrush before adding, "Notwithstanding my appearance today, Belle and I are not men."

"You certainly are not," he said with what could be construed as a glimmer of appreciation.

"Pardon my manners. Please do come in and have a cup of tea and a slice of the pound cake I made this morning."

"Don't mind if I do."

While she busied herself at the stove, putting on the kettle for tea, she was aware of his scrutiny of the cabin's interior. "Quite a transformation. It's downright habitable."

"I owe much of my progress to the Tylers and Harpers. They were a huge help."

"Most of the valley folk are good that way."

"But not all?" She set them each a plate of cake on the table, then turned back to check the kettle.

He straddled a chair and sat down. "Not all. For a time Lord Dunraven's agent was intent on buying up the valley and forcing out the settlers."

"Dear me." Sophie took a seat across from him. "I

had heard of Lord Dunraven's presence and the establishment of his hotel and hunting preserve, of course, but I had no idea his ambition was so pervasive."

"It was. However, it seems to be dissipating in recent months. Perhaps he's lost interest in his toy."

"The hotel may well be a good addition to the area, but riding roughshod over the settlers? I can't abide that."

"All the more reason for some of the rest of us to buy up land he may have his eye on. It's not just an aesthetic matter. It also involves water and grazing rights. In fact, I have just come from looking over some land I intend to purchase. Being so close, I figured I'd check on how you're doing."

"I'm thriving. The next project is planting flowers and vegetables."

"In between your mountaineering and gardening, I hope you'll have time for this." He reached in his pocket and withdrew a leather-bound volume. "It's *The American* by a new writer named Henry James. I would like to know what you think of it."

Dare she hope that in this remote place Tate Lockwood might be someone with whom she could discuss literature? "How thoughtful of you. I shall devour it with interest. Thank you." She leafed through the book, then turned to Tate. "Your Marcus seems to be quite a bookworm."

"He is. Prying him out of the house is difficult. However, you managed nicely on Wednesday."

There was an odd note in his tone, almost as if he begrudged her the time playing with the boys in the snow. "It took a few minutes, but Marcus eventually seemed to enjoy himself. With Toby, of course, there's no problem. He was born to play." She chuckled. "And I forgot I'm a grown woman. Snow angels, for goodness' sake."

He took a sip of the tea Sophie had poured him. "I scarcely know what to do with them."

"Perhaps the best advice I can offer is for you to remember your own boyhood—what you liked to do, what your passions were…"

"I had two and two only. Books and my dog."

Again she sensed bitterness in his voice. "There you are. That's a fine start. Marcus loves to read and Toby enjoys animals."

"Speaking of which, you were right to advocate for the dogs."

"The dogs?"

"Yes. I imagine you wondered why the boys didn't already have one."

She blushed. "I did. I'm sorry if I created a problem for you."

"Actually, you solved it. Tomorrow I'm taking the boys to visit a family with a litter of collie pups."

"That's wonderful."

"But one pup won't do. If the boys can't even agree on a name, I figure we need two dogs."

"Brilliant. It might be hard for Toby to share 'Buster' with Marcus. What does he want to call his? Aeschylus?" Then the man actually laughed. The sound filled the room and penetrated her heart. "Would it be presumptuous to ask if I might call again sometime in the next week or so to meet these two canine wonders?"

"The boys will insist on it."

"I'll look forward to coming, perhaps on Wednesday again."

Tate swigged down the rest of his tea, then stood. Sophie rose, as well. A sudden awkward silence hung between them. "I appreciate your coming by," she said just as he uttered a thank-you for the tea and cake. He added, "I hope I didn't disturb you."

"Not at all." She trailed him to the door.

He clapped his hat on his head before pausing on her porch. "Beautiful view."

"It inspires me."

"It has that power." He faced her. "Good day, Sophie. I'll tell the boys to expect you Wednesday." He made his way down the steps and mounted his horse.

She waited as he paused for a moment, studying her before finally lifting his hand, and then riding off toward home.

She looked down at herself. A paint splotch covered one knee and the bandanna had slipped back on her head. She was a fright. A tomboy spectacle serving tea to a gentleman. What must Tate think of her? She bore little resemblance to the well-bred women he was accustomed to in the East, but at least she hoped she would never prove as faithless as his ex-wife.

Another thought stopped her in her tracks. Why should she care?

Sophie Montgomery was the most puzzling woman he had ever encountered, Tate thought as he galloped toward home. Highly intelligent and spirited, she nevertheless had little appreciation for propriety or decorum. There she stood, her face smudged with paint, sawdust covering her shirt, and her hair pulled back with a bandanna that looked as if it had survived several buffalo hunts, and wearing—of all things—breeches. It was one thing for her to wear bloomers beneath her skirt on the grueling journey up from Denver, but quite another for her to wear trousers as a matter of course. Yet he suspected that scandalizing the neighbors—or him—was the farthest thing from her mind.

Recalling his first sight of her today, he chuckled. He'd stifled his laughter when he came up on the porch to greet her. Momentarily, she'd seemed oblivious to her unseemly attire. Then her expression had changed as embarrassment swept over her. She was not a woman whose face concealed her thoughts. Rather than the artificial coquettishness of most women, she seemed not to care about others' opinions of her. Open and honest, she lived in the moment.

Wednesday. The boys would be excited about her visit. At least Toby would. Who knew what excited Marcus, if anything? Tate hoped the acquisition of his own dog would help bring his older son out of the gray place to which he'd retreated ever since Ramona had packed up and left. It was hard not to pin his hopes on the unsuspecting canine. Or on Sophie or anyone else who could move the boy. Rejection, rather than affection, characterized his son's behavior toward him. He'd tried to be understanding. How hurt Marcus must've been by his mother.

Sadly, Marcus reminded him far too much of himself. In the mansion of his boyhood, Tate had been more decorative than cherished, more rejected than loved, and starved, not for rich food, but for normalcy. Books taught him about others and the world, and Buck schooled him about acceptance and love. He wanted more, much more, for Marcus.

He shouldn't pin his hopes on others, but he prayed the tutor would arrive soon. Surely the young man could appeal to Marcus and engage his considerable intellect, while at the same time helping Toby become more disciplined in his studies. Tate slowed to a trot, recognizing his own shortcomings. Nothing in his past had prepared him for being a model father to his sons, yet he had no more sacred obligation.

Chapter Five

"So what do you think?" Belle Harper sprawled atop a boulder the size of a small building Saturday afternoon.

Sophie leaned back, propped on her arms with her legs dangling from the rocky ledge, and laughed aloud. "It's magnificent." The endless sky stretched in cerulean splendor above the distant snowy peaks. Pure air filled her lungs, and she felt alive in a way she hadn't in a very long time.

"You didn't do badly for your first hike. Not as much huffing and puffing as some, but then, you've had time to acclimate to the altitude."

"How high are we now?"

"About ten thousand feet." Belle gestured toward Longs Peak. "That's over fourteen thousand, and I'm told the last two thousand feet are treacherous. Above the tree line, boulders abound, so some difficult rock climbing is involved. It's by no means impossible for women to reach the summit, although men try to dissuade the 'fairer sex' from the attempt. Yet a couple of our sisters have achieved the feat. I want us to join their number."

"I'm game, although I'll need considerably more experience. When might we attempt the ascent?"

"Depending on your conditioning, I'm guessing early- to mid-September. Weather is a factor. Early snow would knock us out."

"Some will deem us crazy to attempt it."

Belle shoved back her hat and turned to study Sophie. "What do you think?"

The prospect was fraught with uncertainty and danger, but Sophie didn't hesitate. "It would be the most exciting, exhilarating thing I've ever done."

"Let others doubt or mock us. That will just fuel our determination." Belle opened her canteen and took a sip. "Once or twice a week, then, we'll tackle the mountains. Flattop Peak is next."

"I'd welcome the challenge." As she uttered the words, Sophie understood why she was so open to Belle's direction. On today's hike, there had been long minutes when her mind was so focused on the trail she hadn't once thought about Charlie. Yet paradoxically, now touching the pockmarked surface of the rock beneath her fingers, she felt as if she were that much closer to heaven, closer to Charlie.

"Ready to start back?"

Sophie levered herself to her feet. Beyond lay the valley floor, dotted with small settlements. In the distance, the imposing lodge of Lord Dunraven reminded her of Tate's concern for preserving the area. He was right. Such a beautiful place was not meant to be the province of a single individual. She shivered with excitement, knowing how much she wanted to be part of Estes Park's future. She spread her arms as if to encompass the valley. "Look, Belle. Is there any better place on earth?"

"Not in my mind."

Trailing Belle down the mountain, she concentrated on noticing each smell—juniper, pine, spruce—and each animal—the chattering chipmunk, a soaring eagle, the lone doe poised by a small pool. Before she knew it, she was singing to herself and considering the hymn's lyrics.

All things bright and beautiful,
All creatures great and small,
All things wise and wonderful,
The Lord God made them all.

Could it be that here in this mountain paradise she could regain her unquestioning faith? What would Charlie want for her? There was really no question. She knew that difficult and painful though it was, he would want her to embrace life, to climb out of the valley of her gloom and ascend to unknown heights.

What in the world had he done? Any serenity Tate had known within his home had vanished with the arrival of two rambunctious pups. Toby's Buster skittered through the house nipping at his master's legs and yipping excitedly, only quieting when he fell, exhausted, into the dog bed the boys had made of old blankets. Marcus's female was only minimally more sedate and thankfully felt no need to establish supremacy over her brother. When Tate asked Marcus what he'd decided to name his collie, his son had shrugged and said, "These things can't be rushed. The name *has* to be right. In many cultures, a name has great significance, you know."

Tate stood at the window of his office, aware he

should be working instead of watching the road for Sophie Montgomery. Marcus had seemed more light-hearted than usual this morning, and Toby had dogged Bertie about the refreshments before retiring to the back porch to brush Buster's lush coat. Granted, the boys had few visitors, but was Sophie that much of a novelty? Occasionally they attended community suppers, which afforded Marcus and Toby the opportunity to mingle with others their age. Toby knew no strangers, while Marcus tended to stand on the sidelines until another boy made an overture. Had Marcus always been so shy and reserved? Tate cast his mind back. Although quiet, he'd also been a thoughtful, charming little boy. Sensitive. Therein lay the problem, no doubt. Marcus had reacted far more viscerally to Ramona's disappearance than had Toby, who tended to live in the present, while Marcus brooded on the past. Tate shook his head in disgust. He, who could open mines, negotiate with bankers and parlay minerals into wealth, was helpless to deal with his own troubled son.

A flash of color caught his eye. Sophie rode up the road, her red jacket clashing with her copper curls. She sat easily, clearly long accustomed to riding. Living on a ranch had obviously equipped her for pursuits many women disdained. Ramona. Yes, disdain would've been her reaction to someone like Sophie. He hated it when his thoughts conjured his ex-wife from his subconscious. She was out of his life, and he had to move on.

He straightened his suspenders and put on his coat before walking to the front door, where Toby already waited with a grin on his face, Buster right behind him. Even Marcus had closed the book he was reading and stood by the fireplace, his expression expectant, if guarded.

Before she could knock, Tate opened the door to Sophie, who entered with a smile, pulling off her gloves. "What a beautiful day!" she exclaimed, but before she could go on, Toby scooped up his dog and held it out to her. "See, miss? It's Buster."

Tate started to admonish the boy for speaking up before Sophie had even removed her jacket, but she winked and he fell silent. "Oh, Toby, he's adorable. May I hold him?"

Tate helped her out of her jacket as she balanced the puppy against her chest, cooing softly to the animal. "Aren't you a sturdy little fellow? A 'Buster,' indeed."

Toby peeked around the door. "Where's Beauty?"

Sophie smiled. "At home. I wanted your pups to be the center of attention." She entered the living room and nodded at Marcus. "And what of your dog?"

"Sleeping. I'll get her in a minute."

"Have you named her?"

He clasped his hands nervously before answering softly. "I thought maybe you could help me." He swallowed and then went on. "It has to be just the right name."

"I understand. A name marks one forever."

"I like your name. *Sophie.* Are you wise?"

She laughed. "Not always. It's a difficult name to live up to, but I try."

Tate watched their exchange. Sophie had somehow gained enough of the boy's confidence for him to trust her to offer suggestions for his dog's name.

Toby pulled on Sophie's skirt. "Wanna play checkers?"

Marcus looked menacingly at his brother. "We're gonna name my dog."

Tate stepped forward. "Before that, wouldn't it be courteous to invite our guest to sit down?"

"Please sit," Marcus mumbled.

"Here's a chair," Toby offered.

Sophie sent Tate an amused glance before moving to the chair and sitting, still clutching Buster. "Thank you, gentlemen."

"Gentlemen. She called us 'gentlemen.'" Toby giggled.

Bertie entered the room with a tray laden with a plate of cookies, cups and a teapot, and milk for the boys. "Good afternoon, Miss Sophie. I hope you favor sugar cookies."

"I do, indeed."

When they were sitting down with their refreshments, Tate found himself at a loss for words. What could he possibly talk about with her? Did it matter? She was here for the boys.

She settled her cup in her lap and turned to him. "I've been reading in the Denver papers, just delivered, about silver discoveries west of here. That should lure even more settlers to Colorado, I should think."

"We've only seen the first of the influx. I'm in no position to complain about westward expansion since I myself have profited from leaving the East to make my own way."

"That can't have been easy."

"The hardest part was leaving my family behind, but mining camps are wild places, not fit for a lady." He caught himself before saying anything about Ramona.

Sophie covered the awkward silence. "It will be exciting to be part of Colorado's future."

Future? "Does that mean you're planning to stay? You haven't been here long nor have you endured a high country winter."

She smiled impishly. "Why, Mr. Lockwood, I do believe you are trying to discourage me."

"Not 'discourage,' but perhaps protect you from yourself."

"I appreciate the impulse and I'm not unacquainted with the dangers, but in just this short time, the mountains have worked their magic on me."

Magic? What was the woman thinking? It took much more than fairy dust to survive a brutal winter up there.

Marcus had slipped out while they were talking and now returned with his yawning brown-and-white dog. "Here." Marcus held out the pup. Sophie set down her cup on a side table and embraced the animal, who promptly licked her face.

"What a charmer," she said.

Marcus blushed. Toby and Buster drew near and sat at Sophie's feet. "Are you finished with your cookies? Tell me when to set up the checkerboard."

Marcus bristled, and Tate knew it was time to intervene. "Toby, let's you and me play a few games and give Sophie and Marcus time to discuss names."

Sophie shot him a grateful smile. "Marcus, why don't we sit at the library table by the bookshelves? We might need to do some research before you feel right about what to call your dog."

Tate concentrated on the checkers while also trying to eavesdrop on Sophie and Marcus's conversation.

"I don't want a boring name like Queenie or Lady."

"How do you feel about historical or literary names?"

"Like what?"

Toby jumped Tate's black marker and muttered, "Pay attention, Papa."

He was paying attention, all right, but not to the game.

"Well, there are historical names like Cleopatra, Betsy Ross—"

"No. What do you mean literary names?"

"Perhaps from Greek mythology or Shakespeare."

Toby kicked Tate under the table. "Please, Papa."

"Oh, you mean like Athena and Juno or Juliet?"

"Exactly."

"It's your turn." Tate made a move and then strained for his older son's voice.

"Wait! I have an idea, Miss Sophie. Your name means *wisdom*, right? I want my dog to be wise, too." His brow furrowed in concentration. "What about Minerva?"

"Minerva is a strong name. You could call her Minnie sometimes if you'd like."

"Minnie…" The boy seemed to be testing the word. "Yes. I like it." He shoved his chair back and carried the puppy to his brother and father. "My collie has a special name, the same as the Roman goddess of wisdom. Minerva." The pup in his arms looked up at him and seemed to nod her head.

"A fitting name for such a fine animal," Tate said.

"Minerva! That's not as good as Buster," Toby announced.

"It's not a competition." Sophie moved to Marcus's side and laid a hand on his shoulder. "Each dog is unique and deserves a unique name."

With that one statement, Sophie calmed the boys and secured peace. After that, she played two checkers games with Toby and two with Marcus. Tate chuckled to himself watching them vie for her attention. Sooner than he liked she announced her departure.

"Are you gonna come again?" Toby asked as she donned her jacket.

"When I receive an invitation," she said.

Tate hesitated, his stomach in a knot. Courtesy suggested he should follow up on that remark. He couldn't.

It would never do for her to become a fixture in his sons' lives. He was grateful for the time she'd given them, but there was too much likelihood of hurt if they became overly attached to her.

Yet after she'd left, Toby sulked by the fireplace, desultorily stroking Buster. Marcus, cradling Minnie, hunched over a book on mythology he'd extracted from the shelf. With a restlessness he was unable to tame, Tate paced the room until finally he grabbed his coat and hat and headed for the barn, where he hoped lulling sounds and familiar, earthy odors would quiet his racing heart.

When she entered her cabin later that afternoon, Sophie was greeted by a delighted Beauty as well as by the enticing aroma of the ham and beans she'd left simmering in the Dutch oven before visiting the Lockwoods. After checking the fire pit, she brought in fresh wood before removing her hat and jacket. Even though the weather was still wintry for May, she'd found the ride home invigorating and had worked up a healthy appetite. As the renewed fire warmed the room, she washed her hands and was preparing to dish up some supper when Beauty bristled and stalked to the door, where she stood on guard. "What's the matter, Beauty?"

When the dog didn't stir, Sophie moved stealthily to the loaded rifle. She would not make the mistake again of opening the door without knowledge of her caller's identity. Leaning against the door, she called out, "Who's there?" just as a voice boomed, "Open up, missy. It's me. Grizzly."

Limp with relief, she opened the door. "Please come in."

Looking more like his namesake bear than a man,

Grizzly entered with his dog, Sarge, and stood eyeing the weapon in her hands. "Good fer you, missy. Can't get too comfortable here." Then he turned his gaze to the stove. "Smells like I'm just in time for dinner." Without waiting for an invitation, he continued, "Don't mind if I do."

Behind them the two dogs circled each other, made a few playful nips and then settled happily in front of the hearth. "See you've got yerself a partner."

"Her name's Beauty and she's a great companion."

"No substitute for a red-blooded man, I'll wager," he said with a mischievous wink.

"I had one of those, and one was enough."

He tossed his bearskin hat on the table. "Don't quite know how to take that, missy. One was enough to spook you forever or you had one so good he put anyone else to shame?"

In that moment Sophie found she had a need to talk about Charlie, and in a peculiar way, she knew Grizzly was discreet. "I'll dish us up some ham and beans and tell you about my Charlie. Will you be able to stay the night?"

"If it's all right with you, in the barn." He removed his heavy coat, withdrew a packet from one pocket and then threw the garment over a chair. "I stopped by the Harpers' place and picked up some mail. Here." He thrust the bundle into her hands. Spontaneous tears filled her eyes as she recognized her father's spidery hand and Lily's graceful one. It was all she could do to set the correspondence aside and concentrate on Grizzly. These were her first letters from home. She mentally corrected herself. This was now home—that other place was Kansas.

"How does the mail work up here? I've written some letters, but need to learn about posting them."

"Lucky I stopped by, then." He sat down and pulled closer to the table. While she served the piping-hot bowls, he explained. "Those who regularly make trips down to Denver or Longmont take the mail and then fetch parcels and mail back to Harpers'. Joe sorts it and holds it until it's either picked up or until someone passing by can deliver it."

"So I should give you the letters I've written?"

"Best to deliver them to Harper, maybe when you next go to church."

"I rue the time delay on sending or receiving the post."

"One price of livin' in God's country." He took his first spoonful, nodded approvingly and said, "Now, girl. Tell me about this Charlie."

As she explained to Grizzly how they had met, how deliriously happy they'd been and how talented and ambitious Charlie was, she found that speaking aloud about him to another was liberating. So long as she could share their special times, her memories were fresh and comforting—proof that her love for him and his for her was enduring.

"And then what happened?" Grizzly demanded, wiping his unkempt beard with his napkin. "Don't reckon he left you to fend fer yourself in this wild place."

"If only," Sophie said, her eyes focused on a piece of ham swimming in the broth. "At least then he'd still be alive."

Grizzly laid down his spoon and reached for her hand. His warm, rough skin was oddly soothing. "Tell me about it?"

As if floodgates had been breached, the details tumbled out, accompanied by tears she was helpless to stem.

When she finished, he squeezed her hand and shook his head. "Heap of tragedy there. Loneliness, too, I 'spect."

"Unbearable," she added softly, wiping her wet cheeks with her apron. "That's why I said I'd already had one red-blooded man. He was a blessing from God. I don't ask for more."

Grizzly leaned back in his chair and crossed his arms over his chest. "You don't strike me as a quitter or you wouldn't be here."

"Life doesn't stop just because the heart has been ripped out of a person. I had no choice but to live. Otherwise, I would dishonor Charlie's memory."

"Or he'd haunt you from the grave," Grizzly said with a chuckle. They fell silent, and Sophie struggled to swallow the last of her ham and beans. Sometimes it did seem as if Charlie was…not haunting her but… abiding in her presence. Like right now. He would've liked Grizzly and quizzed him about his knowledge of the mountains.

She folded her napkin and was about to rise from the table when Grizzly's next words stopped her. "I think you're selling your God short, girlie."

"Whatever do you mean?"

"I ain't much fer churchgoin', but the Big Fella is a bountiful God. Think of all He created, how generous He was. While there's a powerful lot of wailing and gnashing of teeth in the Good Book, there's hope and promise and love abundant. My God isn't gonna set you here in this Eden and leave you alone. No, ma'am. He's no quitter. Now, your Charlie may have been a wonder of a sweetheart, all right, but I'm gonna be aprayin' for

him and the Lord to send you another man to love. Lord
knows, we all can use a heap o' lovin'."

"But I don't need—"

"You hush now and leave all this in God's hands. It
may not be about what you need, but about what you
have to give. Ever think of it like that?"

She stared at this hulking giant of a man, so filled
with kindness and so unlike any confidant she'd ever
had. Was he, too, a gift from God? "I've not always
been good about surrendering."

His laughter shook the walls. "Do tell," he finally
sputtered after gaining control of himself. "You just
wait. If there's one thing old Terence P. Griswold has
learned in his time on this earth, it's that life is full of
surprises. Yours'll come, mark my words." He got to
his feet, took his hat from the table and smiled down
at her. "Mighty fine supper, missy. Even better palaver.
I'll be long gone by sunup, but I surely appreciate you."
He winked. "And you can cook, too."

After he left, it was as if some of the air had been
sucked from the room, such was his energy. She pondered their conversation. Was she to believe God could
have more surprises in store for her? Grizzly had cred-
ited her with faith, a faith she didn't know whether she
could claim anymore.

With a lightening of spirit, she turned to the bundle
of letters Grizzly had delivered, untied the twine holding them together and arranged them in chronological
order, her fingers trembling with excitement. She recognized missives from her father, from both brothers
and their wives and from her nieces and nephews. A
treasure delivered by a disheveled mountain man. If
nothing else, God surely had a sense of humor.

Later, after banking the fire and changing into her

cozy flannel nightgown and wrapping up in a wool shawl, Sophie settled in the rocker near the hearth and by lantern light began to read the precious letters from her family, beginning with one from her father. His tall, scratchy hand, so familiar to her, recalled his patience as he tried to teach her her ABCs before sending her off to the one-room schoolhouse. Although she knew him as a man of few words, his words, when they came, were wise. This message was no exception.

Dearest daughter,
By now, I picture you settled in the mountains with fresh air cleansing your soul and invigorating your spirit. We are all grateful to the Hurlburts for their hospitality and relieved to know they are nearby should you require assistance. From the time you could walk, there was never any keeping you down. I think God created you to explore and embrace what life has to offer. This is how I deal with your absence—rejoicing instead of regretting. Although I imagine it may still be cool where you are, here the pastures are greening and the spring flowers blooming. Spring has always represented promise for me. I pray it does for you, as well. We eagerly await word from you and a description of your cabin, surroundings and new friends.
Always with prayers and love,
Your Pa

Sophie folded the letter carefully and held it for a moment to her heart. With what nobility and devotion he had cared for his family. How difficult it must have been for him—a widower with two small sons and an infant daughter. Yet never once had she seen evidence of frustration or resentment in his treatment of her brothers or her. Quite the contrary. As she looked back, she suspected his children were the glue that held him together after the loss of their mother.

Next she read a scrawled, smudged note from her adopted nephew Alf, followed by a few lines from his mother, Rose, with an enclosed recipe for venison stew. Then she picked up a letter from her brother Caleb and his wife, Lily. Caleb began with a detailed account of the cattle business in which they were all involved; and then Lily took over, telling about their children and Seth and Rose's. Sophie looked up, nearly overcome by nostalgia. In the family's loving words she could smell the lilac-laden breeze, hear the laughter of little ones playing hide-and-seek, taste Rose's famous cinnamon buns and feel the love that so characterized her Kansas family. It would have been easier perhaps for her to remain cocooned in the circle of their care, but she had known that such a course would ultimately paralyze and change her. No, she had needed to leave.

She glanced around her small cabin, fixing her eyes on those artifacts of home—the quilt, the photograph, Lily's sampler. Even though it had been the right decision to come here, just for a moment tears of homesickness prickled as she pictured each and every one of them—her father, Caleb, Lily, Mattie, little Harmony, Seth, Rose, Alf and Andy. Blinking, she opened the final letter bearing the most recent postmark, one from her brother Seth. She unfolded the single page and tried to take in his few but disturbing words.

Sister, our father has had a small stroke, but seems to be recovering. Doc Kellogg has recommended slowing down, but you know how stubborn Pa can be. We are all keeping an eye on him, so don't fret.

Sophie closed her eyes, trying to picture her vigorous father diminished. In her heart she knew the other family members would do all they could for his benefit, yet she couldn't suppress her initial reaction. She should be there. Once more she blinked back threatening tears. In her planning she had tried to prepare herself mentally for the fact that she would miss important family occasions or health issues, but nothing had prepared her for this blunt reality.

As if sensing her distress, Beauty rose from the hearthside, where she'd been sleeping, and came to Sophie, laying her head in her mistress's lap. That one comforting act provoked what Sophie had so valiantly been trying to restrain—a lonely sobbing that filled the room.

Now what was he supposed to do? Tate paced his office early Friday morning, frustration and helplessness fueling his movement. The solution upon which he had pinned his hopes had blown up in his face. Why couldn't people be counted upon to fulfill their obligations? He went to his desk and reread the offending letter.

The previous evening, exhausted from a ride to and from a meeting on the far side of the valley, he had not read his mail, picked up by his foreman, Sam. Only now had he opened the letter from Wallace Tolbert III, full of flowery language and evasions. Despite their flourishes, the man's words screamed cowardice. Once full of brave, idealistic promises, the young man had "reconsidered the generous offer to serve as tutor and companion" for Marcus and Toby. "Other opportunities of a more civilized nature" had presented themselves, so now Tate was once again faced with the dilemma of educating his sons. He threw the offending letter on the desk, cursing under his breath. He sat down, opened a desk drawer and withdrew several brochures from Eastern boarding schools. For the umpteenth time he studied them: "exceptional young men"; "a remarkable classical education"; "playing fields worthy of Eton." The claims swirled in his brain.

No doubt they were excellent schools. Faraway excellent schools. Parentless schools. He swiped the papers to the floor. No. He couldn't send his boys away. No education was worth their separation.

He wasn't a praying man. Yet he had no other place to turn and no solutions for the problem gnawing at his heart. Could he spare the time from his schedule to tutor them? Not if he intended to maintain his business interests, which would one day, when they were academically prepared, enable him to send his boys to the finest universities. Besides, their needs were so different, and nothing in his education had prepared him to teach anyone. He buried his face in his hands, uttering only the small word, "Please."

Preoccupied, he barely heard the tentative rap on the door. He waited, and the knock came again. "Come in," he called.

Marcus edged into the room, trailed by Minnie. "May I have a piece of paper and some ink for my pen?"

"Of course. Are you writing a letter?" Even as he asked the question, he couldn't imagine to whom his son might write.

"In my mythology book, I found more information

about Minerva. I thought Miss Sophie might like to know."

"I'm sure she would. If you write it down, I could have one of the hands deliver it for you."

He rubbed his right toe over his left boot. "Good."

Tate handed him several sheets of paper and a small bottle of ink.

Instead of withdrawing, the boy hesitated as if wanting to say something more. "Papa, do you think if I send this letter, she'll come see us again? She's very smart. I like talking to her."

As if a knife had lodged in his chest, Tate recognized his son's hunger for knowledge. "In your letter, perhaps you could invite her for another visit."

"Thank you, sir," Marcus said before beating a retreat.

Sophie Montgomery. He'd thought all he had to do was accompany her from the Hurlburts' to her mountain cabin. Mission accomplished. Yet she wouldn't go away. Not out of his home and not out of his mind.

He leaned back in his chair, staring at Wallace Tolbert III's annoying letter. The longer he studied it, the more incensed he became. Until, like a bolt from the blue, an idea occurred to him. Not one without pitfalls, but nevertheless a practical solution in such an extremity. Did he dare? What choice did he have?

Raising his eyes heavenward, Tate expelled a sigh. He'd had no idea God could work that fast.

Chapter Six

Friday evening Sophie marked her place in the book she was reading and stared into the flames licking at the logs. What a different world Henry James depicted in *The American*, one where Americans were viewed as upstarts invading the bastions of European aristocracy. Old society clashing with cultural change. Although James's prose style was challenging, his characters piqued her interest. She longed to converse about the book. Might Tate prove a worthy literary companion? She sighed. Not likely with his many obligations and his circumspect treatment of her. And yet…

She bent to the book once more, fascinated by Christopher Newman's moral dilemma. Should he expose the Bellegardes for who they were or permit them to continue with their pretensions? Reaching the end of a chapter, she reflected that she, like the character, had exchanged one culture for another. In the eyes of some she was defying convention—living alone, riding astride, planning to scale Longs Peak—yet if she and others didn't undertake such challenges, women might forever be confined by prejudice and male societal expectations. It was appalling that as an educated woman, she was deemed too ignorant to vote while ruffians staggering out of taverns were welcome at the polls. She wondered what Grizzly would think about evolving roles for women. And Tate? Based on his reaction to her thus far and what she knew about Ramona, she assumed he'd align himself with those who expected a female to stay in her place. But Charlie? She smiled. He'd wanted her to be her best self, wherever that took her.

The next morning after she'd fed Ranger and Beauty and hung her wash on the line, Sophie pulled out some writing paper and sat at the kitchen table, determined to find the words to cheer her father. Although Seth had tried to reassure her, a small stroke was still cause for concern. Even as a little girl, she had taken care of the "boys." Keeping house and cooking for her father and brothers had been not only a necessity, but a labor of love. Yet here she was, hundreds of miles away.

Knowing her father would be more interested in her situation than in her pity, she briefly addressed his stroke, assuring him of her confidence that with time he would recover fully. Then she launched into what she hoped was a lighthearted account of her Colorado adventures, including her acquisition of Beauty, her friendship with Belle and her amusing encounters with Marcus and Toby. She lifted her pen from the page. She wanted to include something about Tate, but what? He wasn't merely an acquaintance, and she had to admit that in some ways he was important to her. She shook her head, then carried on with a description of the local church services. Tate could wait for another time. After sealing the letter to her father, she wrote a quick note to Seth.

Dearest Brother,

Thank you for informing me about Pa. I'm sure
Doc Kellogg is keeping an eye on him, as are all
of you, but I imagine that he is a stubborn patient.
I feel very far away, although Pa and all of my
dear Kansas family are in my daily prayers. Seth,
I know I can count on you and Caleb to let me
know if I need to come. No journey is too long or
arduous when my loved ones are in distress. The
post is unreliable and erratic, but I'm sure if necessary, you could telegraph the Hurlburts and they
could get word to me in a more timely fashion.

She stared at the words covering the page. How inadequate they seemed. She'd made the decision to leave
Kansas, but perhaps she hadn't fully anticipated what
the emotional cost might be. She carefully folded the
letters and slipped both into an envelope addressed to
Seth. She would deliver the packet to Joe Harper when
she went to church the next day. With a sigh, she pushed
back from the table, determined to clear her mind.

"Beauty?" The dog had been lazing on the front
porch, but stood in response to her call. "It's a beautiful day for a walk. Come."

On the way to a nearby ridge crowned by rocks and
juniper trees, the landscape began to fill her empti-
ness. How she wished Charlie and her beloved family
could share in such splendor. At the top of the ridge a
flat plateau covered by low bushes and colorful flowers beckoned her on. Beauty bounded ahead of her and
then circled back as if soliciting approval for another
romp. As she walked, Sophie felt her worry lifting. Pa
was in good hands and improving daily, she was loving
Colorado…all was well. She paused, turning slowly in

a circle to take in the panorama of the mountains. Then just a few steps away she noticed a bush covered with small red raspberries, then another bush and another. She knelt and plucked one of the sun-ripened berries and put it in her mouth, savoring its sweetness. Beauty nosed her curiously, and she cupped a branch in her hand. "Berries. Perhaps the first of the season," she told the dog. She decided to fill her pockets with them, fancying a dishful topped with fresh cream after dinner. So busy was she moving among the bushes and plucking raspberries that she lost track of time.

Suddenly the hairs on the back of her neck rose, and she had the eerie sense she was being watched. She grabbed Beauty by the scruff of her neck and froze, her heart thumping. A crashing of twigs and a low growl followed. Then before she could react, a lumbering black she-bear, followed by two cubs, was closing in on her, teeth bared.

Tate stood on the porch of Sophie's cabin, frowning. The woman was nowhere to be found. Surely she couldn't have gone far. Whinnying from the barn indicated that wherever she was, she had walked. He'd hoped to arrive, dispatch his business and be on his way. Yet he couldn't be too impatient and end up botching the proposal he intended to put to her. He checked his watch, removed his hat and sank down onto a porch chair, smiling with the recollection of her appearance the day she painted it. He could only imagine the reaction of his aloof, fastidious parents to her hoydenish, paint-smeared apparel. But he had left behind the social constraints of upper-crust Philadelphia and had never been sorry. Rather like Christopher Newman in

The American, he could see the flaws in what passed for high society.

He stretched out his legs and leaned back, enjoying the unaccustomed solitude. With effort, he tried to still his mind, racing with figures, contracts, assay reports and, more immediately, his mission here, upon which so much depended. Of course Sophie enjoyed the boys. That was not in question. But given her independent streak, he had no way to predict how she might respond to the question he planned to pose. He waited, amusing himself with watching a nest of jays. After thirty minutes or so, he checked his watch again. What could be taking Sophie so long? Since he hadn't seen Beauty, he assumed the dog must be with her. But what protection or assistance could a dog offer if something had gone wrong? If she'd fallen, for instance? With that thought, he stood and paced the porch, wondering if he should search for her. But where?

Lost in speculation, he failed to hear her approach. "Tate? What are you doing here?"

He wheeled around, took one look and gasped. Her normally rosy-cheeked face was ashen, her shirtwaist was soiled with dirt and dried vegetation, and her skirt was ripped and bloodstained. He ran to her and grabbed her hands, which trembled in his. "Sophie, are you all right?"

She sighed deeply even as she swayed on her feet. "I am now," she said, relief evident in her voice. Beauty bounded up and sat by her mistress's side.

"Are you bleeding?"

She looked at him dazedly before she finally glanced down. "I don't think so." She picked up her torn skirt. "My, claws are sharp, aren't they?"

"Claws?" He could hardly articulate the word for the tightness in his chest. "What claws?"

"The mama bear's." As she spoke, she allowed herself to be led to a rocker on the porch.

"Bear's?" He sounded like an idiot, but he was having a hard time imagining the danger she'd escaped. Even her hands were crimson. "Let me get a cloth and wash off that blood."

He was not prepared for what happened next. She examined her hands and the fabric of her skirt and began to laugh. How could she laugh? Was she having a hysterical reaction to her ordeal?

"Dear Tate," she said with a weary smile, "it's not blood. It's raspberry juice."

"But you said 'claws.'"

She sobered. "I won't lie. Beauty and I had a close call. We were in a raspberry patch, and that mother bear was not happy with our invasion of her territory."

"Or about the threat that you posed to her cubs. My word, you could've been killed." His stomach churned at the thought. "How did you escape?"

She took off her hat and ran her fingers through her curls in the effort to tame them. "By the grace of God and Terence P. Griswold."

"Grizzly?"

"When he first came to visit me, he taught me some things he thought I might need to know about living alone in the mountains. One was what to do in an encounter with a bear." She paused, clenching her fists as if recalling the terrifying moment. "I had hold of Beauty, so I fell on the ground on top of her, grabbed her muzzle and played dead."

"But the tear in your skirt?"

Sophie closed her eyes. "The bear came close enough to nudge me and swipe at my skirt."

He was speechless. The bear could've mauled her—and the dog. Only her quick thinking had saved them from a fate too ghastly to contemplate. *If only he'd gone looking for her.*

"It was a lesson I needed to learn," she went on. "Perhaps I've been too cavalier about the dangers in these mountains."

He knew better than to agree with her just now. "When I didn't find you here, I was concerned about your whereabouts."

"Concerned?" She attempted a teasing grin. "Are you equally concerned about me when you're at your house? Or riding out on business? Surely I've proved now that, with Beauty's help, I can take care of myself."

He doubted it. What would she have done without Grizzly's information? However, there was no use contesting the point when she needed calming and he needed to gain her cooperation. "You are, indeed, your own woman."

"Thank you." As if suddenly remembering her manners, she said, "Could I serve you a cold glass of lemonade?"

"I'd be partial to that, but not until we clean the, er, raspberry juice off your hands." He followed her inside, where she hung her hat on a peg by the door and set to work pumping cold water into a basin and then soaping her hands.

"You must have been quite frightened," he said as he picked up a towel and gently dried her hands.

"Mama Bear had every right to protect her young. It's nature's way. We were trespassers."

"Does this change your mind about living alone?"

She shot him an indignant look and grabbed the towel from him. "Certainly not. I handled the situation, didn't I? I'm not completely naive, you know. In fact, I'm more determined than ever to prove myself against the elements, including climbing Longs Peak later this summer." She hung up the towel and began pumping more water into a pitcher for the lemonade.

He retreated to the table. "Still harboring that ambition, are you?"

"Not only 'harboring,' but actively preparing for it." She squeezed several lemons into the pitcher and sprinkled in some sugar. "You don't approve, do you?"

"My approval is not the issue, but your safety is. After today, I'd think you would be reconsidering the climb. Even beyond the physical danger of such an enterprise, I hope you're prepared for negative reactions from many folks."

"No progress is made without risk. Old ways have to be challenged." She handed him his lemonade and sat down across from him. "It's rather like Christopher Newman's issue concerning European society. To challenge or not to challenge societal norms."

He couldn't help himself—he grinned. "So you're enjoying *The American*?"

"I'm not sure *enjoy* is the proper word. Let's just say, I find the premise thought-provoking and the characters well drawn."

"What about James's style?" From that point, he was drawn into a lively discussion of the merits and flaws of the novel. Perhaps the topic had served to distract her from her meeting with the bear. During a lull in the conversation, he realized it had been far too long since he'd been so intellectually stimulated by a book or a conversation.

She fetched the leather volume and turned to a particular page. "Listen to this," she said, reading a passage aloud. "Isn't that a clever description?" She smiled at him. "Thank you for loaning me the book. I shall return it as soon as I finish."

Mentally crossing his fingers, he seized the moment. "I am hopeful you will often be at my home to avail yourself of my library."

"Oh?"

"The boys and I need your help."

"Is something wrong?"

"Not wrong exactly. Just missing." Bypassing diplomacy, he went right to the point. "I would like to hire you to tutor Marcus and Toby."

Her eyes widened. "I am no teacher."

"I had engaged a tutor from Ohio who now informs me he is unavailable. Apparently our terrain is too rugged and dangerous, and another less adventurous opportunity tempted the lad to decline my offer of employment. But I note—" he grinned wryly "—that our terrain has not daunted you. If I am to find a tutor before the boys fall victim to even more educational lapses, I must turn to locals." He shook his head. "Few choices here." He covered her hand with his own and looked directly into her eyes. "Except for you."

"Tate, why, I couldn't begin to—"

"Hear me out. Please. I don't mean to imply that I'm so desperate that even you will do. Quite the opposite. After what I've observed when you and the boys are together and considering our discussion of Henry James's work, you may well be the perfect choice. You did tell me you'd been educated at an Eastern academy for women. I beg you to consider my offer."

Sophie withdrew her hand and stood, tucking wayward curls into her haphazard topknot. She walked to the window, remaining there for long minutes before returning to stand behind her chair, gripping its back. Before she spoke, he hurriedly added, "I will pay you what I had intended to pay the tutor, and we will work out mutually convenient hours." Still she said nothing. What was he overlooking?

"The salary, though welcome, is not a factor for me. I need to think about this, Tate. I can't promise any more than that."

He hadn't anticipated such reluctance. He pulled out his strongest argument. "The boys need you. They already think of you as a caring friend. And remember Marcus? How he waited to name Minnie until you could help?"

"They are delightful little fellows."

He seized upon that crumb. "Consider how far behind they already are in their studies. Can either of us in good conscience permit that condition to continue?"

She stared at him. "You cannot. They are your responsibility, but please don't transfer your obligation to me."

"I didn't mean to suggest…" He took a deep breath and started over. "I know you care about Marcus and Toby. And you are superbly qualified. I appeal to you on their behalf, not mine."

She nodded and let her eyes fall on him, compassion registering now where before there had been skepticism. "It must be hard for you, Tate. Your concern for your sons is laudable. And you are correct—I am very fond of both boys. I shall consider your proposal and let you know after I pray about it. As you are aware, I've had a rather distressing afternoon. Will Tuesday be soon enough for an answer?"

What choice did he have? "Tuesday will be fine. Perhaps you could join us for the midday meal. Say 1:00 p.m.?"

"I will be there."

Sensing a new awkwardness between them, he rose to his feet, preparing to leave. "I'll be on my way."

He grabbed his hat as she ushered him to the door. One last appeal. Surely that was all that it would take. He stepped across the threshold and then turned back to her. "By your own admission, you love a challenge. What could be more challenging than lighting up Marcus with ideas and showing Toby that there's more to life than fun?"

He stared deeply into her eyes, willing her to respond. "Until Tuesday," he said. Then suddenly remembering his other mission, he reached into his pocket, withdrew an envelope and handed it to her. "From Marcus," he said before heading toward his horse.

Because Sunday was warm and windless, folks gathered on chairs and blankets in the Tylers' yard for prayers and to listen to the men take turns reading from Scripture. The lack of a preacher made for a shorter service to the delight of the restless children. Sophie had brought Beauty along and planned to spend the night at the Harpers' so that she and Belle could hike together the following day. Besides, although she would never admit it to Tate, the confrontation with the bear had left her shaken. She had, indeed, been foolhardy to disregard the dangers of living alone in a new place. Surely Belle's company would help restore normalcy.

Before the service, Sophie had consigned her letters home to Joe, who was reasonably certain someone would be taking the post down the canyon within the next week. She was relieved they'd already been sealed before the bear attack. Her Kansas family didn't need that bit of news.

Sitting beside Belle on a sturdy carriage blanket, Sophie closed her eyes and tried to heed the droning voice of the reader. Her wandering mind snapped to attention at a challenging verse from Psalm 143: "Teach me to do Your will, for You are my God: may Your good Spirit lead me on level ground." Folding her hands in her lap, she bowed her head. She needed God's guidance to walk on the right path, the one He intended for her. She had not yet made up her mind about Tate's proposal. Was tutoring the Lockwood boys where her "level ground" lay? Or was she beguiled by her need to be of use to the motherless little fellows? Would she run the risk of the boys' growing dependent on her and she on them? Complicating matters was Tate's busy life. Would he distance himself from his sons if she were engaged with them? A danger, since the very opposite needed to happen. Could she be an agent to bring father and sons closer together? Was their relationship even any of her affair?

She would happily obey God's will if she could be certain what He asked of her. One thing she knew with certainty: she could not swoop in from the outside and fix that family. She was confident she could serve as a tutor. But should she? In honesty, proximity to Tate could be disturbing. Something about his prickly persona touched her in confusing ways.

"Sophie?" She felt Belle elbowing her. "Services are over. You were deep in prayer, sister."

Sophie leaned close to Belle and confessed, "Not prayer. Woolgathering."

"Sometimes I think they're the same thing."

Sophie pondered Belle's remark. "I'd never thought of it that way. Maybe God is present in our random thoughts."

"Well, if He's not, He certainly should be." Belle jumped to her feet. "Come on now. Let's get some food."

In the course of the afternoon, Belle introduced Sophie to more of the valley folks. Some already knew about her; others barely concealed their shock that a lone woman would take up residence in such a place. Just as they headed out for the Harper home, Belle left her side and ran after a tall, wiry man with a long beard and a deep tan whom Sophie recognized as the talented tenor who'd led the hymn singing today. "Bill, wait up." Belle paused to catch her breath and motioned Sophie to follow.

"Can't stop now, but you two gals can walk with me a spell if you're on your way home." Just as Sophie reached the twosome, the man set off at a rapid pace. "Gotta get to my place in time to feed the animals."

"This is my friend Sophie Montgomery. Sophie, this is 'Wild Bill' Porter, one of the best mountain guides hereabouts."

Without missing a step, Bill tipped his hat. "I've heard tell of you, Miss Sophie. And about how Belle has convinced you to try Longs Peak with her. A grueling task, not one for women to undertake."

"Others have done it," Belle challenged.

"Are you talking about Isabella Bird, who, rumor has it, practically had to be dragged up to the summit?"

"Don't forget about Addie Alexander and Anna Dickinson," Belle said, reminding him of two other women who had made the ascent.

"That's hardly a convincing number," Bill muttered. "And you fillies?" He eyed Sophie. "Look, she's just a little bit of a thing, and you, Miss Harper, are full of big talk."

"We're going to do it." Belle's tone was full of conviction. "With or without your help."

The man stopped in his tracks and looked from one to the other. "You can't do it alone."

Belle relented. "I know that. May we hire you as our guide?"

He stroked his beard. Sophie watched with bated breath as he considered Belle's request. "You." He nodded at Sophie. "You're scrawny, but Grizzly tells me you're full of fight."

Sophie squared her shoulders and looked him straight in the eye. "He's right. I will not quit."

"Nor I," Belle promised.

Bill shook his head. "Call me crazy. I'm making no promises today. But come late August or September, mayhap I'll consider pulling you girls up the peak."

Before he took off, Belle leaned toward him and kissed him on the cheek. "Done!"

"We won't let you down, sir," Sophie added.

"No need for the 'sir.' Just Bill."

After he'd left them, Belle squeezed Sophie's hand. "He was the only guide who would have considered us."

That night Sophie shared Belle's bed. They whispered about their hiking plans and then Belle fell asleep. Sophie, however, remained wide-awake, discomfited by the unfamiliar mattress and recurring images of Toby and Marcus. Toby, whose enthusiasm was contagious, and dear Marcus, who had sent her detailed information about the goddess Minerva. What should she do? Would agreeing to tutor them solve problems or create more? She rolled over on her side, staring out the window at a full, white moon. "God," she whispered, "please. Show me Your will."

Tuesday morning came, the day of reckoning. Sophie quickly finished her chores in preparation of the ride to Tate's place. She still had no idea what answer she would give him. Scary as it was, she was relying on God to send her a sign. When she had first settled here, she had needed the days of hard work and solitude to continue her healing and to contemplate the future. Now, though, she was finding the quiet days sometimes palled, and she was increasingly drawn to the people who had befriended her. From that standpoint, interaction with the Lockwood boys could be a tonic, but she would never accept a position simply for the company.

She took extra pains with her hair, braiding it and coiling it around her head. Still, the stray, unruly curls escaped as they always did to frame her face. Over her bloomers, she wore a denim skirt. A simple white waist and red jacket completed the outfit. Glancing around the cabin, she was arrested by the words on Lily's sampler, "Trust in the Lord with all thine heart…and He shall direct thy paths." Sophie shook her head, also remembering Sunday's psalm passage. She was to surrender—that was the message. She put on her hat, locked the door and headed for the barn. God knew all about her rebellious spirit. And now He wanted her to yield her will to Him? Well, maybe she could, but the question remained: What was His will?

Beauty trailed behind Ranger as they made their way to the Lockwood ranch. Sophie scanned the peaks ahead of her, longing to be high among them. With each strike of Ranger's hooves, she continued her prayer: *Lord, prepare my heart and show me the way.* By the time she dismounted in front of Tate's house, a calm had settled over her. Somehow she would receive her answer shortly.

Since breakfast, Tate had barricaded himself in his office, trying to bury himself in work. Yet even as he stared at the assayer's report, the figures failed to penetrate his brain, so addled was it by anticipating Sophie's decision. She had to say yes. If his will could coerce her, he would exercise it. But he knew her better than that. If anything, further pressure from him could be fatal to his ends. He was accustomed to getting his way—miners worked extra hours, bankers extended loans and ranch hands followed his orders to the letter. How could one tiny, redheaded female be so contrary?

He had requested Bertie to prepare a lavish lunch. He had seen that the boys were presentably dressed and had reminded them to be on their best behavior. Sitting back in his chair, he stared out the window. All he could do was let the day unfold as Sophie would direct.

Restless, he stepped to the window and studied the landscape. Aspen leaves shook in the breeze and sun glinted off the river. Then, in the distance, he spotted her approaching the bridge. He wondered how long it had been since she'd ridden sidesaddle. Yet even astride, she rode in an expert and ladylike fashion. This time she'd brought Beauty, who ran ahead of the horse as if scouting the trail. With dismay, he noted the rapid pounding of his heart. So much was at stake. He loved his sons. An education was vital. Surely Sophie wouldn't disappoint him. If she could face a charging she-bear, surely she could handle two young boys.

He watched her approach, fighting an unforeseen pleasure that rose amid his anxiety. When he observed her tying up her horse, he straightened his cravat, took a deep breath and left the sanctuary of his office. In the front hall, he was met by the clamor of barking pups and excited boys. "Papa, she's here!" Toby exclaimed, but to Tate's astonishment it was Marcus who threw open the door and greeted their guest with an exuberant, "Miss Sophie, we're glad you came. Did you like my report?"

"I did, indeed, Marcus." She paused in the entryway, beaming at the boys. "What a delightful welcome! May Beauty come in? I'd love her to meet the puppies." Just then Minnie circled her legs while Buster tugged at the hem of her dress.

"Yes, yes!" came the chorus of approval.

"Follow us," Toby ordered, taking off for the living room.

Amid laughter and yipping dogs, Tate took Sophie's hat and cloak. "May I add my more sedate welcome?"

She glanced up at him, her eyes dancing above a smattering of pale freckles. "You may, indeed, Mr. Lockwood."

"Luncheon will be served shortly, but for now, your presence is clearly required by two boys and three dogs."

Tate leaned against a wall, observing the scene. Sophie sat on the rug in front of the hearth with the boys gathered around her, while Beauty lay a bit apart, her tail happily thumping on the floor. Both pups were crawling all over Sophie. He hoped they wouldn't soil her clothes, but any admonishment died on his lips as he studied the pleasure on his sons' faces. Fragments of conversation penetrated his thoughts.

"Look what Buster can do."

"Minnie really is a wise dog."

"I do believe my Beauty likes her new puppy friends."

Unquestionably Sophie had been right about the pups. They had made a difference for both Toby and Marcus.

Bertie tapped him on the shoulder. "Luncheon is ready, sir."

He clapped his hands to summon the group to the table, where a delicious potato soup awaited them. "Boys, you know the rule. Please confine the dogs while we are eating." The usual groans greeted his directive, but they complied without complaint. As he seated Sophie, he was uncomfortably aware of a faint floral scent.

Marcus leaned forward, his spoon suspended halfway to his mouth. "Miss Sophie, did you know that once people thought the world was flat?"

"That's silly," Toby blurted.

"I did know that, Marcus." She turned to Toby. "Why do you think that's silly?"

"'Cuz everybody knows it's round."

"How do they know?" Sophie prompted.

Toby wrinkled up his nose. "How? I guess 'cuz somebody told them."

"But what made them believe that somebody?"

Dumbfounded, Tate watched the deft way she prodded Toby.

"You need to know about Ptolemy and Copernicus and Columbus and—" Marcus faltered.

"Do you know about them, Marcus?" Sophie asked gently.

The older boy hung his head. "Well, kind of." Then he peered up at Sophie, longing evident in his expression. "But I'd like to learn more."

Toby kicked the table leg. "I still don't believe folks could've been so dumb."

"Are there things we are still 'dumb' about, do you think?" Sophie challenged.

As the meal went on, Tate interjected only rarely, preferring instead to watch Sophie deal with the boys. The woman was a natural teacher, and they hung on her every word. He liked how she didn't merely give them answers, but stimulated their thinking. Surely she could see the impact she was having. He found himself admiring once again the quick intellect she'd exhibited in their discussion of Henry James. The more he watched her interact with his sons, the greater his dread that she would turn down his offer of the tutoring position. Finally after a dessert of warm oatmeal cake, he ordered the boys and dogs outside and escorted Sophie to his office. His massive desk and familiar furnishings provided him with at least the illusion of confidence. He indicated she should take the leather armchair opposite his. "Sophie, thank you for coming today and engaging my sons in such a delightful and thought-provoking manner. It is my hope that you have favorably considered my offer to tutor the boys."

"As yet, I am not prepared with an answer. Allow me to lay before you my concerns."

Not trusting himself to speak, he merely nodded.

"In no way must Marcus and Toby look upon me as a substitute mother. Nor must you. That is not the role of a tutor. Although I can befriend them, I would regard our sessions as purely academic."

"Agreed."

"I should also like regularly scheduled tutoring sessions and the freedom to pursue my mountain climbing. How often had you thought I would meet with the boys?"

"That would be up to you, based on your assessment of their needs and progress."

She brushed a stray curl behind her ear. "This is a difficult decision for me. I care for the boys, but this is not how I envisioned my time in the mountains."

"Is there anything I can say to influence you further? I will pay you handsomely, as I mentioned previously. Would there be other inducements I could offer?"

"I would ask you to order supplies and books of my choosing. I would also require the loan of a horse and cart on occasion, so that the boys and I could make forays into nature or spend time at my cabin, if needed."

He took heart. "Both reasonable requests." She said nothing. The clock on the wall chimed the half hour. Still she remained silent. He could no longer abide the impasse. "What, then, is preventing you from accepting my offer?"

She looked up at him, her eyes full of unshed tears. "I fear I may be unable to maintain a proper professional distance with the boys."

"Why is that?"

She shrugged as if mystified by her own answer. "Because I have come to love them."

He breathed a sigh of relief. "Sophie, that is precisely why you are the very one to teach them."

Another moment passed before she finally whispered, "Very well, then, I accept the position."

Chapter Seven

After agreeing to tutor the boys, Sophie had remained at Tate's long enough to make a list of needed books, maps and supplies and to receive overwhelming affirmation when Tate told Marcus and Toby the good news. Toby had hugged her exuberantly while Marcus stood back, smiling shyly, until she was just about to leave. Then he stepped forward to shake her hand. "Miss Sophie, I believe you will be a most effective teacher."

"I shall do my best for you and Toby," she said.

Tate handed Sophie her hat and cloak. "Your best will be of great benefit to the boys." He caught her eye, and in that glance, communicated his relief. Outside, he helped her mount, although he knew she needed no assistance. Holding the reins, he looked up at her. "'Thank you' is hardly adequate."

"I'm doing it for the boys," she said rather more sharply than she'd intended.

"Yes." He studied his feet. "For the boys." Then he turned over the reins, and she wheeled Ranger toward home, the forlorn sound of *for the boys* echoing in her ears.

Riding along, she was oblivious to the gray clouds

forming over the mountains, so consumed was she by the enormity of her decision. *Dear God, are You sure I have this right?* She had never taught anyone, never even considered such a path. Although most of her fellow students at the female academy had been preparing to teach, she had buried herself in her studies primarily to distract herself from her grief. Lessons in pedagogy had held little interest for her then. And now? How could she possibly live up to Marcus's expectations? Or address Toby's curiosity?

Yet, at the moment of decision, God *had* sent her a sign, not a starburst or thunderbolt, but rather an all-encompassing peace within her heart. Playing with the puppies and discussing theories about the earth had filled her with both excitement and a sense of…well, purpose. She had seen the longing in the boys' eyes and had known that, whatever her inadequacies or reservations, she would do her best not to disappoint them.

Beneath her, Ranger tensed—and it was then she noticed lightning across the valley. She kicked him into a canter, hoping they would arrive at the cabin before the heavens opened up. In the race for home, she found herself wanting to escape Tate's ranch—or, more specifically, Tate. Marcus and Toby were one thing; Tate Lockwood was something else altogether. Despite her determination to let God guide her, she had fought against tutoring the boys, but not because of them. Grimacing, she admitted her reluctance was born out of the unsettling realization that she was attracted to the handsome, complicated Tate Lockwood. Surely that was not part of God's plan for her. God understood she had known one true love—Charlie. Then amid an awful thunderclap, Grizzly's words rang in her ears: *I'm gonna be aprayin'…for the Lord to send you another man to love.* She remembered protesting such an absurdity— and Grizzly's admonishing her to leave everything to God and to understand it was not her needs that mattered, but what she could give.

She frowned. Why did she have a disturbing feeling that she might have something to give Tate? Confusion and concern consumed her all the way home.

Ranger arrived at the barn just as the first raindrops fell. By the time Sophie unsaddled him, wiped him down and poured out his oats, a cloudburst had descended. She raced for the cabin and moved directly to the woodstove to warm her hands. After stoking the fire and adding wood, she took off her outer garments and wrapped up in a shawl. She knew storms arrived suddenly in these parts, generally in the afternoon. She should have started for home sooner. She laughed derisively. She should have done a lot of things, none of which would involve Tate Lockwood, whose wariness was often belied by the yearning in his soulful brown eyes. Well, there was no undoing her promise, but she vowed to keep her professional distance from the master of the house.

She sank into the rocker. No doubt about it, though, she did love the boys, who tugged at her heartstrings and reminded her of her precious nieces and nephews in Kansas. She laced her fingers in prayer. *God, I am Your servant and will go where You lead. Forgive my impertinence, but are You sure You know what You're doing?*

Tate had left for Leadville the day after Sophie had agreed to tutor the boys, but not before he'd charged Sam with the errand of going to Denver to obtain the supplies she required. Now homeward bound after eight days away, he realized it had been a relief to travel on

business without the nagging worry of the boys' education. Now Sophie's presence would afford him more
freedom from the confinement of the ranch. As much
as he'd resented the burden of escorting her from Denver, she had proved a godsend. He had actually been
able to enjoy the ride to Leadville and his meetings
with prospectors and metallurgists. He was excited by
the possibilities of a growing silver boom and the opportunities for profit available to those who, like him,
had funds to invest. Wryly, he reflected on his parents,
who had scoffed at his Western ambitions and had told
him he would never amount to anything if he left the
East. He wondered if he would have taken any satisfaction in proving them wrong had they still been alive to
notice—if they would, in any sense, have been proud
of him and the uses he was making of his inheritance.

No matter. *He* took pride in his success. He was
able to provide his sons with a bright future, especially
now that Sophie would be teaching them. On this ride
home, his thoughts had often turned to her. Too often.
He would never forget the warmth in her eyes when
she finally agreed to tutor Marcus and Toby. Although
they would, of necessity, be spending time together, he
needed to guard against becoming personally dependent
on her. He had admitted to himself from the beginning
that despite her unconventional ways, she was appeal-
ing, challenging—and enchanting. He wished he could
focus on her intransigence instead of on his memory of
the beautiful, spirited young woman in a stunning blue
satin gown he'd met in Denver.

Arriving at the ranch, he was eager to see the boys
and hear how the tutoring was progressing. He burst
into the house and called out, "Marcus! Toby!" He was
greeted by silence. He threw his hat aside and strode

into the living room—empty. In the library alcove he found a map of the valley open on the table alongside two slates. "Bertie?" He was walking toward the kitchen when the housekeeper came rushing downstairs, a load of linens in her arms.

"Sir? We didn't expect you until tomorrow."

"I was eager to see the boys. Where are they?"

"Miss Montgomery took them on what she called a 'nature excursion.'"

Nature excursion? "I see. When are they expected home?"

"I don't know, but I would imagine this afternoon in time for her to return to her cabin before dark."

"Very well. I will be in my office."

He fumed. He didn't want to go to his office. He didn't want to be cooped up wondering where his sons were or what the baffling Miss Sophie was up to. Pacing the floor, he decided to go find them. To evaluate what was going on. *Nature excursion?* What did that have to do with the classics? With mathematics?

He grabbed his hat and set forth to find his sons and assure himself of their well-being. After all, their tutor had recently barely escaped mauling by a bear.

Sophie had set up headquarters on a flat outcropping and assigned each of the boys a plot of ground to serve as their "laboratory." The goal was for each to sit quietly for fifteen minutes and record their observations. Marcus had fallen swiftly to the task, but Toby had required gentle guidance. In the past week, Sophie had come to understand that while Marcus thrived on intellectual challenges, Toby needed to be caught up on reading, writing and arithmetic basics. She rather imagined he had charmed previous tutors instead of taking his lessons to heart. While they worked quietly, she, too, studied her surroundings, so different from Kansas. Colorful mountain flowers bloomed in nooks and crannies causing her to marvel at their beauty, variety and resilience—alpine fireweed, forget-me-nots, mallow and buttercups, but none so arresting as the delicate columbine. She consulted her watch and called for the boys to bring their notes and gather for lunch and discussion. While they made their way to the rock, she unwrapped the hard-boiled eggs, ham and biscuits Bertie had prepared for their lunch.

"That was hard," Toby said, presenting her with his smudged paper.

"Hard? Nor for me," Marcus boasted.

Sophie laid a restraining hand on the older boy's shoulder. "What made it difficult, Toby?"

"Sitting still for so long. Being quiet. Thinking up what to write down."

"Yes, scientific observation requires discipline. Did you notice anything you might not have had you merely walked across your plot?"

Toby shrugged. "Prob'ly."

Sophie distributed the food. "While we eat, let's talk about what we each noticed and whether what we saw raised any questions. I'll start. I found a tiny, white mountain flower poking out of a rock. I wonder how it got there."

"I think—" Marcus began before Sophie raised an eyebrow to forestall his comment.

"Toby, how would you explain that? Do flowers grow out of rocks?"

"Rocks aren't alive."

"Correct. So how would a flower get there?"

Toby bit into his biscuit, frowning in concentration,

while Marcus squirmed eagerly beside her, but said nothing. "From a seed, I guess."

"And how would the seed get there if the rock didn't produce it?"

The boy chewed thoughtfully.

"Marcus, could you give your brother a hint?"

"What might carry a seed to this place?"

Toby's eyes lit up. "A hiker, maybe, or an animal." He stared into the distance before grinning in understanding. "I think the best idea is a bird. He could pick up seeds in his beak and spill some as he flew along. Birds eat seeds, you know."

Sophie clapped her hands. "That's a fine scientific conclusion."

"Con-clu-shun?"

"A reasonable answer to a question based on careful thought and observation."

"I saw some things," Toby said with newfound interest. "A little trail in the dirt."

Marcus could refrain no longer. "We have pinecones at home, and I found another and wondered how it was formed."

"Where might we find answers other than by observation?"

"Books!" both boys answered at once.

"And experts we might meet," Marcus added.

Sophie finished her hard-boiled egg and took a sip from her canteen. "All right now. Show me your list of observations and then let's begin thinking of questions for which we might research answers."

Engaged in discussing the project, none of them heard a rustling in the bushes until Tate burst out of the brush, his face red with exertion. "What's going on here?"

Sophie cringed at his accusatory tone. She rose to her feet. "Lessons."

"It seems more like a picnic to me." He glared at Sophie. "I presume there have been no bear sightings." Before she could answer, he leaned over and picked up a piece of paper on which Toby had drawn a bird flying over rocky ground. "And this? Tomfoolery."

Noticing Toby's quivering lip, Sophie took the picture from Tate and shot him a cautioning look. "Quite the contrary. This is Toby's scientific conclusion concerning the manner in which seeds are distributed over varying terrains."

Marcus thrust out his detailed sketch of the pinecone he'd discovered. "We are taking this home to study conifers."

Tate's initial temper seemed to fade, but he still looked confused. "This outing is not what I had in mind when I engaged your services."

"And what did you have in mind? Mere book learning without actual exposure to the world in which we live—the world that is our laboratory?"

He studied her as if she, like other specimens, had been found under a rock. A mixture of emotions crossed his face, but finally he merely shook his head and muttered, "Most unconventional."

"And you expected less from me?" She struggled to conceal a grin. "Trust me, Tate, what is going on here is in the name of education. We must learn from observing everything in our environment. And that does, indeed, include field study as well as books." She faced her two young charges. "For now, gather up your things and walk back home with your father." She sent Tate a warning glance. "Along the way, tell him what you observed this morning as well as pointing out what you observe on the walk home."

"I already spotted that hawk." Toby pointed toward a tall tree. "See, Papa. Maybe he dropped the seed."

Tate glanced skeptically at Sophie, before turning back to his son. "What seed?"

And the three walked off, Toby jabbering and Marcus offering explanations. Perhaps Tate was learning from his sons that education can happen anywhere at any time. His mistrust of her motives had stung. Yes, she was new to her role, but before he confronted her, she had thought the lesson was going well. Extremely well. She trailed along behind them and only occasionally did their chatter intrude upon her thoughts. She could justify her lesson from the standpoint that her students should not always be cooped up, but she was also forced to admit she had not yet had time to digest the academic materials Sam had procured for her in Denver. In her next session with the boys, she would assess their readiness for the lessons she had in mind and begin working with Toby on his reading. That ought to satisfy their father.

When they all arrived back at the house, Tate disappeared into his office. Masking her irritation, Sophie continued discussing the boys' observations; then together, they made a list of questions for further inquiry. How is a pinecone formed? Why do boulders break apart? How do plants and animals survive cold winters?

After dismissing the boys to play with the puppies, she straightened the library table and found Bertie in the kitchen. "I'll be on my way. Thank you for the delightful picnic fare."

"My pleasure. When will we see you again?"

"I will be hiking for the next two days. Then I'll

return. Meanwhile, I've given the boys some assignments. In my absence, perhaps they can spend more time with their father."

The housekeeper pursed her lips. "One can hope."

Sophie heard resignation in Bertie's voice. Determined to remain cheerful, she said, "He has just returned from a long journey. After he rests, he will surely give them his attention."

Bertie's sigh followed Sophie as she went to get her wraps. As she was putting on her hat, she heard footsteps, and when she turned around, Tate was standing there studying her. From his impassive face to his clenched hands it was impossible to guess what he might say. When he finally spoke, he surprised her. "I was wrong. Please forgive me."

She had no idea what his apology had cost his pride, but she was grateful for it. "It is not my place to forgive you, although you are welcome to forgive yourself."

He took one step toward her, and despite her rapidly beating heart, she was determined to stand her ground. "You are right. The sphere of learning is broad, indeed. I shouldn't have assumed a frivolous purpose for your outing or implied you had put the boys in danger. On our walk home, they quite amazed me with their perceptions."

She stared into the depths of his brown eyes, afraid of losing herself there. "You are not a man for whom apologies are easy."

"Another one of your 'scientific' observations?"

Looking at him, she thought he might actually be on the verge of a smile. "That…and a strong hunch."

"I fear you are coming to know me rather well."

"And to like you."

She had no idea she'd uttered those words aloud until

he murmured, "And I you." After a long moment that grew exponentially more uncomfortable, he stepped back and held her cloak for her.

Flustered, she sought comfort in the mundane. "You shall find us working from books next time. You are welcome to come and oversee."

A softer expression replaced the intensity in his eyes. "You do not require supervision. Proof of the boys' learning will come soon enough. Good day, Sophie."

When the door closed behind her, she stared off into the distance, more confused than ever. The man was an enigma.

"How's the tutoring going?" Belle asked the next morning as they set off on a rugged trail with a steep rise in elevation.

Sophie, trudging behind her friend, inhaled deeply. "It's too early to tell, although both boys seem enthusiastic and willing to learn. I still can't believe I allowed myself to be talked into the position."

"Tate Lockwood can be quite persuasive when it's to his advantage," Belle said drily. "And getting you to tend to his boys' education will relieve him of the responsibility."

Sophie took a few more steps. "You sound critical of him."

"I haven't walked in his moccasins, as the saying goes, but those motherless boys don't need an uninvolved father."

"It's my perception that beneath his stern exterior he cares deeply for them."

Belle paused, leaning on her walking stick to catch her breath. "Perhaps you can bring some of that paternal love out in the open."

"Me?"

"Face it, Sophie. You are a lively, caring young woman. Even Tate can't help but notice and respond to you. I figure you will lead him into a more loving relationship with Marcus and Toby."

"My, that's quite an assignment." Yet even as Sophie doubted her abilities to effect such a change, she remembered the earnestness of Tate's recent apology.

Belle waved her arm and they resumed their hike. Along the way, Sophie examined her surroundings. The gnarled junipers that resembled old men, the stately spruce spearing toward the sky and the industrious chipmunks scampering from rock to rock in search of food. Each time she and Belle rested, she was transfixed by the rocky peaks. Iced by snowy crevices, they gleamed in the sun like nature's El Dorado.

In the early afternoon when they reached the timberline, Sophie shivered in delight. Above and beyond were boulders and rocks that bespoke of time eternal. Looming in the distance, even higher, was massive Longs Peak. Belle interrupted her thoughts. "There it is, sister. Magnificent, isn't it?"

"I can imagine the thrill of setting foot on the summit. Such a triumph shouldn't be reserved for males."

Belle handed Sophie a piece of jerky. "Are you sure you want to make the attempt?"

"Do you doubt my abilities?"

"No, but now that you've gained some hiking experience, it's your commitment of which I must be assured. The ascent is arduous and subject to unanticipated danger."

It was only reasonable that Belle satisfy herself regarding Sophie's motives and will. Her friend was undoubtedly trying to prepare her for rigors of which she herself was ignorant. "I would be foolish to disregard the challenges of the ascent, but it is those very challenges that make me even more determined."

"Well, then, thanks to Wild Bill, we will set our sights on a grand adventure." Belle sat down on a protruding rock. "Beyond the physical challenges, are you prepared for the disapproval, even censure, we may reap for ourselves?"

Sophie looked down at Belle, in whose eyes she read the importance of her compelling question. "You think two young women climbing to the summit of Longs will result in an outcry?"

"I don't *think*. I *know*. Word will get out. The press may even descend, and naysayers will be gleefully waiting for us to fail."

Sophie had to admit she had given little thought to the repercussions from what she viewed as both an adventure and a showcase for women's capabilities. She laid a hand on Belle's shoulder. "If not us, then who? I will not falter, Belle, and if real or symbolic rocks are thrown, then so be it. Nothing worthwhile was ever achieved without risk."

Belle covered Sophie's hand with her own. "All right. It's the two of us against the world." She lowered her eyes. "I didn't want the uproar we may cause to come as a shock to you."

"Thank you, Belle." Sophie studied the sky, telltale wisps of cloud clinging to the farthest peaks. "Looks like we need to head for our horses."

On the descent, they were accosted by two men who stood blocking their path and eyeing them with distaste.

One, dressed in the tweedy alpine garb of a tenderfoot, muttered to his companion. "I say, old chap, who are these wild women?"

A bearded giant of a man, apparently the guide, snorted. "Hussies who think they can brave the treacherous heights of Old Man Mountain."

"Hussies!" Belle exploded. "Virgil Dennis, you know very well, I am not a hussy." She turned to Sophie. "Nor is my companion, who happens to be the tutor of the Lockwood boys."

"That's supposed to make it right?" The guide rolled his eyes in disgust.

"Where I come from," the first man drawled in his aristocratic British accent, "upright, civilized women do not wear…uh—" he raked his eyes over Belle and Sophie, clad in their hiking bloomers "—masculine garments. Most irregular." He sniffed as if at some noisome odor. "Pray tell, do permit us to pass."

"Nobody's stopping you," Belle said with a scorching look.

"And where we come from," Sophie added, "men are not so rude and narrow-minded."

"Then you don't come from around here," the man called Virgil Dennis barked. "You're both a disgrace." He urged the Englishman forward. As the two passed Belle and Sophie, Dennis muttered under his breath, "Don't be thinkin' the likes of me will help get you out of any trouble you get yourselves into."

"And a good day to you, too," Belle snorted, throwing Sophie an I-told-you-so look. After they had put considerable distance between the men and themselves, Belle commented, "That, my dear hiking companion, is the least of what we can expect from the populace when word gets out concerning our Longs Peak aspirations."

"I don't know about you, but their censure has only hardened my resolution. Nothing would give me greater

YOUR PARTICIPATION IS REQUESTED!

Dear Reader,

Since you are a lover of our books – we would like to get to know you!

Inside you will find a short Reader's Survey. Sharing your answers with us will help our editorial staff understand who you are and what activities you enjoy.

To thank you for your participation, we would like to send you 2 books and 2 gifts – **ABSOLUTELY FREE!**

Enjoy your gifts with our appreciation,

Pam Powers

SEE INSIDE FOR READER'S SURVEY

For Your Reading Pleasure...

We'll send you 2 books and 2 gifts
ABSOLUTELY FREE
just for completing our Reader's Survey!

YOUR READER'S SURVEY
"THANK YOU" FREE GIFTS INCLUDE:
- ▶ **2 FREE books**
- ▶ **2 lovely surprise gifts**

PLEASE FILL IN THE CIRCLES COMPLETELY TO RESPOND

1) What type of fiction books do you enjoy reading? (Check all that apply)
- ○ Suspense/Thrillers   ○ Action/Adventure   ○ Modern-day Romances
- ○ Historical Romance   ○ Humour   ○ Paranormal Romance

2) What attracted you most to the last fiction book you purchased on impulse?
- ○ The Title   ○ The Cover   ○ The Author   ○ The Story

3) What is usually the greatest influencer when you <u>plan</u> to buy a book?
- ○ Advertising   ○ Referral   ○ Book Review

4) How often do you access the internet?
- ○ Daily   ○ Weekly   ○ Monthly   ○ Rarely or never.

5) How many NEW paperback fiction novels have you purchased in the past 3 months?
- ○ 0 - 2   ○ 3 - 6   ○ 7 or more

YES! I have completed the Reader's Survey. Please send me the 2 FREE books and 2 FREE gifts (gifts are worth about $10) for which I qualify. I understand that I am under no obligation to purchase any books, as explained on the back of this card.

102/302 IDL GH6M

FIRST NAME	LAST NAME

ADDRESS

APT.#	CITY

STATE/PROV.	ZIP/POSTAL CODE

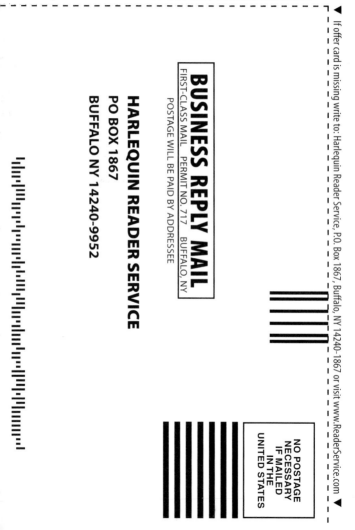

satisfaction than for us to make a statement by waving a flag from the summit."

Belle stopped and held out her hand to Sophie. "You carry it to the top, and we'll both wave it!"

Sophie saluted her friend. "That's a deal." Then looking down at herself, she couldn't help it. She burst into giggles. "I think it was the bloomers that did those fellows in."

Belle's accompanying laughter echoed across the valley below.

Chapter Eight

Tate sat in front of the fire, an open book in his lap. From the library alcove, he could hear the murmur of voices—Toby reading from a primer, Marcus asking a question, Sophie affirming their efforts. In less than two weeks, she'd made significant strides with the boys. Toby had actually crawled into his lap one evening as he was reading a recently delivered Denver newspaper and proudly pointed to words he recognized. "See, Papa?" he'd boasted. "I'm getting to be a good reader. And I computed the size of this house." *Computed?* Clearly that word sounded more sophisticated to the boy than "doing sums."

"Did you know that music is based on mathematics?" he heard Sophie inquire of her students.

"That can't be true," Marcus objected.

"It's just singing and fiddling," Toby added.

Curious, Tate leaned forward.

"Look here," she said.

From his chair, Tate watched her make notations on a piece of paper, the boys clustered around her,

Tate turned back to his book, but found himself re-reading the same paragraph. Any remaining concentration was broken by the sound of a lilting, clear soprano. "Lullaby and good night, with roses bedight…" Her voice held him in thrall, but it was the final words of the song, dying away, that brought tears to his eyes. "…Lay thee down now and rest, May thy slumber be blessed." Who had ever sung lullabies to his sons? Maybe a nanny early on. Certainly not Ramona. Then another equally disturbing thought occurred to him. Who had ever sung him lullabies?

"…and this song is by a wonderful new German composer, Johannes Brahms. Did you like it?"

Both boys gave enthusiastic assent.

"Look, now, at the mathematics. You see that I have drawn lines and symbols on this paper. This is the way music looks on a page."

"Why?" Toby's voice was mystified. "Just sing it."

"If we only heard music, it would be much more difficult to pass it on to others far away or to perform it the way the composer intended."

"That makes sense," Marcus said. "Toby, think about it. Mr. Brahms lives in Europe. How could we know his music unless there was a way to communicate it in writing?"

Tate couldn't help himself. He stepped into the alcove, and after securing Sophie's nod of approval, took a chair at the other end of the table. He watched in wonder as she explained the mathematical timing involved in the shape of the notes and the vertical bar lines. Then she tapped out the rhythm, drawing out *by* longer time than *lulla*, and showed them how the notes reflected the timing. Then she reached for another piece of paper and quickly sketched four bars of a score. "Now, then, boys. How would you tap out this rhythm?"

Tate watched in amazement as the boys quickly grasped the concept.

"Enough for this lesson," Sophie announced. "Let's finish by singing Brahms's 'Cradle Song' together." She nodded to him, soliciting his participation, yet he could hardly utter a sound, so moved was he by his sons' sweet voices raised in song. When the notes died away, silence hovered in the air until Sophie clapped her hands. "Bravo, young men!"

Tate noted how his sons gazed at her with delight. Even though he had engaged Sophie reluctantly, he doubted a male tutor from the East could have aroused such curiosity and adoration. Yet caution was needed, lest the boys become overly attached to her. He couldn't bear the thought of their being crushed once again by a female who, for whatever reasons, might walk away from them.

Released from their studies, the boys ran off in search of the pups. Sophie gathered up the papers and stowed the writing utensils. Finishing, she turned to him. "It was good of you to join us…to show the boys your interest. I hope you know you are always welcome."

"It's not often I have the time," he hedged. "Business occupies me."

"I understand your myriad enterprises require your attention, but so do your sons."

He winced. "Is that a criticism?"

"I did not intend it as one, but as a reminder. Children are not forever, and what happens to them as youngsters has a great bearing on what kind of adults they become."

The woman had pricked a sore. What had happened to him as a child should happen to no one. He wanted his boys to know they were loved. Sophie was right. He had been too detached, too afraid his influence would more closely resemble that of his own mother and father rather than that of a more loving parent. He swallowed back his hurt and self-insight.

"Tate?" He looked up into Sophie's quizzical glance. "Are you all right?"

"Just lost in thought. You…you opened a wound."

She sat down and folded her hands on the table. "I'm listening."

Could he bring himself to say what he was thinking? In the distance a puppy yipped, a boy laughed, the fire crackled. "I don't know how to be a good father." She raised her hand in protest, but he rushed on. "Please, no demurrals. I had no parent after whom to model myself."

"They died when you were young?"

"No. But I never felt wanted or appreciated. I couldn't do much of anything right in their eyes. Now, as an adult, I understand that they were cold, unloving people. I doubt there was much, if any, affection between them. Our home, our so-called family, was all for show."

He looked away from Sophie, whose eyes were awash with tears. "I was foolish to expect Ramona to be any different. Once she and the boys moved to Colorado, no matter how hard I tried to create the loving, stable home of my boyish fantasies, I failed. So—" he sighed deeply "—here we are."

Sophie covered his hand with her own. "My dear man, you are too hard on yourself."

He curled his fingers around her hand, as if it were a lifeline. He cleared his throat before daring to look at her. "I appreciate how you so effortlessly give Marcus and Toby the love they need. They soak it up. I don't seem to know how to do that."

"It's natural to want to make men of them, I suppose, just as my father did with my brothers. He didn't want them to be soft. But that does not mean you should withhold your approval and affection, as your parents obviously did. Discipline is necessary, of course. But always, first and foremost, is love."

"How did you become so wise?"

Her smile lit up the room. "I owe any wisdom I possess in this regard to scientific observation. This ornery, outspoken sister and daughter learned a great deal from the school of experience. As for you? You don't need my help, you just need to allow yourself to love. To let go of an unhappy past and embrace the present. Trust me, God desires the best for you."

He stared at her, caught between wanting to believe her and longing to retreat to the comfort of his customary isolation. Her eyes never left his, and in them, he read both challenge and caring. Finally he mumbled to himself, "What's God got to do with anything?"

Before she could respond, Toby burst into the room followed by Marcus, who carried a spoon and large tin can covered with canvas. "Listen to this! We made it ourselves. Bertie helped."

Marcus began slowly beating on the makeshift drum, the tempo slow-slow-quick-quick-slow. Then both boys chanted in rhythm, "We-like-learning-things."

When they finished, Tate held out his arms. "Great job!" The boys came and nestled within his embrace. Only when he looked up did he note that Sophie had slipped from the room.

"Wanna hear more, Papa?" Toby whispered, his face alight.

Tate inhaled the outdoorsy smell of his son's hair. "I do," he said quietly. "That was quite remarkable."

"It's because of Miss Sophie," said Marcus.

Even as he listened to another drum performance, Tate understood that it was too late for any of them to view Sophie Montgomery as merely a tutor.

The next day while Beauty played in the yard, Sophie knelt beside a row of lettuce in her small garden. It seemed she had only to turn her back before weeds encroached or animals enjoyed the leafy delicacy. The day was warm and perspiration dampened her brow. Busy with tutoring Marcus and Toby and hiking with Belle, she'd neglected her own home. Now everywhere she looked another chore demanded her attention. Mending, dusting, grooming Ranger, blacking the stove— the list was endless. When she was occupied with the Lockwood boys or with Belle, she didn't have so much time to think. Or remember.

Today the loss of Charlie was a weight crushing her spirit. By now they'd not only have been married but would surely have had a child or two. She pictured his strong, tanned hands, the way they had caressed the limestone of the Flint Hills, as if he intuited how it would perfectly suit the buildings he had in mind. Those same roughened hands had ever so gently traced the line of her jaw and lifted her fingers to his lips. Savagely, she rooted out a weed. Memory. Sometimes she could keep it at bay. Other times, like now, it intruded, threatening to overwhelm her with what might have been. Little Reuben and Jessica remained only fantasy—the future children she and Charlie had named in their daydreaming. Listening to the water rushing over the rocks in the nearby stream, she sometimes thought she heard

Charlie's robust laughter, and every time she contemplated the stony faces of the mountains, she imagined discovering them with Charlie, whose affinity for all things geological had been moving to observe.

She sat back on her heels and removed her bonnet. In moments like this, she was forced to acknowledge that she had failed to foresee the challenges involved in setting up housekeeping by herself in the middle of an untamed environment. Nights when a fearsome, cold wind rattled the wooden shingles or when the baying of coyotes sounded close, she wondered what she had been thinking to cling so stubbornly to her vision. Not to mention one protective she-bear who had destroyed any illusion of control. She didn't even want to think about winter—the snow, the isolation, the sheer boredom. Although it wasn't in her nature to give up, the thought of wintering in the cabin was increasingly unappealing.

Disgusted, she retrieved her bonnet, stood and focused on the scene before her. Meadows green with waving grass, peaks bold and timeless and the silver of the rushing stream. Where would she rather be? At home, pitied and protected in the bosom of the Kansas family who loved her dearly? Being a schoolmarm in a small New England town, like so many of her fellow academy students? Suddenly, nothing seemed more important than soaking her tired feet in the icy stream. She went into the house, set her bonnet aside and picked up the latest book she'd borrowed from Tate's library—the fascinating *Around the World in Eighty Days* by the Frenchman Jules Verne—then walked to a rock beside the stream and sat down. The bracing massage of the water over her bare feet coupled with the exciting story made for pure indulgence. Not for the first time, she was thankful for Tate's standing order with a Philadelphia bookseller, since new titles arrived with almost every post. She wondered about the neglected little boy he'd been whose main companions, by his own admission, were books and a dog. She pulled her feet out of the water and sat back on the rock. She would simply have to discipline herself in order to accomplish her domestic chores and also fulfill her obligations to the Lockwoods and to Belle. As she finished a chapter, the sun settled over the western mountains and a cool breeze raised goose bumps on her arms. How could she consider being elsewhere? Her place was here in this special valley.

Tucking the book under her arm, she strolled toward the house, determined to iron the shirtwaists she'd washed yesterday, but just as she reached the porch, she heard someone approaching on horseback. Tate's foreman, Sam, slid from the saddle and waved. "Got letters for you, miss," he called.

She hurried toward him. "It's thoughtful of you to deliver them."

He shifted from foot to foot. "Not my idea. Mr. Lockwood's. Sent me for the mail down to Harpers'. Said if there was anything for you, I was to deliver it." He reached in his saddlebag and pulled out a pair of envelopes. "Here," he said, thrusting them at her. "Duty's done. I'll be takin' my leave."

He remounted and started off at a trot. She stared at the letters—one from Lily and one from Rose, her sisters-in-law, so different from one another and yet so loving and dear. The tears she'd been fighting throughout the afternoon tempered her joy at receiving messages from her family. She pulled a rocker nearer the edge of the porch where the light was better and settled with the letters. She started with Rose's.

My dearest Sophie,

Seth joins me in sending you our love and also our thanks for your recent communication concerning the wonders of Estes Park, both natural and human. We are grateful you are thriving. I know you are curious about your father.

Living with him on the ranch has been a blessing, since he does require some attention. Although his speech is getting easier to understand, he has trouble with his right hand and arm and needs assistance with things like buttoning his shirt and holding a cup. That has not stopped him from trying to help around the place. He is able to ride, which is a blessing since it gives him pleasure and makes him feel useful.

Our Alf is growing into such a fine boy and enjoys helping his grandpa, and of course little Andrew is a joy to us all. Seth tells me to convey how much he misses you and your feistiness. I miss you, too, dear.

Sophie stared into space, letting Rose's words wash over her. It was difficult to imagine her vigorous, vital father impaired in any manner. He would fight to get better—that was his nature—but not without a great deal of frustration. Rose hadn't said much about her responsibility in caring for him, but that was just like her—self-effacing. Yet Sophie knew Rose was devoted to all the Montgomerys and would spare nothing to ease their lives.

She set Rose's letter aside and opened Lily's.

Dearest Sophie,

I know how worried you must be about your father. Truth to tell, he has had quite a time of it. In Father's medical opinion, he thinks Andrew is making progress, but it seems slow to us, and Andrew often is quite impatient with himself and others. He doesn't blame God, but he does question why he has been afflicted. As you might expect, Rose is a saint with him, and Alf and Andy follow him like puppies. But, in truth, it is Aunt Lavinia who keeps him from giving up.

Sophie sighed, picturing her father's impatience. Who would ever have thought that Rose and Lily's sophisticated aunt Lavinia Dupree would play such a vital role in their lives, especially Pa's? They had all been surprised when the newly widowed Saint Louis socialite had visited her Flint Hills family and then made the stunning announcement that she was building a summer home there. The woman did not suffer fools lightly, and Sophie could well imagine Lavinia's intransigence in putting Pa through his paces.

She comes to the ranch at least three times a week and barks at him until he does some of the therapeutic exercises and movements she claims to have read about. If the situation weren't so sad, it would be almost comical, yet beyond her badgering and his recalcitrance, I believe they have deep respect for one another. Caleb and Seth do what they can, but their hearts are sore, so it is understandably more difficult for them to be stern with their father. I am sorry to have begun with news which may distress you. On a lighter note, our daughters are thriving and growing like weeds.

Sophie finished the news concerning her nieces, then set the letters aside, lost in worry for her father as the sun finally slid behind the mountains, leaving her in the shadows.

After church the following Sunday, Sophie and Belle huddled together, studying a rudimentary map of Longs Peak. "See here," Belle said, pointing to a line on the paper. "This is where the boulder field begins, and I am told the ascent through those obstacles can be rigorous."

Sophie leaned forward. "Boulder field? You mean nothing but rocks?"

"We will be above tree line there and, yes, guides say it's nothing but rocks, some so big they defy belief. So I propose that in the next month or so we find areas where we can practice rock climbing."

Sophie nodded, but before she could comment, Martha Tyler bustled over. "You girls, I declare. If I'm hearing right, folks are saying you two plan to climb Longs Peak."

Belle smiled up at her neighbor. "We are."

Martha glanced around as if fearing to be overheard. "I'm not one to say you've lost your senses. I get mighty tired of menfolk always thinking they know what's best for women. But I do hope you'll be careful. That mountain can be treacherous."

"We're doing our best to prepare," Sophie said.

"I surely couldn't do it myself, but I just wanted you to know I'll be praying for your success." Then Martha beamed at them both before rejoining the others.

"Well, that's one supporter." Belle held up an index

finger. "On the other hand, Mabel Hawes pulled me aside before church to tell me that rumors of our intentions were 'scandalous' and 'against God's natural order.'"

"I imagine it's always been thus with pioneers, male or female. Think about how his countrymen scoffed at Columbus."

"For me, all such negative comments serve as motivation." Belle nodded at Sophie. "We have to succeed."

Riding home, Sophie was charged with excitement. Belle's enthusiasm was infectious, and the idea of proving naysayers wrong stoked her determination. Her brothers had learned over the years that she was fearless, even unstoppable. Yet she knew what they would say if they were here. *You're doing what? Are you crazy?* That had always been their initial reaction to the unconventional things she undertook, like riding in the roundup, but in the end, they had clapped her on the back and crowed, *That's our girl!*

Hearing a horse approaching, Sophie slowed to a walk and pulled Ranger to the side of the road. Around the bend came Tate, mounted on his large chestnut. He drew close and reined in his horse. "Where have you been?"

"Good day to you, too," Sophie said with asperity. What business was it of Tate Lockwood's where and how she spent her time?

"I couldn't find you at your cabin."

"Of course not, it's Sunday."

"What's that got to do with it?"

"Along with many others, I attend services at the Tylers'."

"Oh, that," Tate muttered dismissively.

Sophie held her tongue, sensing that Tate Lockwood

was in no mood for a sermon. "Is something wrong with one of the boys?"

"Why would you assume that?"

"You apparently came to the cabin to fetch me. I can't imagine another reason."

He leaned over his saddle horn as if cowed. "I've botched this conversation. Let's start over."

"A splendid idea."

"I've come to invite you to spend the afternoon with us. The boys have planned some games to celebrate Toby's birthday."

"Birthday? I had no idea. If you had told me earlier, I would have prepared a gift."

"Bertie has baked a cake. When the boys realized this morning that I had failed to invite you, they were quite upset."

Irked, Sophie didn't want to make it easy for him. "I have other plans for the afternoon."

He raised a skeptical eyebrow, but his tone was gentler when he said, "Surely you won't disappoint the boys."

"Why do I feel as if I'm being manipulated?"

He grinned. "If that's what it takes…"

"You know very well I can't ignore Toby's birthday, even if his father does lack social graces."

Trotting alongside Tate toward his house, Sophie couldn't decide if she was more galled or amused. Verbal sparring stirred up her competitive instincts. She was annoyed to have had no advance notice of Toby's birthday, but she looked forward to celebrating with him. Once again, though, Tate Lockwood had caused her consternation. Worse yet, he'd gotten his way.

What a buffoon! Of course his approach to Sophie had been rude. It was only when Toby asked him this morning if he'd remembered to invite Sophie that Tate realized his oversight, so he'd lit out to find her. He'd been concerned she might turn down his request and thereby devastate his son. Yet his invitation to Sophie had made him sound like an insensitive fool. When they reached the house, she leaped from her saddle before he could assist her. "I'm sorry if I've offended you," he said as they walked to the front door.

"This isn't the first time and I doubt it will be the last," she said saucily. She laid a hand on his arm. "But considering the occasion of your delightful son's birthday, you are forgiven."

With those words, Sophie flashed a mischievous grin and hurried ahead of him through the door, where a noisy crush of dogs and boys greeted them. In that moment of disorder, an inexplicable happiness enfolded him.

Toby threw himself at his teacher. "Miss Sophie, you came!"

"Happy birthday, young man. So now you are nine years old?"

"I am, and we're gonna have cake and games now that you're here."

Marcus corralled Minnie and sidled up to Sophie. "My brother thinks he's so big, but he's not as big as me."

"And he never will be," Sophie said, "but older brothers needn't lord it over younger brothers."

Marcus cocked his head. "I guess you're right."

Tate never ceased to be amazed by the woman's instinctive skill in handling the boys. After gathering for Bertie's delicious spice cake, they adjourned to the library for a few games of dominoes, during which Tate noted how Toby's mathematical skills had improved under Sophie's tutelage. Next, Toby wanted to play jack-straws, but after only one game, he tired of the concentration and dexterity demanded to lift a slender stick from the pile. Then Marcus suggested they draw the shutters and make shadow finger puppets. Tate soon learned Sophie was adept at creating shadow figures on the wall. She had the boys giggling over the bird that flapped its wings and the pig that opened and shut its mouth.

"Show me how," Toby demanded after she'd depicted a cat. Both boys watched intently and then repeated the pattern.

"Would you like to see a bear?" Tate asked, entering into the fun. He formed the image of a bear on its hind legs and growled in accompaniment.

Marcus approached his father to study the position of his hands and fingers. "How come you never showed us that?"

The boy's question pierced Tate's heart. Why hadn't he played with the boys, taught them games? Had he really been that preoccupied with business? Or had he been afraid of making a mistake with them? Had his aloofness been self-protective? What kind of father puts his own selfish needs ahead of those of his children? When the answer came, his heart fell. He was just like his own father.

He turned to Marcus and put his arm around him. "I should have, son. I should have." He swallowed. "From now on, we'll try to have more fun."

As his son turned away, Tate heard him mumble, "We'll see."

The challenge in those words was clear. Tate would have to prove himself, but at least the door was open for change.

* * *

After the games, Tate opened the shutters and Sophie noticed long afternoon shadows on the floor. "Oh dear, I'm afraid I have overstayed my welcome. I have just enough time to get home." She gave each of the boys a hug and hurried to the door.

"I can't tell you what your being here meant to Toby," Tate said as he accompanied her outside.

"I'm glad you insisted." She hesitated, wondering whether to speak her mind and, as usual, honesty overcame tact. "I hope you're aware of what happened this afternoon when you relaxed and let yourself play. Your boys saw a new side of you, one they liked. One I liked."

"I don't want to appear unapproachable. It's time I realize my parents' mistakes should not be repeated in the next generation. Thank you, Sophie, for showing me a different way."

Glancing up at him, Sophie was arrested by the raw longing in his eyes. "You are a fine father, and you'll only get better," she murmured, laying a hand on his chest. She gasped then, as he suddenly enfolded her in his arms and rested his chin on the top of her head.

"With your help," he whispered. "You are working wonders with the Lockwoods."

The scent of wood smoke and pine clinging to him made her light-headed. She should step back. Yet it had been so long since she had experienced the comfort of a masculine embrace. Not since…Charlie. And then Tate was twining her hair through his fingers, and she could feel the rapid rhythm of his heartbeat. *Now. Retreat now.* She wrenched herself from his grasp, shaking her head. Somehow she found her voice. "I can't do this."

Tate, too, stepped back. "Forgive me. My gratitude

overcame common sense. I meant only to show my appreciation."

Clasping her trembling hands behind her, she sought the right words. "Of course. I'm delighted I could help." She couldn't get away fast enough, but even as Ranger put distance between her and Tate Lockwood, her breath caught in her chest. For that brief moment, she had experienced not only a powerful attraction to the man but a sense of coming home. No! He was her students' father, nothing more. Besides, he had none of Charlie's sense of fun and passion for life. *Charlie, Charlie, Charlie*—her homeward mantra. Yet instead of succeeding in redirecting her thoughts, it only reinforced her memory of that terrifying and wonderful embrace... and of Tate.

Chapter Nine

No matter how hard he tried to distract himself with work or how much he tossed and turned at night, in the three days since Toby's birthday, Tate had been unable to banish Sophie from his thoughts. It was insanity. He'd been helpless to keep from embracing her, and now the memory of her silky hair, her light floral scent and her soft body yielding in his arms was pure torment. Couldn't he have governed his emotions? Resisted a need that rose in him like an unquenchable flame? He admitted he was vulnerable with her in ways that both surprised and unnerved him. Never before, certainly not with Ramona, had he revealed details of his childhood or been so aware of his need for approval.

He assuredly had spooked Sophie. So far this week when she'd come to tutor his boys, her greetings to him had been impersonal and professional. This afternoon that had changed. The boys, oblivious to any tension, had challenged the two adults to a checkers match— Sophie and Marcus versus Toby and Tate. So here he sat watching Marcus and Sophie formulate strategies while Toby squirmed beside him, awaiting their turn at the board. "We're gonna beat them, right, Papa?"

Tate tousled his son's curls. "'Triumph' is our middle name."

"Really? I thought mine was 'Philip.'"

Tate laughed softly. "And so it is."

"But we will triumph, I hope."

"It's all about strategy, son."

But what strategy was there to deal with the feelings he experienced each time he looked across the table at Sophie? Sun streaming through the open window highlighted the gold strands in her hair, and he longed to touch the faint freckles on her cheeks. He stood and walked away from the table as if a few feet of distance could protect him from her appeal. Even if he could act upon his attraction to her, he wouldn't. Too much was at stake: a relationship with Sophie could risk scarring his sons if it didn't work out. That settled, he returned to his seat, vowing to enjoy Sophie as a tutor and friend and nothing more.

Toby pointed to the checkers board. "Our turn, Papa."

Once his decision about Sophie had been made, Tate relaxed into the playfulness of the afternoon, which ended with singing. There was no reason why he couldn't enjoy these pleasant times after the boys' lessons were finished. Besides, Sophie wouldn't be their tutor forever, and it was up to him to learn how to interact with them in a more positive way.

As Sophie was tying her bonnet in preparation to leave, she approached him, though he noticed she kept several feet between them. "Do you recall on the occasion of my employment when I requested use of a horse and cart from time to time?"

"I do."

"I ask your permission to bring the boys to my cabin

this coming Friday afternoon, where I plan to keep them overnight until I return them Saturday around four o'clock."

"Why would that be necessary?"

"I would like them to learn gardening and the uses of plants, as well as some rudimentary knowledge of baking and cooking. That is more easily achieved at my place."

Tate mulled over her unusual suggestion. "Would they be safe?"

"I assure you they will be. Don't forget that I know how to protect myself."

He remembered not only her boasts about marksmanship, but her quick thinking when faced with an angry bear. "I plan to be working in the high pastures those days. You would alert Bertie or Sam to any problems, if necessary?"

"Naturally." She hesitated before adding, "The boys could profit from a change of scene and some education in practical matters."

For the life of him, he couldn't come up with a sound reason to refuse her. "Come for the midday meal Friday, and one of my men will have a horse and cart waiting for you afterward."

Then she smiled, and all his good intentions where she was concerned nearly went up in smoke. Controlling himself, he nodded curtly and walked away, determined to keep their relationship businesslike.

After lunch on Friday, Sophie loaded the boys into the cart and checked to be sure Bertie had packed a change of clothes, coats and nightwear for each of them. Pancho harnessed a small mare called Sallie to the cart and tied Ranger behind. It was a day of blinding blue skies and warm temperatures, perfect for the lessons Sophie had in mind. Toby couldn't stop asking questions and even Marcus looked happy. Wondering if the boys had ever been away from home, Sophie asked if they were looking forward to spending the night. "I'm excited," exclaimed Toby.

Marcus gave a more reasoned answer. "We left home when we moved to Colorado and then again when we left Central City to come here."

"But you've never left just for fun?"

Both boys shook their heads. "I thought Papa would say no," Marcus added.

"Why is that?"

Marcus frowned. "He thinks we're babies. That we'll get hurt or something."

"Yeah, he's a scaredy-cat, Miss Sophie."

"He loves you both," Sophie explained. "He doesn't want anything bad to happen to you."

"He doesn't want *anything* to happen to us at all," Marcus muttered. "I'm sick of it."

Sophie sighed. Already this adventure had hit a sour note. "Your father wouldn't have given his permission if he didn't think our outing was something you'd enjoy."

Toby snuggled closer. "I like being with you, Miss Sophie. And I never spent a night in a cabin."

"It's not fancy, you know."

"We know," Marcus said. "But you'll make it interesting."

Later when the three of them were kneeling on the ground in her garden, she thought she had succeeded in engaging their curiosity. Sophie demonstrated the difference between root vegetables and those grown from seed. "You mean some plants grow under the dirt?" Toby asked, incredulous.

"They do. Some of those have to be planted in the fall."

Marcus looked up from the onion he held. "Don't they freeze in the snow?"

"Not if they're buried deep enough. Think of the bulbs as being like bears hibernating in the winter."

Toby stood up and moved to a different row. "Why are these vines climbing poles?"

"Those are beans and they would fall in a heap on the ground and rot if we didn't help them." Sophie handed each boy a basket. "Why don't you pick some and we'll cook them for dinner."

When they returned to the cabin, Sophie set the beans to boil, throwing in some onion and salt pork for seasoning. Then while they waited for supper to cook, Sophie pulled a botany book from a small shelf and handed it to Marcus. "See how many of the plants we discussed today you can find. After you read about them, maybe you could tell us what you learned. And, Toby, we are going to need to double the cookie and bread recipes we'll be making tomorrow." She passed him a sheet of paper, a pencil and two recipes. "You are getting very adept with numbers. Can you compute how to change the recipes?"

It was sweet how conscientiously each boy went about his assigned task. Their eagerness to please her touched a place deep in her heart. After a rollicking supper during which the boys couldn't stop chattering about the differences between their house and the cabin, they adjourned to the front porch just in time to watch the sun dip behind the mountains. Darkness fell quickly, and soon the sky was spattered with pinpoints of starlight. "I would like to know more about stars," Marcus said quietly.

"The study of stars is called astronomy, and if you would like, we can add that subject to your studies." Sophie laid a hand on the boy's shoulder. "But there is mystery as well as science in the stars."

"What's mystery?" Toby asked.

"That which is so beautiful or moving it is beyond our power to explain. Look there." Sophie guided his arm to a point in the sky where an especially bright star shone. "Do we have any idea how far away that is? Or how a single star can shed such brilliant light for us to see? And even if we wanted, we couldn't count all those stars." She let a silence fall. "The unknown—that is the nature of mystery."

Toby snuggled closer. "You're really smart, Miss Sophie." He tilted his head back and gazed at the heavens. "I like this adventure."

It was late when she tucked the boys into the pallets she'd prepared for them. Marcus did not look pleased. "I've never slept on the floor."

"We're like soldiers, right, Miss Sophie?"

"Snug as bugs in a rug, gentlemen." She knelt between them and, holding their hands, murmured, "Dear God, watch over these Your children that they may be protected through the night and find their rest in Thee. Amen."

Toby smiled, but Marcus looked uncomfortable. "We don't pray at bedtime."

"Never?"

"We just go to sleep."

"Who tucks you in?"

Toby tugged at her sleeve. "What's 'tuck in' mean?"

Sophie fought tears that would only confuse the boys. "It means this." She pulled up the covers around each child, then leaned over and kissed each precious forehead. "Sweet dreams, you two, and roses to your pillows." When she stood to go to her bed, she added softly, "That's what it means to be tucked in."

Tate rode the ridge, surveying the landscape for stray cattle. The morning was overcast and the air hung unusually heavy. He would meet up with his hands and head for home as soon as he satisfied himself there were no motherless calves in the nearby box canyon. He glanced once more at the sky, hoping the rains would hold off until Sophie returned the boys this afternoon. Ever since he'd given permission for them to visit her and spend the night, he'd had misgivings. Her reason for inviting them was valid, yet it was one more tie the boys would have to her. The balance between her effectiveness as a teacher and their growing emotional attachment to her was worrying him. He had never seen his sons so happy and productive nor had he ever seen them cotton to a woman with such enthusiasm and affection. However, the likelihood of Sophie's enduring the winter here was slim. He didn't expect her to stay in the valley after her fantasy of independence played itself out. As for her determination to climb Longs Peak? For reasons that escaped him, she seemed intent on proving herself in a man's arena, despite the danger involved.

Glancing toward Longs, he noticed that in just a few minutes it had been obscured by a cloud cover of nimbus formations. On the horizon jagged streaks of lightning speared the distant mountains. He wheeled his horse and galloped toward Curly and the other hands, who were engaged in counting the herd. As he neared them, he hollered and waved his hat. "Leave off. Storm's coming." Ordinarily he would have insisted they hunker down and weather the storm, but he didn't like the looks of this one. From past experiences with storm runoff rampaging down streambeds, Tate did not want to be stranded in the high country.

It was only as they took off at a gallop for the ranch house that his thoughts turned to Sophie and the boys. A stream ran close to her cabin. Would they be safe? Yet as the first fat raindrops fell, he knew his chances of crossing the river before it swelled with rushing water and reaching Sophie's cabin were infinitesimal. Even as he spurred his horse to greater speed, the boom of thunder drowned out his cry of frustration. All he'd ever wanted was to keep his sons safe. How could he have let Sophie remove them from the solid ranch house built to withstand precisely such a cloud buster? Her cabin was a mere reed in the wind, but it was all that protected those he loved. Then as lightning forked less than a mile away, a stunning thought blazed across his consciousness—those he loved just might include the headstrong Sophie Montgomery. His "No!" was lost in another roll of thunder echoing across the valley.

At the first sound of thunder bellowing from mountain to mountain, Sophie had understood two things. She must get Ranger and the cart horse into the barn with plenty of food and water. At the same time she had to prevent the boys from panicking. This was no ordinary thunderstorm. Everywhere she looked, she witnessed nature unleashed. Rugged pines shook in the gusts of wind ushering the front toward them. Angry gray clouds scudded across the sky as if driven by a malevolent power. Ordering Beauty to stay, she settled the boys with drawing paper and pencils, before racing to the barn to secure the animals. The crack of thunder deafened her, and the horses' eyes rolled in alarm. The first raindrops hit her in the face as she ran back to the cabin. When she opened the door a violent wind wrenched it from her grasp and banged it into the wall. The startled expressions on the boys' faces conveyed their terror. She secured the latch and drew a deep breath, willing herself to a calm she didn't feel.

"Is it raining, Miss Sophie?"

No sooner had Toby voiced the question than a deluge descended, howling around the house and pelting the roof and windows with curtains of water.

Marcus stared down at his brother. "What do you think, dummy?"

Sophie stood over Marcus, sensing the fear that had motivated his barb. Placing her hands on his shoulders, she said, "There's no need for belittling your brother, Marcus. In stormy times, it's more important than ever to be kind to one another."

Toby sniffled.

"Sorry," Marcus mumbled.

A roar of thunder seeming to come from directly above made the boys jump. Toby looked up at Sophie, his eyes wide. "I'm scared," he said in a thin voice.

"It is, indeed, a gigantic storm, but we are snug and warm. We have plenty of food and, most important, we have each other." She moved a chair so that she could sit between them. "Now, then, let's forget the rain. I have an idea." She handed them each two pieces of paper. "Take the scissors and cut these into strips. Marcus, on each strip, write a verb."

He nodded and went to work.

"Toby, remember what a noun is?" He nodded. "You are to write a noun on each strip."

"Why?"

"You'll see shortly."

While they worked, she moved to the window, almost totally obscured by slashing rain except when lightning illuminated the dismal scene outside. Kansas had ferocious storms, but she didn't know when she'd seen one as unrelenting as this. She shuddered to think what would happen to the river unless the rain let up soon.

She hoped the humor of the word game she had in mind would relieve some of the tension. "Turn your nouns and verbs facedown. When I pause and point to you, pull one from your pile and read it." She fought off her concerns to proceed as normally as possible. "Once upon a time a large, old—" She pointed to Toby.

"Elephant."

"—was lost in the woods and didn't know what to do. Finally he decided to—"

She smiled at Marcus, who said, "Dance."

Once the giggles began, they continued throughout the duration of the story.

"Let's do it again, please?" Toby had apparently forgotten about the storm outside. "I have some good ideas for words."

Marcus shot her a look, wise with understanding of the necessity for diversion. In this fashion the afternoon passed. Finally Toby raised the question she'd been avoiding. "We're not going home today, are we?"

"No, dear. We will have to wait for the storm to pass."

"So we get to spend another night with you?" He beamed. "Yippee."

After a cold dinner of biscuits, ham, cheese, pickles and the sugar cookies the boys had made earlier in the day, they huddled by the woodstove, blankets draped over their shoulders. Beauty lay on the floor, her head resting on Marcus's feet. "Tell us a story about when you were little like us," Toby said.

"Yes," Marcus agreed. "It's important to know a person's history."

Sophie put her arms around each boy and drew them closer. "Once upon a time, I lived in Missouri near a big river. My father owned a gristmill, where he ground grain into flour with a huge millstone. I used to love going there and listening to the rumble of the wheel as the weight of the stone ground the grain. I was the youngest child. My two older brothers, Seth and Caleb, were heroes to me. They could ride, shoot, climb trees and fish. So when I was just a little girl, I decided I wanted to be like them."

"Girls don't do that stuff," Toby said.

"Maybe most girls don't, but I did. I knew I could do anything I set my mind to. My brothers thought it was funny that I wanted to tag along, but they took me anyway and taught me all kinds of things."

"That was nice of them," Marcus observed.

"It was. But I did nice things for them, as well. I cooked, cleaned the house and washed and ironed their clothes."

"Wait. Even when you were a little girl, not like a, uh, woman?" Toby looked perplexed.

"Yes, even when I was barely tall enough to reach the pump and the stove."

Toby grinned. "That's *really* little. Younger maybe than me."

Marcus furrowed his brow. "But where was your mother? Didn't she do all those things?"

Sophie paused to gather her thoughts. She didn't want to upset the boys. "I had no mother."

"No mother?" Toby exploded. "How did you get borned, then?"

"My mother died right after she gave birth to me." Her throat clogged, and she was unable to continue.

"That's quite sad," Marcus said. "You never even knew her, right?"

"Not in person, but I knew a great deal about her from stories my father and brothers would tell. They told me she was a wonderful mother. I'm sorry I never knew her."

Toby patted her hand. "You're kind of like us. We don't got a mother, either."

The steel in Marcus's voice took Sophie by surprise. "Oh, we have a mother, Toby. She just doesn't want us. I'll bet Miss Sophie's mother would've wanted her. I'm glad our mother left. I don't care if I never see her again."

While Sophie ransacked her brain for a meaningful reply, Toby hung his head. "Sometimes I don't remember exactly what she looked like. Was she pretty?"

Marcus rolled his eyes. "I suppose, but what difference does it make? She's gone now."

"Growing up without a mother is difficult," Sophie began. "All three of us would like to have known a mother who told us stories and fussed over us. For some of us, life just doesn't turn out the way we think it's meant to."

"Sometimes I get very angry," Marcus said quietly.

"I don't blame you. It must've been so hard when she left."

Marcus wiped his nose on his sleeve. "I don't understand what I did to her."

She had never heard a more forlorn remark. "My dear boy, it wasn't your fault."

Toby leaned closer, but she had eyes only for Marcus. "Then why did she leave?"

"I betcha you were naughty," Toby suggested.

"No, Toby, neither you nor your brother bears any responsibility for what happened. When you are older, you will understand that relationships between adults can be complicated. Sometimes one person has a dream, but the other person cannot share it. God intends us to live our lives as the best person He created us to be, but sometimes we put ourselves in situations where it's hard for that to happen. I think perhaps your mother had to leave to find herself."

"I miss not having a mother," Toby said, snuggling even closer. "Maybe you could be our mother, Miss Sophie."

Sophie's heart plummeted. She could not give these hurting little fellows any hope of such an outcome. "It's a little late for that, dear. What matters when one is disappointed is to go forward trusting that God will bring us to an even better place."

"How can God do that when He took our mother away from us?" Marcus's tone was bitter.

Sophie gently took his face between her hands and guided it close to hers. "God did not take your mother away, nor does He punish anyone with such cruelty. Instead, it is God who has been with you two and your papa so that you can make a better life. God was present with my family through the years, and with the love of my father and brothers, I never felt alone."

She could barely hear Marcus when he finally whispered, "I think Papa blames God."

Sophie felt as though her heart had cracked in two. Such misunderstanding and pain for ones so young... and for a man still embittered by betrayal.

Even late into the night the rain beat down in torrents, but neither that sound nor Beauty's snores could silence her rioting thoughts. Her heart ached on behalf of these darling boys and the father who loved them so. Finally the downpour changed to a gentle drizzle. In the sudden lull she whispered to the God she hoped was listening. *Bless, O Lord, these innocent boys and their father that they may come to a place of peace, secure in their knowledge of Your love and care.*

Brilliant sunshine and cloudless blue skies greeted Sophie when she woke the next morning. She dressed quietly, stoked the woodstove and mixed up pancake batter. Just as Marcus sat up, looking around and rubbing his eyes, Beauty raced to the door, and with a single yip alerted them just as a loud knock sounded. "You all right, miss?"

She'd know that loud, raspy voice anywhere. Grizzly. She opened the door, her arms raised in welcome. "My, you are a sight for sore eyes."

"You're not the first woman to tell me the 'sore' part." He reached down to hold Sarge. "You get through the storm all right? I notice the water came up close to your privy and barn."

"Who's there?" Toby padded barefoot across the wooden floor.

Grizzly threw back his head and laughed. "Well, what have we here, little fella?"

Toby clung to Sophie's skirt. "Me and Marcus, we spent two nights here with Miss Sophie."

Marcus, now dressed, came up to stand behind his brother. "My father knows you."

"That he does. Tate Lockwood is a good man."

"Please come in, Grizzly. We'll eat shortly and you'd be mighty welcome."

As he stepped across the threshold, Beauty slipped past Sophie to join Sarge in the yard. Then after wolfing down their pancakes, the boys hurried outside to play with the dogs.

Only then did Grizzly lean forward and speak confidentially. "The river is way up. Some folks are stranded on the other side until the water recedes."

"Tate?"

"Yes, miss. I figure those little ones will be a mite anxious when they learn that news."

"And Tate will be beside himself."

"I figure you could use a little outing today, so here's what I propose. I'm not much of a churchgoer myself, but I reckon after that gully washer, I could use a dose of the Almighty. How about I escort you and the boys down to the Tylers' for services. I notice you've got a cart out there."

"I do." She thought over the proposition. If the boys were still unable to go home, she needed to forestall their worry, and the church gathering, including other children, might be a useful diversion. Besides, she was anxious about her neighbors' well-being.

Later, after helping the boys wash up, Sophie picked up Sallie's reins and followed along behind Grizzly. It was fortunate that her stream had come no higher, but when they came alongside the river, overflowing its banks, she couldn't believe her eyes. Brush and limbs washed over the rocks, slowed only by large boulders or man-made barriers.

"Look, Miss Sophie." Marcus pointed upstream to the wooden bridge that led to their home. "It's underwater."

"How will we get home?" Toby's lower lip quivered.

"The water will subside, although it may take a day or two."

"How can Papa get to us?"

Marcus straightened up. "Toby, he'll find a way. Maybe he'll have to cross at another point. We're safe with Miss Sophie."

"But I want to see Papa."

Before Sophie could say a word, Marcus put an arm around his brother's shoulders. "Papa will come for us. You'll see."

Sophie allowed herself a brief moment of satisfaction. Apparently Marcus had registered her remark about the necessity of kindness. Yet in Toby's voice was proof of his anxiety.

She hoped the church service would get his mind off his worries. He was such a little boy to carry so much concern. At least he verbalized his. With Marcus, she was never sure what wounds festered beneath the surface.

Awake at dawn to survey the storm damage, Tate paced in a frenzy from window to door to window. Tree limbs scattered the earth, and in the distance he spotted debris hung up on the small portion of the bridge that was still above the waterline. The roar of river was audible even behind closed doors. He'd barely slept, worrying about Marcus and Toby. He knew Sophie would do everything in her power to keep them safe, but what did she know about the ferocity and unpredictability of mountain cloudbursts? As soon as it was feasible, he would find a safe place to cross the river and get to them. He had to assure himself that his sons were safe. The thought of losing them filled him with terror. What if they'd been playing near the streambed when the flash flood came? What if Sophie's cabin had been inundated? He couldn't bear imagining how terrified they must've been in a strange place during a wild deluge.

Over breakfast, Bertie had looked at him sympathetically. He didn't want her pity. "Fret not, sir. Miss Sophie will have known what to do."

Miss Sophie. She could ride like a man, handle a firearm, discourage a bear and scale mountains. But did that qualify her to keep two frightened boys from panic? He sincerely hoped so.

Finally, after helping Sam and the others settle the animals and begin clearing the land, he saddled his strongest horse and set out upriver shortly after noon, noting with irony the serenity of the sky in contrast with yesterday's violence.

At the first point of entry into the river, seething waters discouraged him. Gritting his teeth in frustration, he realized he would have to ride even farther upstream, thus delaying his reunion with Marcus and Toby. Finally he came to a place where the river normally meandered through a flat stretch. Today there was no "meandering," but riding up and down the water's edge, he decided this was his best chance of crossing. At first his horse balked, but with urgent spurring and guttural commands, Tate succeeded in getting his mount into the swirling waters. Once the horse realized his hooves could make contact with the riverbed, he valiantly fought the currents, resorting to swimming for only a few yards before again finding solid footing. As if sheer verbal exhortation could propel his steed forward, Tate leaned over his neck and let loose a string of commands—"Easy, fella" and "Go!"

Finally the horse emerged on the opposite bank,

snorting and shaking off the icy water coating his body. "Good boy." Tate exulted, halting long enough to catch his breath. Shivering, he reached in his pocket for the ham sandwich Bertie had pressed on him. "Now don't you go doing anything foolish," she'd said to him as he left for the barn. He crammed a bite into his mouth and followed it with a long drink from his canteen. Then, figuring his horse had had sufficient rest, he nudged him forward in a steady trot until they reached a trail west of the Harpers' and Tylers' places. He calculated it would take him a little over an hour to reach Sophie's cabin.

Approaching his neighbors' small settlement, he was dumbfounded to see a number of horses, carts and buggies assembled in front of Jackson Tyler's place. Had there been a tragedy of some sort? Nearing the home, strains of music floated on the air, and he made out the words of "Our God, Our Help in Ages Past" and was immediately transported to the hard-backed pews of his childhood where his father's sharp elbow prodded him into wakefulness and the preacher's voice rained down jeremiads liberally laced with words like *sin, eternal punishment* and *hellfire*. In his boyish helplessness, it always felt as if he, a defenseless child, were being pounded by the preacher's oratory into worthless bits of flesh and bone.

His stomach tightened. He shook his head to dispel the distressing memories. Then he saw it. The cart. Hitched to Sallie. He abruptly halted his horse. Were the boys safe? Surely Sophie had not taken them to the Sunday services he'd heard talk of. Relief warred with dismay. She had no right to bring them here.

Paralyzed by the impossibility of such a thing, he roused only when people streamed from the building, the sound of their excited chatter setting his teeth on edge. And then, bursting from the crowd was Toby, racing toward him. "Papa, Papa!"

Dismounting, he knelt on the ground, his arms open in welcome. The next thing he knew Toby had leaped on him, holding him tight around the neck. "I knew you'd come," his son whispered.

"I'm glad you're safe, son." He swallowed back the tears threatening to embarrass him.

Over Toby's shoulder he saw Marcus rapidly approaching followed by Sophie and Grizzly. He lifted Toby with him when he stood, making one arm available to embrace Marcus, who, though normally undemonstrative, clung to him. "Miss Sophie knew you would come for us," the older boy said.

"I wish I could have gotten here sooner."

"Guess what, Papa?" Toby took his cheeks between his hands. "We learned about Noah. Did you know God told Noah a big flood was coming, so Noah built a boat and loaded all these animals and birds and floated on the flood for many days and then he let loose a dove and—"

"Enough," Tate said.

"But don't you see? God saved Noah from the flood and he came to dry land and lived happily ever after. And God saved us, too, and so we gave Him thanks this morning and—"

"I don't want to hear about it," Tate said.

Marcus looked up, his face contorted in a frown. "But we haven't finished the story and it was really interesting and made me think about God. Why don't we ever talk about Him like Miss Sophie does?"

Barely controlling himself, Tate carefully set Toby down and asked them to wait for him at the cart.

Sophie stood beside Grizzly, both of them looking stunned.

Tate took a step forward, his mind churning with unpleasant memories of his childhood church experiences. "I am grateful to you, Sophie, for keeping my boys safe. However, you had no call to bring them to services without my permission. God is a convenient myth. Someone to blame when things go wrong. Someone to inspire false hope. Scriptural fairy tales have no place in my home."

Grizzly scratched his head. "Now, son, aren't you being a bit harsh?"

Sophie still had not spoken, but the stricken look on her face threatened his resolve. "God may be a presence in your lives, but I can't see that He's ever done much for me, so I'll thank you not to involve my sons in religious teaching or observances."

Sophie looked straight at him, her eyes full of tears. "Oh, Tate, how can you possibly say God has never done much for you when you have the proof right in front of you?"

"Where?" he barked, louder than he'd intended.

"There," she said, pointing to Marcus and Toby. She paused a moment before stepping forward and placing a hand on his chest. His breath caught. "I'm sorry you aren't able to open your heart to God. Perhaps that will come with time. Meanwhile, I shall endeavor not to influence your boys in matters of religion."

"I'm sure you meant well, but…" He couldn't finish the sentence. He started toward the cart, but then turned back. "Thank you for keeping my sons safe during the storm."

"They were very brave," she said softly.

He couldn't look at her further and stand accused by

her eyes, brimming with compassion. He didn't need her pity. Didn't need anything. Except his boys.

So why did the word *liar* consume him all the way home?

Chapter Ten

A week passed, during which the waters ebbed and Sophie went about restoring order to her garden. Just this morning Pancho had brought word that the Lockwood bridge had been repaired and it was safe for her to resume the boys' lessons. It was just as well some time had elapsed. Tate's rebuke outside the Tylers', so obviously born out of disappointment with and misunderstanding of God's purpose, had left her stymied. Even as she fumed, she admitted that she herself had questioned God on occasion, especially after Charlie was taken so cruelly from her. In fairness, Tate had known loss, too. Yet his inflexible position concerning religion not only vexed her but, far more important, concerned her. He was limiting the boys' knowledge of God and imprisoning himself in his disbelief. She felt helpless in the face of such obstinancy, even as she ached for the deep hurt the man must've experienced throughout his life. Could they ever regain the easy camaraderie the four of them had enjoyed on occasion?

Approaching the ranch house this Monday morning, Sophie had no idea what kind of welcome awaited her. Setting aside her trepidation regarding Tate, she had missed Marcus and Toby and was eager to see them. From now on she would stick to the business of education and disregard any fancies she had permitted herself concerning her charges' father. Her mind set, she knocked on the door, hoping she would not come face-to-face with Tate. Bertie answered with a huge smile. "Do come in. We've missed you here. The boys are eager to see you."

Almost before Bertie finished her sentence, Toby and Buster came running around the corner. "Miss Sophie! I knew you'd come." He pulled on her arm. "I gotta show you what I did."

Trailing him into the library alcove, Sophie knew that whatever her relationship with their father, she couldn't abandon the boys. Marcus rose when she neared the table. "You are most welcome. I fear the direction of my studies has suffered without you."

Toby produced a full two pages of addition and subtraction problems he'd worked on in her absence. After she'd assigned him a new story in his primer, she turned to Marcus. "Where are you having difficulties?"

"I've been studying about plants in one of my father's botany books, but even though I know some of the scientific names, it would be good to study Latin so I would know the meaning of those names." He looked at her with hope in his eyes. "Do you know Latin? Could you help me?"

"I'm no expert, but when I studied back East, Latin was among my subjects. I will ask your father to order a few Latin grammars."

Marcus eyed Toby as if to assure himself he would not be overheard. "I'm sorry for what happened."

Sophie waited, unsure about the meaning of the boy's comment.

"Papa shouldn't have spoken to you like that." His chin jutted forward. "Besides, it's my business what I think about God, not his. I'm interested in knowing more."

"I can help you with Latin, but you heard your father. He has requested I not discuss matters of religion with you or Toby."

Marcus folded his hands on the table. "Well, then. I'll do it myself. In this library are books about theology—is that the right word?" She nodded. "And a Bible. Nothing can prevent me from studying on my own, right?"

Sophie groaned inwardly. Marcus was putting her in an awkward position—not openly soliciting her help with such studies, but making her privy to information of which Tate would disapprove. Yet she couldn't discourage the lad, not given the resolve shining from his bright eyes.

"You are your own person, Marcus."

There. She had neither encouraged nor discouraged him. His wide-ranging intellect had once more proved itself. If only he could release some of his inhibitions.

The day passed swiftly with a review of previous lessons and the introduction of new skills. Just as she was preparing to depart, Marcus came to her side. "Before you leave, will you ask Papa, please? About the Latin books?" She faltered, knowing she couldn't disappoint the boy.

"Very well. Is he in his office?"

"Yes. I'll go with you."

Did he intuit the awkwardness of her meeting with Tate, or was he merely eager to obtain the means to study Latin?

Tate answered Marcus's knock, then did a double take when he noticed Sophie. "What do you want?"

"I'm sorry to interrupt you, Papa, but we have come to ask about getting a book. Miss Sophie will explain."

Then the boy fled, leaving her alone to face Tate. With a gesture of surrender, he bade her take a seat. He stood in front of her, leaning against his desk, arms folded across his chest. She noted the set of his jaw and the bags under his eyes. "What's this all about?"

Tersely, Sophie explained the need for Latin primers.

"They will be ordered," he said when she'd finished.

She made as if to stand, but he stopped her with one word. "Stay."

She was not a dog to be ordered about, but the look in his eyes implored her to remain. Her throat was dry, but she managed to speak. "For what purpose?"

He pulled a chair near hers and sank into it. "I need to apologize to you. You have done nothing but try to take care of my sons to the best of your ability. Grizzly told me it was his idea for you to take them to services."

"Perhaps so, but I might well have thought of it myself." So...he was absolving her of the motivation, but not the actual experience.

"The service must've made quite an impression. The boys cannot stop talking about it."

"I don't imagine you are disposed to listen, however."

"I wish to put this as gently, yet clearly as possible. I cannot permit my boys to nurture belief in a God who fails them."

"Like He failed you?"

"What do you know about it? Yours seems to be a glib and easy faith."

She stood up, glowering at him. "What knowledge do you have about the trials I've experienced? There has been nothing either glib or easy about the fact that

I've come to recognize I'm nothing without God. And you would do well to arrive at that understanding, too."

"You didn't have a cold childhood or see the looks on your children's faces when their mother killed their spirits."

"No, I did not. But let me tell you something. You can either spend your life in bitterness and, dare I say it, loneliness, or you can come to realize that in and of yourself you are powerless without God."

"And what's He done for you?" Behind his sarcasm, she sensed he truly needed her answer.

She sat back down. "If you are serious about that question and will do me the courtesy of listening without comment or derision, I will tell you what I have rarely confided in anyone. I ask only that you listen with an open heart and promise to think about what I will say."

Moments passed, during which Tate steepled his fingers under his chin and stared at her as if weighing her comments. Finally he sat back and, with a deep sigh, folded his hands in his lap and said quietly, "Begin."

Tate had known Sophie was feisty, but he'd never seen such indignation spark from her eyes as when she leaped up to confront him about his assumptions concerning her faith. *Faith.* The very word made him cringe. He'd had faith once, too, if not in God at least in his wife, and look what had happened there. Beyond that, how had faith ever helped him as a child? If God was supposed to embody love, why had he experienced only tepid tolerance and rejection? He gripped the armrests of his chair. A man made his own destiny, so enough of his self-pity. But God? He'd had no experience of Him. And yet…that day in front of the

Tylers', Sophie had offered his children as evidence of God's gift to him. And he was powerless to deny their importance.

"You must think I've led a charmed life and that faith is as natural to me as breathing." Sophie's head was bowed as if to study her hands, which lay gracefully in her lap. "Perhaps for the fortunate few that may be what faith is. But steel is forged by fire, and I think our lives are no different. It is the very trials we endure that help us see God's hand in our lives and deepen faith." At that moment she looked up. "You are not the only one to be tested."

He sensed she was getting to the crux of the matter and hoped she would spare him the kind of sermonizing he'd so often heard from his overbearing father, *Spare the rod and spoil the child* being one of his favorite texts. He shouldn't look at her. The conviction in her eyes was undeniable. But he'd agreed to hear her out, and so he must.

"Each story is different, but here is mine. I grew up in a home filled with love, even though there was always the regret of what might have been. My father and brothers at least had the comfort of memories of my mother. I had none. Only a few faded daguerreotypes and their stories of her. Do you suppose it was easy when I went to school to be taunted as an orphan, even though technically I was not? Or that I enjoyed staying home from the church mother-daughter picnic? My eighth-grade graduation dress was one of my mother's I had clumsily altered—nothing like the beautiful gowns of my friends. Listening in church to the preachers, I decided I had done something to offend God—that it was my fault He'd taken Mother. Yet all around me I heard the platitudes about God deciding He needed her in heaven. God needed her?" Sophie's voice rose. "*I* needed her."

"I had no idea," said Tate quietly.

"Of course you didn't. That was all a long time ago. As I approached womanhood, I came to recognize that God doesn't rain down punishment on the innocent, act capriciously or abandon His children. We are human and therefore subject to human joys and sorrows. What I thought I had learned as time went by was that God was not a distant, indifferent being, but a companion who walked with me and held me up. In essence, God loved me."

"You said you 'thought' you had learned that kind of faith?"

"Yes, it's easy to get complacent where God is concerned."

"Something happened." Tate waited for what he suspected was the worst of her story.

"I'd lost my mother and had finally arrived at a sense of peace about that." Suddenly Sophie rose from her chair and went to the window, seemingly transfixed by the view of the mountains. "Yet my testing was far from over. When the new courthouse was being built in our town back in Kansas, a young stonemason from the East came to supervise the cutting and placement of the Flint Hills rock. Charlie Devane. Handsome, fun-loving, passionate about his work—he burst into my heart with fireworks and roses."

Tate fidgeted, unsure if he wanted to hear more.

"What he saw in me, I'll never know, but from the moment I met him, I was besotted. All I could think about was Charlie. I longed for those times when we could be alone together. To my everlasting amazement, he saw me as his soul mate, just as I regarded him as mine." She turned around as if to assess his reaction.

Tate hoped his conflicting emotions were not visible in his expression. He envied her that kind of love even as he recognized the jealousy raging in his heart. How could she possibly know the extent of his fantasizing that she might be such a sweetheart for him? Yet he couldn't hope to compete with the kind of love glowing on her face. He'd agreed to hear her out, but to what end now? "So what happened?"

She paced in front of him. "If you wanted to, you could say God had other plans. Charlie and I agreed to be married. No two people could have been happier. When he had the offer of a lucrative job in Chicago, we agreed to postpone our wedding until he finished that work." She withdrew a handkerchief from her pocket and turned aside, seemingly overcome with emotion. When she faced him again, she had composed herself enough to continue. "In short, a rope snapped and Charlie's scaffold fell to the ground. He was killed instantly."

The mental picture she'd created for Tate was one that would remain seared in his brain. "*Sorry* seems inadequate, but I regret that you ever had to face such tragedy."

"Thank you." Now she took the place he'd formerly occupied, leaning against his desk, arms folded across her chest. The intensity of her gaze pierced him. "So don't talk to me about God's absence from your life. Nor His seeming irrelevance. I've been there. Do you think you're the only one who ever raised a fist and shouted at God, 'Why me?' When I lost my Charlie, I had no voice loud enough to scream out my questions. Whatever faith I had leaned upon growing up proved ephemeral. I raged at God and blamed Him for my loss."

Tate rose to his feet. "So why are you arguing with me about faith and insisting I'm wrong to have turned my back on God?"

"Because it is the sinful human part of us that has to find a scapegoat for the bad and ugly things that happen in our lives. And God is handy for such purposes."

"So how did you recover your faith?"

"Not having it locked me in the prison of my own unhappy thoughts. Slowly I recognized that others around me were tending to me, encouraging me, sitting with me as I mourned. And in them I ultimately found acceptance. Through them I came to understand that they were the agents of God. That far from abandoning me, He had been there all along. Few of us escape pain and disappointment in this life. But when we look around, we can always find evidence of His consoling presence."

"Like Marcus and Toby for me."

"Exactly like that. We can wallow in the past and in our perceptions of injustice, or we can embrace our humanity and find God all around us—in nature, in people, wherever."

"You make a powerful case…for your experience." He couldn't voice his continuing doubts about his own faith.

She approached him and put a hand on his shoulder. "Let me give you a story to consider. In Jerusalem there was a pool at Bethsaida where many invalids came to bathe in the healing waters. These included a man who had been there every day for thirty-eight years awaiting the arrival of someone who would lift him into the pool. Then one day Jesus appeared and realized what a long time the man had been lying there. He said to him, 'Wilt thou be made whole?'"

Tate felt his face flush with discomfort, yet he couldn't lower his eyes.

She picked up his hands in hers. "How was the afflicted man to answer? He'd grown accustomed to his situation. Saying yes to Jesus would involve a huge change in his accustomed way of being. Could he risk an unknown future? What might be expected of him were he to be healed?" She paused, letting the questions hang in the air. "Isn't that the issue for you, Tate? Do you want to be made whole? Do you want to leave behind the injuries of the past and see the myriad ways God is working in your life? Or do you prefer to remain imprisoned by doubts and blame-seeking?" She gripped his hands tightly. "No one can answer those questions but you. As for the man in the pool of Bethsaida?" She dropped his hands and smiled, blessing him with the affection in her eyes. "Jesus healed him. Jesus made him whole."

After she left, Tate remained in his office, pondering what she had revealed. In the end, what stayed with him was the unlikely outcome, both for her and for the man lying beside the pool. Jesus could make them both whole.

How he ultimately answered her questions would impact not only his own life, but the lives of his sons. He sighed and moved to the window where she'd stood gazing at the distant peaks. He remained there for long minutes lost in his thoughts. The heart of the matter was this: Did he have the courage and the will to face her questions?

Two days later when Sophie had left after her session with the boys, Tate came across Marcus sprawled in front of the fireplace, Minnie resting beside him. In front of him was a thick volume. So engrossed was the boy that he failed to notice Tate's approach. "Whatever you're reading must be very interesting," he observed.

Marcus sat up quickly, shoving the book away, his face red with guilt. "It's all right."

"May I look at it? Perhaps you'll tell me what you find so fascinating."

Marcus hung his head. Finally, with a shrug, he retrieved the book and held it out for his father to take.

Tate looked at the title spelled out in gilt letters. *Holy Bible.* With a roiling stomach, he realized that what he did at this moment might forever alter his relationship with his son.

Minnie sat up on her hind legs, and Marcus threw his arms around the dog as if to enlist an ally. "Don't blame Miss Sophie. She didn't give it to me."

Tate winced. "I didn't say she did. But you are interested nevertheless?"

"It is one of the great books of all time. I should read it. Many poets and even Shakespeare use biblical references."

"No doubt it does have literary value."

"Papa, it's full of exciting stories. I already learned about Noah at the Tylers', but did you know a man named Abraham took his son to a mountain to be sacrificed to God? That was scary."

Tate choked back a sarcastic retort. It was exactly that kind of subject matter that made him skeptical of the Good Book. "What did you learn from such a story?"

"That people should put God first and then He will be merciful. He was testing Abraham's obedience and faith."

Put God first? "You realize the Bible is an account not only of history but of a belief system."

"Yes." Marcus hung his head, but when he looked up, his voice was tinged with defiance. "We don't talk about God, do we? Why not?"

Why not? Tate's life experience hadn't exactly made him predisposed to entertain a God of love. "It's complicated."

"I wish we could talk about God. He teaches lots of important stuff, it seems to me." Marcus stood up and held out his hand. "May I please have the book back? I would like your permission to continue reading it."

He had never seen Marcus so willing to challenge him, at least in such a mature manner. Between Sophie and Marcus, Tate had the distinct impression he was being sent a message. "Two conditions. You may read it only after you've finished the lessons Miss Sophie has set for you. Second, if you have questions about any of the stories, you are to discuss them with me."

"Thank you, Papa."

As Tate left the room, he shook his head, wondering when he'd lost control. But he knew—when Sophie came. Sophie, who had revealed a past that put his fantasies about her in even greater jeopardy. Charlie Devane. Even the way she'd said his name spoke of the depth of her love for him. How could he hope to compete with such a paragon?

Late that afternoon he watched a rider approach, slip from the saddle and stride toward the house. When Tate hurried outside, he was dumbfounded to see his cousin Robert Hurlburt approaching, his face grim. "Robert, what on earth? You look as if you've been leading a cavalry charge." He clapped a hand on the older man's shoulder. "Please, come inside and let me fetch you something to drink."

"How I wish this was a social call, but as soon as you can be ready, we need to ride to Sophie's. I presume you know the way."

"I do, but whatever occasions the haste?"

"I have come to fetch her. We must leave for Denver in the morning. Her father is gravely ill. The family has sent for her."

Tate's knees nearly buckled. The death of a mother and a sweetheart to be endured, and now this. Sophie's faith would be tested yet again, just as Abraham's had been. He gathered himself. "Of course, we'll go. While you refresh yourself, I'll prepare to leave posthaste. Is Sophie expecting such news?"

"She has been informed of her father's earlier stroke, but doesn't know of this latest life-threatening stroke. The family is praying she will arrive as soon as possible. I have booked her a train ticket, but there is no time to lose."

It was nearly dark when they rode to the cabin. Tate couldn't help thinking that Sophie's life, too, was about to fall into darkness. What would become of her faith now?

Roused from her reading just before bedtime by approaching horses, Sophie grabbed the rifle and stood inside the door. Beauty's guard-dog stance reinforced her unease. Then she heard men's voices. Not Grizzly this time. Others. Strangers or friends? When she heard the thud of heavy footsteps on the porch, she shouldered her weapon. A loud knock followed. "Who's there?" she cried out with as much courage as she could muster.

"Tate and a friend."

She lowered the gun and cautiously opened the door a crack. Tate filled the line of her vision, but when he stepped aside, her mouth fell open. What was Robert Hurlburt doing here? Propping the rifle by the door, she stood aside to allow the two men to enter. Beauty went to Tate, her tail wagging. Sophie stared at Robert. His normally erect posture sagged and his bearded face was drawn. Suddenly she knew. Bad news from Kansas. There could be no other reason for this unexpected nocturnal visit. "Robert?" She didn't even recognize her own tremulous voice. "Why…why are you here?"

She felt Tate's arm around her, just as her legs started to give way. He ushered her to a chair and knelt at her side, holding her hand. Robert pulled up another chair and sat facing her. "It's your father, dear."

She stifled a wrenching sob. "Is he…?" She couldn't complete the thought.

"He's alive, but he's had a massive stroke. Your family has sent for you."

The silent scream rending her chest was surely audible, yet neither man flinched. Frantically she looked from one to the other. "But when? How?"

The compassion in Robert's eyes compelled her to look at him. "I will come for you in the morning and we will make our way to Denver. I've made a railroad reservation for you three days hence. While Dr. Kellogg urges haste, he is hopeful you will arrive in time."

In time. In time? The words battered her soul. Andrew Montgomery—her precious father, who had never done anything but care for her and love her. A world without him in it seemed unimaginable. Charlie and now Papa? Lost in memory, it was only the comforting grip of Tate's hand on hers that restored her to the present. She got to her feet, her eyes scanning the room.

"There is so much to do. I must be about my preparations."

Tate placed both hands on her shoulders. "Sophie, all you need to do is pack. Beauty can return home with me. The boys will enjoy looking after her in your absence. Curly or Pancho will check on the cabin while you're away. Please clear your mind of any worries about this place."

"And Belle?"

"I'll send word to her."

Robert stood. "I'll call for you at sunrise. Effie will be waiting to greet you in Denver. Meanwhile, she sends you her love."

Such kindness on all sides was her undoing. The tears she'd valiantly tried to withhold burst forth in a hiccuping rush. Dimly she was aware that Tate had gathered her to him and that she was dampening the front of his shirt. That concern evaporated with the onslaught of her grief. Brave, undaunted, independent Sophie? That persona had collapsed under the weight of her worry. Right now, her only shred of comfort came from the shelter of Tate's embrace.

Chapter Eleven

And so it was that a few days later Sophie found herself staring out the window of a passenger train heading east across the vast open spaces of Kansas. With every muscle tensed in a vain effort to speed the locomotive toward her destination, the passing landscape held little interest. Would she arrive in time to spend precious hours with her beloved father? Or would she be too late? She prayed not. The ride down to Denver had been both an emotional and physical challenge, and only Effie's soothing ministrations after they arrived had renewed Sophie's energy sufficiently for her to undertake the remainder of the trip. Now, in diabolical concert with the rhythmic clanging of wheels on rails, questions pecked relentlessly at her brain: *Should I ever have left Cottonwood Falls? Was I selfish to follow my dream rather than concerning myself with my family's needs? Can Pa forgive my absence? Will I be able to forgive myself?*

A debilitating dread sapped her energy, energy that would be sorely needed when she arrived. Her brothers and sisters-in-law had borne the brunt of her father's incapacitation. Now perhaps she could lend a helping hand, God willing. But the thought of saying a final goodbye? Unbearable.

Only the breeze blowing through the open window kept her from expiring in the beastly heat. Laying her head back and closing her eyes, she tried to capture the majestic Colorado peaks, the melody of icy stream water, the fragrance of fresh mountain air. She must've dozed off, because she was suddenly awakened by the sound of her book falling to the floor. Retrieving it, she held it to her chest, cherishing the memory of Tate's thoughtfulness.

He had joined Robert and her in the ride across the park to the point where the descent began. The three had dismounted briefly to exchange farewells. Tate had drawn her aside and thrust a small volume into her hands. In the early-morning light she had made out the title—William Wordsworth's *Lyrical Ballads*. When she'd looked at him inquiringly, with one finger he'd traced the line of her jaw and said in a low tone, "So you don't forget the mountains—or us. I've marked a passage or two in the 'Tintern Abbey' poem." Then, as if he'd revealed too much, he took a step back and studied the lightening eastern horizon. "You'd best be on your way. I wish you well on your journey."

"Thank you."

"There's one more thing." He cleared his throat. "The boys wanted me to ask if you're coming back."

In that moment, she saw the raw hope in his eyes. Yet, in honesty, she could make no such promise. Instead, she'd lowered her head and whispered, "I don't know, Tate. I...I don't know."

A mournful train whistle punctuated her reminiscence, bringing her back to the reality of the looming decisions threatening to overwhelm her. As she had often done since leaving Estes Park, she opened the book of poems and turned to the first passage Tate had marked.

Once again
Do I behold these steep and lofty cliffs,
That on a wild secluded scene impress
Thoughts of more deep seclusion; and connect
The landscape with the quiet of the sky.

In the margin he had written "May the memory of the beauty and wonder of nature bless you."

With care she closed the volume and grasped it tightly, a kind of lifeline. She bowed her head in recognition of a truth. Perhaps this was as close as Tate could come to prayer. Yet it was, for her, just that—a prayer.

Six days had elapsed since Sophie's departure, time marked by Toby's daily question at breakfast: "When is Miss Sophie coming back?" Tate tried to remain optimistic, but could ill afford to give the boys false hope. He'd carefully explained to them the reason for her sudden departure. Toby had accepted the explanation, but Marcus was more perceptive. This morning he had asked Tate to follow him into the library alcove. There he proudly opened the Latin primer that had arrived earlier in the week. "I'm getting some of this, Papa, but without Miss Sophie, it's really hard. She is coming back, isn't she?"

"I hope so."

Slowly closing the book, Marcus sighed. "She might stay in Kansas." It wasn't a question. "Her family is there. They may need her. She likes it here, I know, but she has no family in Estes Park." He shrugged in resignation. "Except for us."

Tate was at a loss for words. He could neither encourage that line of Marcus's thinking nor deny it. Sophie had become far more than a tutor to the boys and, if he was honest, far more than a friend to him. If she failed to come back? It didn't bear contemplating. Yet if she did return, what would that mean? Was he prepared to think of her as family as Marcus obviously did? "We'll have to wait and see. For this afternoon, how about riding over to her cabin to check on things."

"Can Beauty come with us? She's probably missing home."

"Good idea."

Later as the two trotted down the road, Tate marveled. Marcus was not an outdoorsman and often rejected offers to go riding. Today, though, he'd accepted with alacrity. As soon as they arrived at the cabin, they went to work airing it out. Then with Beauty following closely behind, Marcus helped stack firewood and joined Tate in sweeping and dusting. All the while Tate did his best to avoid looking at the sampler on the wall and its words of challenge: "Trust in the Lord with all thine heart; and lean not unto thine own understanding." He didn't want to think about the questions that message raised for him. Was there really a God he could trust? As for his own understanding, was his confidence in his abilities and decisions justified...or arrogant?

Marcus pulled him from his introspection. "Toby and I had fun the nights we stayed here," he volunteered as he pushed a broom around.

"Despite the flood?"

"I knew we'd be safe with Miss Sophie."

Safe. Tate wondered if Marcus had ever felt that with his own mother.

"If she comes back, Papa, it won't be for a while, right?"

A lonely pang shot through Tate. "No, son. It will take time for her to settle her affairs."

"I miss her."

All the way home, Tate's chest was tight. The very thing he'd worried about had happened—had been happening all along. Nor had he been powerless to stop it. He could've done something. But, just like his sons, he was captivated by Sophie. And he wanted more.

When they arrived home, Tate was surprised to see Joe Harper's gelding tied to the hitching post. After suggesting to Marcus that he brush Beauty, Tate headed for the house. Bertie told him Joe was waiting in his office. Tate hung up his hat and entered the room. "Harper, good to see you."

After shaking hands, they both sat down. Joe nodded in the direction of Tate's desk, where several letters were stacked. "Thought I'd bring those along."

"You didn't need to."

"I know. But I wanted to talk to you about that citified crowd over at Lord Dunraven's place. Some bigwig who owns a London newspaper is summering up here and has gotten wind of Belle and Sophie's plan to climb Longs Peak. Scuttlebutt has it that now editors from papers all around Colorado and beyond may send reporters and photographers up here, and that to a man, they are hoping for a failure, no doubt so they can ridicule the women." He leaned forward. "I've done everything in my power to get Belle to drop the idea, but she's determined. Perhaps you can persuade Sophie to give up their summit ambitions."

Tate knew Sophie. An attempt to dissuade her from any goal to which she had set her mind would be doomed. "I don't have that kind of influence, Joe. What she does in regard to scaling Longs is her business." Even as the words left his mouth, frustration mounted—frustration with the idiots who would set women up as sources of ridicule, with Sophie for being so reckless and headstrong and with his own helplessness in the matter. "At the moment, of course, she is in Kansas with her dying father. Whether she returns is a matter of speculation."

"Rest assured, we would all like her to come back, Tate. She's a delightful young woman, which—" he winked "—surely has not escaped your notice. Belle is very fond of her. But I shudder to think what might happen if their Longs Peak climb results in a journalistic frenzy. Belle claims she and Sophie have discussed what they might be up against, but…" He lifted his hands in consternation.

Tate frowned. "They may think they know how to handle the attention they will attract, but I don't have a good feeling about this."

"Nor do I." Harper stood. "Those of us with their best interests at heart will have to be vigilant." The two men, preoccupied by their concern, walked in silence to the front door. There Harper spoke again. "The personal letter on your desk has a Denver postmark. Maybe it brings news about Sophie."

After his neighbor rode off for home, Tate stood in his office, staring at the mail lying on his desk. He picked up his letter opener and slit the top envelope. One sheet of paper fell out. Dread mixed with eagerness as he unfolded it and quickly assured himself of Sophie's signature.

Dear Tate,

When I arrived at the Hurlburts', a telegram had
come saying Papa was weak, but hanging on to
life. I will not know until I get to Kansas what the
future may hold for me. I miss the boys and hope
it will be possible for me to return and continue
tutoring them. Time will tell. I have also written
Belle Harper with this news of my indefinite stay.
Whether it happens this year or next, I have told
her not to give up on our plans to climb Longs
Peak. I send the boys my love and ask you to be
patient with me.

Patient? Easier said than done when all he wanted to
do was follow her to Kansas and make sure she returned
with him to the mountains she loved. And to somehow
dissuade her from the perilous trek up Longs.

At last. As the train slowed for her stop, Sophie blew
the dust off her hat before putting it on. For the past
hour, she had reveled in the sight of her beloved Flint
Hills, her heart pounding in anticipation. And there!
Tears flooded her eyes when she spotted her brother
Caleb standing on the platform, with Lily beside him.
How she had missed her family. She clenched the handle of her reticule. *Dear God, what news have they
brought?*

Assisted by the porter, she climbed down from the
train and was immediately engulfed. "Sophie, dear,"
Lily whispered, while Caleb held her by the shoulders
studying her intently.

"Colorado seems to agree with you," he said.

She looked from one to the other, scarcely able to
believe they stood before her. "I'm so relieved to be

here." Then gathering her courage, she asked the question that had plagued her throughout her journey. "Pa? How is he?"

"Eager to see you," Caleb answered solemnly. "Come along now. I'll gather your bags and we'll talk along the way."

Sitting between the two on the buggy seat, Sophie scanned the familiar countryside, so different from the Rockies. With each turn of the wheels, not only did her concern for her father increase, but so did the sudden, spontaneous ache of Charlie's loss. This stony land had been her beloved's workshop...once.

Caleb spoke just loudly enough to be heard over the road noise. "There is no way for me to soften the blow, Sophie. Pa is near the end. He goes in and out of consciousness. Aunt Lavinia and Rose are with him now, and when he's not working, Seth hardly leaves the bedside."

Sophie grabbed her brother's knee in an effort to hold herself upright. "I should've been here."

Lily placed an arm around Sophie's shoulders. "Please don't blame yourself. My father has assured us that medically there was nothing any of us could have done to prevent this last stroke. None of us ever knows what a day will bring, yet there is consolation in knowing that God is with us everywhere, even in the valley of the shadow of death."

It was as if only with those words had the finality of her father's situation hit Sophie. She sagged into her sister-in-law's comforting embrace and let her pent-up tears flow. As they neared Cottonwood Falls, Sophie straightened, willing herself not to look at Charlie's courthouse building, wiped her streaked face with a handkerchief and found her courage. "All right. That's enough of that. Tell me what I must do, how I can help."

For the rest of the trip to the Montgomery ranch, Lily outlined the schedule of care aimed at making Andrew comfortable. "Your father hasn't much time, Sophie, but I know at some point he will be aware of your presence. Having all his children surrounding his bed should soothe his agitation."

"We've arranged for you to stay in your old room," Caleb added, "so you can be in the house with Pa. We are taking Rose and Seth's boys home with us for a few days."

"I hate to inconvenience anyone."

Lily smiled. "Our girls are excited about the prospect of having their cousins come for a visit." Her smile faded. "Given the circumstances, it's probably best that Alf and Andy are away during this time."

When the buggy rolled to a stop in front of the house, nostalgia nearly overcame Sophie—for gardens planted together, chess games contested, stories told around a winter's fire. Rose came running toward her, followed by Seth, and hugged her close. "Dear girl, what a joy to see you, despite these sad circumstances."

Then her tall, broad-shouldered brother took her fingers in his work-roughened hands. "I don't have words, sister." When Sophie looked into his warm, hazel eyes, she saw the quiet heartache in them.

Sophie studied the sturdy limestone house with its riotous flower beds surrounding the deep porch. "There's no place like home, is there?" she asked without expecting an answer.

"Come freshen up," Rose said, "and then I'll take you to your father. Lavinia is sitting with him currently." Lavinia, Lily and Rose's aunt, was a wonder—the grand

Saint Louis society woman had been transformed by family into a Flint Hills fixture.

Seth carried Sophie's bags to her old room under the eaves, its comforting furnishings so full of reminders of her girlhood. When he left her there, she slipped off her travel jacket and used a soft cloth to soak up cool water from the basin. Heat, unlike any in the mountains, suffused this second story. She wiped her flushed face and neck and redid her hair, lifting it higher off her neck. Before she went to her father, she uttered a silent prayer that she might be a source of light and comfort to this dear man who had so valiantly undertaken to raise three motherless children.

Lavinia stood at the bottom of the stairs. "My dear," she said, "we are so glad you have come." She nodded toward the downstairs bedroom door. "Rose and Seth are with Andrew." Then she cupped Sophie's cheeks and kissed her on the forehead. "Go with God, child."

No amount of imagining could have prepared her for what greeted her upon entering the sickroom. Her sturdy, muscled father had been reduced to a fragile wraith laid out on the bed beneath a light counterpane. His sunken cheeks and pale skin bore no resemblance to the tanned, laughing face she held in her memory. Seth yielded his chair at the bedside, and Sophie rushed forward. "Papa, Papa," she said as she sank into the chair and gathered his cool, dry hand in hers. "It's Sophie." She leaned even closer. "Papa, I'm home."

His ragged breaths filled the silence. Sophie waited for what seemed an eternity for his eyes to flutter open. "Swee-har," he mumbled. Then he repeated the mangled word in a more demanding tone. "Swee-har!"

Sophie stood and leaned over him, her fingers smoothing the hair off his forehead. "I'm here, Pa. Your Sophie."

"No," he rasped. "No. Swee-har." He thrashed impotently, then once more fixed his rheumy eyes on Sophie. "You. Bride. Love."

Seth came up behind her and ran his hands up and down her arms, which were suddenly pebbled with goose bumps. "It's all right, Sophie. He thinks you're Mother."

Sophie could have wept with the sadness of it all. Now, in his final hours, her father was turning to the sweetheart he'd lost to childbirth all those years ago. The woman he had continued to love. And loved now.

"Swee-har," her father whispered, just before closing his eyes. "I see you."

"He'll sleep now," Rose said. "Let's get you some supper, and then, if you wish, you can sit with him for a time before bed."

Worn-out from the trip and the emotions of the day, Sophie hadn't realized how hungry she was. As usual, Rose had prepared a delicious meal. Sophie ate quickly, anxious to get back to her father's bedside, praying he would recognize her before slipping off to eternity to join his "Swee-har." *Just once more,* she begged God, *let him see me and hear me tell him how much I love him.*

Despite her exhaustion, Sophie remained at her father's side until ten, when Caleb was due back to relieve her. Rose and Seth had retired earlier, and the house was eerily quiet except for occasional ghostly creaks and the relentless ticking of the hall clock. Fighting drowsiness, Sophie passed the long minutes by recalling her many happy times with her father—from his clumsy attempts to braid her hair before she learned to do it herself to his mischievous teasing about Charlie's courtship. Occasionally Pa would stir, even reach up and claw the air as if searching for something—or someone. Then his arm would fall limply back to the bed. She had so hoped he would open his eyes, recognize her, and... what? Forgive her for her absence?

Just as the clock struck ten, Caleb entered the room and stood at the foot of the bed. "You should get some sleep. I promise to call you if he needs you." With that Caleb helped her to her feet and walked her into the hallway. There he paused and drew her into a brotherly embrace. "I'm glad you're here, dear Sophie. It's not just Pa who needs you. Seth and I do, too. You are, and always have been, our gift from God." Then with what sounded like a muffled sob, he turned and reentered their father's room.

Lying in her bed, Sophie was convinced she would never sleep, the events of the past few days whirling in her brain. Heavy-eyed, she tried to think what the morrow would bring. And the day after that. She wanted to keep her father here on earth, to hold him ever closer to her heart. Yet simultaneously, she prayed to be able to release him, for him to arrive at a peaceful end.

Finally, she dozed off, only to be awakened at dawn's first light by Rose, gently shaking her and whispering, "Come, now, Sophie. It's time." She hastily donned a robe and followed Rose down the stairs. Lantern light from the bedroom cast long shadows on the floor and in the distance a cock crowed. Seth and Caleb stood one on each side of their father's bed. Seth turned and led her to the chair. She picked up her father's hand, calloused from a lifetime of hard work. Across the bed, she noted Caleb's lips moving in a silent prayer. Pa's mouth was open and the sound of each irregular breath wounded her.

Then he roused, and another garbled "Swee-har" escaped his lips. Sophie clutched his hand and stood up, leaning close. "I'm here, Pa." Then a wondrous thing happened. He turned his head. His eyes were open and clear. "Sophie?"

She kissed his hand. "Yes, I'm here."

"Good girl," he mumbled.

"I love you, Pa. So very, very much." She was aware that Caleb now sat on the bed and Seth was supporting her.

The old man looked then at each of his children. "Good boys. Good girl."

Just before he once more closed his eyes, he looked straight at Sophie. "Mountains. Your dream. Be happy there."

Caleb cleared his throat and Seth tightened his grip on her. Minutes passed where words were unnecessary to express the bond of love blessing them all.

Then, almost without their notice, the labored breathing ceased and the wrinkles on their father's face relaxed in such a peaceful expression that Sophie could not help but murmur a relieved "Amen," even as her heart broke.

"He was waiting for you," Seth whispered.

Chapter Twelve

Tate looked around at the folks seated on the ground outside Martha and Jackson Tyler's place. He realized it was more people than he'd ever seen at one time in one place in Estes Park. He'd resisted coming and had been embarrassed, even a little irritated, by the welcome so many had tendered. Nor was he oblivious to the surprised looks some had tried to conceal when he'd arrived with Marcus and Toby in tow. Rapscallions. Nobody but his sons could have convinced him to attend a Sunday service, something he had not done since leaving Philadelphia. But, for better or worse, here he was.

Without Sophie's lessons, the boys had grown restless. Particularly in Marcus, Tate sensed a loneliness that took him back to his own childhood. As the days had worn on, he knew his sons needed exposure to other young people. It was Marcus who had first brought up the idea of the church service. "I'm learning lots from the Bible. The preacher can prob'ly teach me more."

Toby had jumped right on the suggestion. "I know about Noah. I want to hear another story about those Bible people. Come on, Papa. Let's go."

When Tate had offered lame excuses, Marcus had

shrewdly looked right through him and said, "What are you afraid of, Pa?" He had not answered. How could a mere boy understand a fear of losing control, of accepting a God who had created a world in which bad things happened?

For the benefit of his sons, though, coming to the community church service had been a good idea. Toby was playing tag with several other children while Marcus and a trapper's son about his age huddled together on a rock examining some bird feathers. For Tate, though, the experience bordered on torment. Seeing his friends and neighbors, all seemingly quite at ease, made him feel distinctly out of place. He looked about for somewhere to sit and perhaps become less conspicuous. Just then Martha Tyler sidled up to him. "The world hasn't come to an end, you know," she said with a smile.

He grinned ruefully. "Because I'm here, you mean?"

"People come to the Lord at different ages and stages."

"I merely brought my sons to a community gathering. My coming to the Lord is an entirely different matter and not likely to happen anytime soon."

She patted his shoulder. "The way I figure it, that's more up to the Lord than to you. Would you join our family for the service?" She glanced around. "It's about to begin."

Grateful to be part of a group instead of a lone curiosity, he allowed himself to be led to a large blanket spread on the grass near the Tylers' front porch, where Jackson, Dolly and John were already seated. Across the way, a farmer he recognized rang a large cowbell and the children scampered to join their families. "Isn't this fun?" Toby panted, settling beside him. Marcus sank down on his other side and poked him. "I think I'm going to like the service."

Then to Tate's surprise, John Tyler stood up, extracted a tuning fork from his pocket, hit a note and commenced singing, "To God be the glory, great things He has done…" From high sopranos to deep basses, other voices joined in. Martha pressed a hymnal into his hands opened to the correct page. Marcus and Toby leaned closer, found the place and were ready to sing when the chorus came.

"Praise the Lord, praise the Lord, Let the earth hear His voice!" Tate remained silent despite Toby's tug at his sleeve. All around, people sang with enthusiasm, finally finishing with, "O come to the Father, through Jesus the Son, and give Him the glory, great things He has done." *Great things?* Tate inwardly scoffed. Wars? Floods? And was he expected to give God credit for the benefits derived from the sweat of his own brow? From shrewd business decisions? Should he be giving God the glory for leading him into a doomed marriage with the wrong woman?

By the time the preacher started with several Bible readings and prayers, Tate was more than edgy—he was ready to bolt. Yet with Marcus's and Toby's hands in his, he was anchored to the spot. "Listen, Papa," Toby said rather too loudly a few minutes into the sermon, "he's telling us about some men in a lion's den. I like lions."

"Daniel," Marcus snapped at his brother.

Tate could relate to the story. He felt rather as if he, too, were confined in a lion's den of others' expectations that he should suddenly "come to the Father," as the hymn suggested and plead mercy. He hated to disappoint Martha Tyler, but God was not tapping him on the shoulder this day.

A stray thought startled him. Did Sophie truly believe all of this church haranguing? After what she'd been through? What she was currently enduring? That would be faith, indeed. He wished he knew what was happening with her father. With her. Then with an inner groan, he owned up to his greatest fear—what if she didn't come back?

Dimly he became aware the congregation was now singing "Blessed Assurance." He squirmed in the hope this unendurable service would soon be over. *Blessed assurance?* He could almost bring himself to pray if he thought God would assure him of Sophie's swift return. And not just for the boys' sake. Despite all his efforts to the contrary, he was pretty sure he was falling in love with the irrepressible Sophie. But he'd be a fool to voluntarily step once more into the lion's den of romantic love. Look where that had gotten him before. "I like the singing," Toby said when the service concluded, "and the stories and all the people and—"

"Promise we can come back again," Marcus said, fingering Tate's sleeve.

What were the boys experiencing that he wasn't? Yet how could he deny them something they so clearly enjoyed with people who were offering them a broader sense of community?

Tate relented. "I suppose we could."

Toby jumped up and down at his side. "Yippee! Maybe Miss Sophie will be here next time!"

"If she comes back," Marcus reminded his brother.

"She'll be back," Toby responded with confidence. "I got the blessed insurance about it."

"Assurance." Marcus was quick with the correction.

Tate started walking the boys toward the buggy. *In-*

surance or *assurance*, what was the difference? What mattered was the ever-deepening bond they all felt with Sophie and what they were going to do about it.

Only the sheltering presence of Caleb and Seth on either side of her kept Sophie grounded in the present moment. All she wanted to do was float far beyond this crowded church and the suffocating reality of her father's death. For the past two days well-wishers had arrived at the ranch in a steady stream, sapping her energy and allowing little outlet for the private grief building within her. This morning's funeral, conducted in lieu of the regular Sunday service, was nearly over, and though she appreciated the outpouring of sympathy from their friends, she felt an overwhelming need to be alone—to run up into the hills and give vent to her own sorrow. As if from a great distance, Pastor Dooley's words flowed over and around her. On the other side of Seth, a sob erupted from Rose, and Sophie bit her lip to keep from crying out. Caleb maintained a soldier's erect composure, but she could see his leg jiggling with tension. The reading of the twenty-third psalm preceded the final prayer. Sophie clung to the verse "Yea, though I walk through the valley of the shadow of death, I will fear no evil: for Thou art with me…" Her father had feared nothing except the loss of those closest to him. He had always faced adversity and tragedy through faith and hard work. He would expect nothing less of her.

"What a friend we have in Jesus, all our pains and griefs to bear…" Caleb helped her to her feet. From every side, loud, imperfect voices sang the concluding hymn, but all Sophie could do was wonder how Jesus was planning to help her bear the weight of her losses. Outside the church, the ladies began laying out dishes for the funeral luncheon. Sophie nearly gagged on the odors. She couldn't imagine putting a bite in her mouth, much less swallowing it.

Lavinia Dupree came up to her, placed a firm hand under her elbow and led her to the shelter of an overhanging tree. "I expect you've had enough of community rites. These events too often take on a life of their own."

Sophie sagged against Lavinia, permitting herself to rest in the older woman's embrace. "They mean well," she finally said.

"Of course. But they are not your concern. Or mine. Sometimes you have to forget everyone else and concentrate on your own needs."

Sophie stepped back and turned her head to watch the funeral goers, who now seemed more like relieved banquet guests than consolers. *Meaning well* was nice, but it wasn't enough.

"Sophie?" Lavinia spoke softly. "What about you?"

Sophie searched her heart. "I can't cry. I need to, but tears won't come. I should be crying."

"Grief has no 'shoulds' and crying isn't required." Lavinia picked up Sophie's hand and gently stroked it. "If you could do whatever you wanted right now without a thought for propriety, what would it be?"

Sophie lifted her eyes to Lavinia's. "I would go out into those hills and walk and talk to God. Question Him. Plead for answers."

"And maybe shake a fist or two?"

For the first time all day, Sophie managed a smile. "That, too."

"All right, then. When we get back to the ranch house, you do just that, and I'll keep everyone else at bay."

Sophie knew the imposing woman could handle any objections. The entire family loved Lavinia, but rarely crossed her. "How did you know how I'm feeling?"

"Funeral rituals have suffocated me on occasion, too."

"Thank you," Sophie murmured, finally feeling a sense of direction.

After arriving back at the ranch, Sophie went to her room and exchanged her black dress for a shapeless gingham one. She donned a wide-brimmed sunbonnet and after giving each of her brothers and sisters-in-law a gentle word, slipped out the kitchen door, passed through the barnyard and started up a cow path leading toward a rocky flat-topped hill. The buzz of insects and the earthy smell of prairie grass soothed her. The faster she walked, the more deeply she breathed, the better she felt—as if finally her lungs could once again expand and contract without the grip of worry. She realized her body, too, had long been coiled with tension. She was accustomed to the out-of-doors, to challenging her stamina in the Rockies. The past few days had been uncharacteristically confining.

One of the ranch dogs trailed her, much as Beauty might. Sophie experienced a sudden spasm of longing for the solitude of her cabin and the majesty of the mountains. Reaching the top of the hill, she sat down on a limestone outcropping, letting her legs dangle over the side. Below, nestled among the trees, was the ranch house built so lovingly by her father and Seth. She pictured them, their shirtsleeves rolled up, toting the stone blocks and sawing boards for the framework. She had thought her pa one of the ablest, strongest men in the world. Fearless, yet gentle. Determined, yet flexible. And always loving. She closed her eyes, recalling him carrying her as a toddler on his broad shoulders, pushing her in the rope swing he'd made for her and holding her on his lap as he told tales of his boyhood. She sat, remembering him, for a measureless time. When she opened her eyes, she was surprised to feel teardrops on her cheeks. Then she saw it—the Chase County Courthouse—her Charlie's grand achievement. Charlie. Pa. There was no holding back. The floodgates opened and raw pain poured forth in an overdue catharsis.

When she could finally breathe again, she wiped her tear-streaked face on the soft hem of her dress. *God, what am I to do now? So much has been taken from me.* And then the questions came, one piling atop the other. Could she possibly leave this place again? The place where so many memories lived. The place where she would always be enfolded in a loving family circle. She had been far away when her father needed her. What if she was needed in the future? Had she sacrificed family to indulge her love of adventure? Yet there was no denying the powerful lure of the mountains or the liberating sense of being on her own. Being…true to herself.

She stood and gazed around the comforting mounds of the Flint Hills. Beneath her feet, wildflowers peeked from between rock crevices. There was beauty here, too. Not the wild, rugged beauty of the Rockies, but a more subtle kind. She recalled her father's dying words. *Mountains. Your dream. Be happy there.* But could she? Of course, she'd have to return to close the cabin and collect her things. But stay?

Turning for home, she was startled to spot the figure of her ten-year-old nephew, Alf, sitting still as a stone a few yards down the path. How long had he been there? He faced the west, his legs folded, his arms at his sides, his raven's-wing hair shining in the sun. At the sound of a rock dislodged by her foot, Alf turned. "I was worried," he said simply.

This was far from the first time that the boy had seemed to intuit the feelings of his elders. "I needed to be alone."

"I know. Me, too." In one graceful movement, he got to his feet.

It occurred to Sophie that far too often adults underestimate the grief of children. And this one? He had witnessed the murder of his Pawnee mother at the tender age of four. He knew sorrow deep within his bones. "Are you ready to go home?"

He nodded. "Now I am."

They walked in companionable silence for a ways. Then in a voice so small she had to lean closer to hear him, Alf said, "I want to know about the mountains. Are there eagles there? And bears?"

In that moment Sophie experienced a flash of recognition. Alf wanted the same kind of answers Marcus craved. She was overcome by her deep affection for both boys. And for Toby. Tate's sons posed another consideration. How would she balance her affection for them, and theirs for her, with a possible decision to leave Colorado?

"Aunt Sophie?"

Returning to the present, Sophie tucked Alf's hand in hers as they trudged along. "I have seen a bear, quite close actually, and I have a friend named Grizzly, who wears a bearskin coat and hat. I have yet to see an eagle, but there are hawks aplenty, and—"

"One day might I come visit you in Colorado? I should so like to see the mountains."

His question tore at Sophie. Soon, she would have to

decide where she belonged. "You are always welcome, Alf. I believe you would find the mountains as beautiful and compelling as I do."

"Someday I will come," he said with resolve.

"Yes, someday," Sophie whispered. *God willing.*

Sophie would surely come back. If for nothing more than to reclaim her belongings and say goodbye. Tate tried not to be obvious, but Joe Harper must surely wonder why he so frequently checked for his mail. Today he'd manufactured an excuse concerning business matters. But standing in Joe's tiny wooden post office, Tate experienced yet another disappointment. Still no word from Sophie. Only a brief telegram from Robert Hurlburt announcing Andrew Montgomery's death. It had been two weeks now since Sophie had departed. Tate rationalized that settling affairs and being with her family would take some time, but if she was still set on Longs Peak, she would have to return soon lest weather prevent the attempt. Belle remained convinced the two of them would persevere, although she, too, had received no post from Sophie, whose determination to make the ascent was Tate's best reason for hope.

"Get what you came for?" Joe asked as he continued sorting envelopes.

"Yes and no."

The postmaster looked up, studying Tate closely. "Belle didn't hear from Sophie today, either."

The valley was full of mind readers and gossips, Tate thought sourly. "Am I that transparent?"

Joe chuckled, but had the grace to say no more.

Changing the subject, Tate asked, "Have you heard anything further about those journalist fellows?"

"Two of them were in here yesterday, nosing around.

Wanted to talk with Belle. I told them no. They got a bit hostile, asking why I thought I had to protect a grown woman fully capable of speaking for herself." He paused. "I tell you, Lockwood, I didn't like them or their attitude, and I'm afraid there are others like them, itching to get a big story."

"If Sophie comes back and she and Belle attack Longs, I'm thinking we need to have a plan. Feisty as they are, two young women may be no match for a pack of ravening opportunists."

"Their ilk are relentless."

"You can count on me and my hands, and I'm sure Jackson and John Tyler will help."

"I'll talk with some of the other valley men, as well," Joe promised.

"There's a part of me that wishes Sophie would stay safely in Kansas."

"A mighty small part, I reckon," Joe said, winking broadly. "She's good for you and the boys."

Tate chafed at the personal turn of the conversation. "Yes," was all he said before lifting his hat in a gesture of farewell.

He rode home slowly. He couldn't recall when anyone had occupied his thoughts as Sophie had these past interminable days. It didn't help that the boys talked about her incessantly and clamored for the information he couldn't give. In truth, he had no idea whether she would return, and if she did, for how long. He was in a bad way and knew with certainty that if she didn't come to him, he would go to her.

Sophie woke up in an unfamiliar bed. Dawn was just breaking through the east-facing window and the curtains rustled in the gentle breeze. As she roused to full consciousness, she remembered how she'd arrived exhausted at the Hurlburts' Denver home the previous evening after a fortnight in Kansas. Effie had fed her a light supper and packed her off to bed, assuring her there would be plenty of time to talk after she'd had a good night's sleep. Sophie turned on her side to watch the sun rise. It had been so difficult leaving her family and the familiarity of the Flint Hills. They had, of course, implored her to stay. In her heart of hearts, she knew she could not. She had to finish what she had begun, both with Belle and the Lockwood boys. Then... then she would decide where her future lay.

Before she returned to Colorado, she'd made herself face once again Charlie's death and the loss of his love. The day before her departure from Cottonwood Falls, she went to the courthouse. She walked around the magnificent building, touching the stones that Charlie's strong hands had sculpted, marveling in his vision and his talent. She prayed for the magnificent limestone facade to reveal a message, to direct her decision. The silent stones yielded nothing. Yet as she concluded her circuit, her father's voice echoed in her mind: *Trust in the Lord.*

That was all she could do. And now, lying here, nothing was any clearer to her than it had been that day at the courthouse. *Trust.* Somehow, someday, she would be shown the way. Meanwhile, she had a goal that might get her through the coming weeks—the ascent of Longs Peak.

After breakfast, Robert left the house on business he needed to accomplish before accompanying her to Estes Park. Effie poured them each another cup of coffee and suggested they retire to the front porch with its grand view of the Front Range. For a few minutes, they sat in silence. Sophie let her beloved mountains calm her while the taste of fresh-brewed coffee spoke to her of the blessing of friends like Effie.

"My dear, you have been through a difficult time. The death of a parent is a stab to the heart."

"I never knew my mother," Sophie said in a soft tone. "My father was my everything—nurturer, confidant, protector, playmate. Even at the grave site, I found it impossible to believe he had vanished from the earth."

"But never from your heart."

Sophie clutched her cup for its comforting warmth. "No, never from my heart."

"Trite as it must sound, somehow life does go on, but any semblance of normalcy takes time. Permit yourself that time."

Silence ensued in which Sophie pondered the demands on her life—the desire of her family to have her return to Kansas, the tug of Toby and Marcus on her heart, the daunting but energizing task of trying to scale a 14,255-foot-high peak, the need to decide whether to winter in the mountains.

Then Effie homed in on the one thing Sophie had tried to avoid thinking about. "And what of Tate Lockwood? Robert seems to think he has more than a passing interest in you."

Being in Kansas with all its rich memories of Charlie's courtship had made it easy to block any thought of Tate…and her attraction to him. Yet seeing the mountains had stirred feelings in her she had not until this moment fully admitted to herself. "I don't know, Effie."

"He's a complex man, but I do believe he is one capable of great love if he will give himself over to another." Effie cocked her head inquiringly. "Could you be that one?"

Sipping from her cup, Sophie delayed replying. How could she answer? Her emotions were confused in a way she'd rarely experienced. She was both eager to see Tate and at the same time terrified of misreading his intentions. And guilty at the thought of being, in any way, unfaithful to Charlie's memory. "Dear Effie, I'm grateful for your interest and affection. But I cannot answer you. I don't even know my own mind."

Effie set down her cup and took Sophie's hand. "Then go to the mountains, child. Be open to their lessons."

"Thank you, Effie." With the sun warming the porch, Sophie tipped her head back, experiencing a peace that had eluded her for many days.

Chapter Thirteen

Sophie's jaw dropped. She'd expected to find a musty, dirty cabin. Instead, the windowpanes had been cleaned and nary a speck of dust was to be found on any surface. In the center of the table was a bouquet of mountain wildflowers and simmering on the stove, a pot of chicken and dumplings. She whirled to face Robert Hurlburt. "Who? What? I'm flabbergasted."

He removed his hat and stepped toward her, grinning broadly. "Elves, do you suppose?"

She shot him a knowing look. "Fess up. I think there's a plot afoot."

He pointed at two notes on her bed. She immediately recognized Marcus's precise hand and Toby's scrawl. "The boys?" She hastily read their welcome-home messages in which they took credit for the appearance of her home.

Robert winked. "And their father."

It was hard to grasp the idea of Tate Lockwood bent to mundane housekeeping tasks. "Tate?"

"He wrote me that he and the boys were hatching this plan to welcome you."

Before she'd left, Tate had promised to look in on the

cabin, but this was beyond her expectations. Just then Beauty bounded inside, her tail wagging an exuberant welcome. Behind her raced the two boys followed by Tate. "Happy homecoming, Miss Sophie!" her students shouted before catapulting into her arms.

"We missed you," Toby said.

Marcus, nodding vigorously, added, "Please, don't leave us again."

Moved by their embrace, Sophie could barely contain her emotions. Then her eyes caught Tate's. He stood across the room, motionless, taking in the scene before him. As if a magnet had fixed her gaze on him, she couldn't look away. "Welcome home, Sophie," he said, taking a step toward her. "I'm so sorry for your loss."

"Thank you," she murmured, kissing each boy on the top of the head and then casting an approving glance around the cabin before extending her hand to Tate. "I'm overwhelmed by your care of my home." The pressure of his thumb grazing the back of her hand sent a spark through her.

Before releasing her hand, Tate explained that he and the boys had prepared the cabin for her arrival and Bertie had cooked the meal. "I picked the flowers," Marcus added.

"Anyone else famished?" Robert asked. "Let's eat."

As they gathered at the table, Sophie had a clear view of the mountains, lush with their varied hues of green. She took a deep breath, then, looking around, said, "It's good to be here with all of you."

Tate caught her eye. "I hope it may always be so." In his fond glance, she read something beyond his customary reserve. "Colorado isn't the same without you." At the other end of the table, the boys were laughing at something Robert had said. Tate leaned closer and lowered his voice. "Sophie, *I'm* not the same without you, either."

His admission caught her by surprise. It wouldn't do to acknowledge how often he'd been in her thoughts on the trip back or how rich her hopes were for a new beginning. "I missed you," she said, and then quickly added, "and the boys." Tate's words seemed to imply a shift in their relationship, but given her recent poignant memories of Charlie, she needed time before she was ready to explore the deepening affection between her and Tate.

Shortly after their meal, she was further surprised by a hubbub in the yard. When she went to investigate, the Tylers, Harpers and Grizzly shouted, "Welcome back!"

Belle ran toward her, arms outspread. "We're so glad you're home."

That was not the last time the word *home* was used to describe her cabin. Throughout the rest of the early evening as her friends offered their sympathy for her father's death and caught her up on local news, she wondered once more where *home* really was. Could it be here? From somewhere deep inside, the next question demanded her attention: *With Tate?*

The following Sunday was one of those perfect days travel writers draw upon to extol the beauty and benefits of mountain living—blue skies, warm temperatures and just enough breeze to carry the fragrance of alpine meadows. Sophie arrived at the Tylers' in plenty of time to greet the neighbors and thank them for their condolences. She and Belle cornered one of the old-timers and peppered him with questions about Longs Peak. Despite his clear disapproval of their motives, he warmed to the topics of the boulder field, the chasm view of the lake far below the east face and the challenges other climbers had faced. So engrossed were the women in his tales that at the cowbell's summons, they could hardly tear themselves away. Hurrying toward the assembled congregation, Sophie was distracted by the sight of Marcus and Toby waving at her. What were they doing here? Then, unbelievably, she spotted Tate seated behind them, a self-conscious grin on his face. He shrugged, as if acknowledging the novelty of his attendance.

Belle grabbed her by the arm and they quickly found a spot just as John Harper began leading the opening hymn, which, with a kind of blessed synchronicity, was "What a Friend We Have in Jesus." The music immediately transported Sophie back to her father's funeral and the voices raised there in sweet communion. Glancing around at her neighbors, who were clearly intent on praising the Lord, she thanked God that faith could be found both in Cottonwood Falls and in Estes Park. She sneaked a look at Tate, who, though not singing, was holding the hymnal for his sons. She assumed it was they who had led him here, and for that, she was grateful. He had fought so fiercely to avoid acknowledging God's work in his life, yet here he was. She folded her hands in her lap, praying that no matter what happened between her and Tate, he might, at last, come to know the Lord and find peace.

She grew drowsy with the long-winded sermon and was grateful when it came to an end. Hardly had the last *Amen* been chorused than Toby and Marcus came to her side. "I'm pleased to see you here," she said.

Marcus nodded sagely. "It's the best place to learn more about the Bible."

"I usually like the stories," Toby added. "Not today,

though. How could those mean brothers leave Joseph in a pit?"

Sophie patted his head. "Just wait. You'll like the ending."

Tate joined them. "Good morning," he said, doffing his hat. "I'm wondering if you know when you can resume the lessons?"

"Not before Tuesday or Wednesday. Belle and I are planning a strenuous hike tomorrow. We have so little time left to prepare for Longs Peak."

"Ladies don't climb tall mountains," Toby announced.

"Now, then, you know I've set a goal of climbing that one—" she pointed to the tallest peak "—and I intend to achieve it."

Marcus nodded. "'Anything is possible,' that's what you always say."

Tate edged closer. "I trust you'll exercise caution." When the boys ran off to join their friends, he drew her aside. "I must warn you about a distressing development concerning your summit attempt."

She cocked her head in inquiry. "Go on."

As he filled her in about the gathering interest of newspapermen and other naysayers, she waited patiently until he finished. "We are aware of such folk and have even encountered a couple of them."

"It might be best if you didn't reveal the specifics of your plans. I would hate to think any of them would try to sabotage your efforts."

"Thank you for this word of caution."

He lifted her hands in his. "I don't suppose there's any possibility of dissuading you from this venture?"

She laughed. "You know me better than that. When I'm determined—"

"—wild horses can't stop you." He smiled. "Your spirit is part of what makes you so endearing."

Endearing? "And your protectiveness reveals genuine concern."

He stepped closer, gathering their joined hands to his chest. "I beg you to take care. What you call 'concern,' I call—" he faltered before going on "—affection."

From somewhere in the chaos of her emotions, Sophie heard Toby's insistent voice. "Papa, Papa." His abrupt appearance saved her from the necessity to speak. Just as well. She had no words with which to respond.

"Papa, wanna see a lizard?" The boy held out his cupped hands.

Sophie mentally shook her head. Nothing like a lizard to save her from a moment of intimacy for which she wasn't sure she was ready.

Belle joined them and Tate repeated his warning. She nodded. "Joe says the same thing. We'll be careful."

"But undaunted," Sophie added. "And tomorrow we have a big test—the longest, most ambitious of our hikes so far."

Toby set the lizard on the ground. "You can do anything, Miss Sophie." His adoring look humbled her.

Please, God, keep me from ever hurting this boy or his brother.

In the cold light of dawn, Sophie and Belle set out on horseback for the trailhead. They were attempting not only Flattop Peak, but the two adjacent ones, all three connected by a narrow ridge. As they rode along, it seemed sacrilege to break nature's silence with words. Sophie had scarcely slept for the excitement of once again scaling heights she had only been able to dream of in Kansas. Just as they passed a tarn, the sun rose, silvering the surface of the water. Kinnikinnick and lichen-covered rocks blanketed the ground beneath scrubby junipers as they approached the spot where they would tether their horses. "Today will test us," Belle said as she dismounted.

As eager as they both were to climb Longs, Sophie knew neither would make a foolhardy decision just to save face. "Let's go, then!" Sophie said, strapping two canteens around her chest. They had gone scarcely a half a mile when a greasy-haired young man with a notebook in his hand jumped from behind some bushes and blocked their way.

"Sophie Montgomery? Belle Harper?" He had the inquisitive look of a well-fed weasel.

"Sir, let us be on our way," Belle said, attempting to brush past him.

The man merely backed up and held his ground. "I mean no harm. I just want to interview the Longs Peak Beauties." He handed Belle a card. "Rupert Stowe, reporter for the Denver paper."

Sophie bristled. "First of all, this is highly inappropriate. You, sir, are essentially accosting us, hardly a ploy guaranteeing our cooperation. Second, we are not a sideshow. We are two women setting out to prove our mettle against the mountain."

"And third," Belle joined in, "we have no intention of giving you or any of your so-called colleagues an interview at this point. So you have a choice. Either let us pass or follow along if you can keep up with us, asking your questions as you will, knowing we will not answer."

With that, both women left the trail, skirting the man, and began climbing at a rapid pace. Neither looked back for some time, although from the gasping behind them, they knew the reporter was trying to follow. "He won't last another five hundred feet of altitude gain," Belle snorted under her breath.

"This will be his first lesson in how a determined woman can be equal to a man," Sophie said, planting one booted foot in front of the other.

When they were certain the interloper had been left far behind, they rested briefly and drank from their canteens. "This is what my brother and Tate warned us about. I don't know who has been bandying our plans about, but the press is clearly on our trail."

Sophie grinned. "Even if Mr. Stowe couldn't keep up." Then she sobered. "Neither of us wants this to turn into a spectacle."

Belle screwed the lid back on her canteen. "Perhaps it is best if only those close to us know the date of our attempted ascent. When we have succeeded, then it will be time for interviews to help further the cause of emancipating women."

After a difficult last few feet to the top of the second peak, they sat down and extracted lunches from their packs. The views in all directions were spectacular. Belle broke the silence. "Have you decided whether to stay for the winter?"

Sophie shook her head, aware she would have to make that decision before early snows blocked her escape route.

"Much as I would prefer for you to be here, I have to say I'm concerned about how you would fare, removed as you are, in your cabin. You're brave and resilient, but our winters make victims of the uninitiated."

Sophie knew it would be foolish to underestimate the elements. "I haven't decided." She paused, gathering the will to voice her confession. "Belle, I'm afraid once I leave, I may never come back." There. It was out. The tug of family and Kansas was strong, yet no matter how she rationalized living in Cottonwood Falls, it didn't feel right. Yet how could she reasonably stay in Estes Park?

"You love it here, don't you?"

Sophie lifted her arm and swept it across the landscape. "It's not only beautiful, it's sacred."

"You tutor the Lockwood boys. Perhaps you could board there for the winter. Bertie would be a suitable chaperone."

"Still tongues might wag."

Belle tilted her hat back and looked squarely at Sophie. "Might they have cause to wag?" When Sophie blushed, Belle laughed. "I knew it. You're sweet on Tate. And come to think of it, he's mighty attentive to you."

"I don't know what to do." Belle sat quietly, waiting for her to continue. "I had a sweetheart once." Then Sophie told her friend about Charlie. "I came to the mountains to start over, but everywhere I look, I see the rocks and think of Charlie's talent. He would've thrived here." She leaned over to relace her left boot. "Maybe I'm due only one love in this life."

"Nonsense," Belle replied. "You're not in control of love. And if God has seen fit to send you another, as I believe He has, who are you to object?" Rising to her feet, Belle added, "Time to move, sister."

As Sophie struggled to the third mountaintop, she reflected on Belle's words. Where was the line between being rational and stubbornly ignoring God's will? Charlie would want her to be happy, if such a thing was within her grasp. He would've loved Tate's boys, she thought, imagining how they would have charmed him. Then with each step, she pictured Tate as he had stood in her cabin to welcome her home. In his expression had been such longing and quiet joy that she could scarce believe the evidence of her sight. And then his heartfelt words—*Sophie, I'm not the same without you, either.* She had replayed them over and over in the past few days. If she trusted his words and the feelings they stirred in her, how could she leave this place? Yet daring as she might be, could she reasonably brave a high country winter?

So rapt by her mental questioning was she that it was only when Belle grabbed her arm and pointed to the sky that Sophie became aware of the lightning forking just beyond the next peak. And of the wind, suddenly gusting furiously and carrying with it a chilling drop in temperatures.

"Hurry, Sophie. We must find shelter and find it quickly. A freak snow is not beyond the realm of possibility."

Tate had done his best in Sophie's absence to help the boys with their studies. He had set aside time this afternoon to listen to Toby's reading and to discuss the Trojan Wars with Marcus. Before they gathered, he had added more logs to the fire. A wild wind howled around the house and the sky looked ominous. "Papa, I checked the barometer, and just like you predicted, it's going down," Marcus told him. "A storm is coming."

"So it is," Tate said. "But we're safe and warm here."

"Not like last time when the floods came," Toby reminded them. "Do you think they'll come again?"

"Remember, son, not every rain causes flooding. Besides, rain is good for the grasslands."

"I wish Miss Sophie was here with us," Marcus said as he sprawled on the floor beside Minnie.

Tate nodded in agreement. Belle and Sophie had been hiking today, but surely they had arrived safely back at the Harpers' by now. This would be no night for anyone to be up in the mountains. Toby climbed into his lap, holding out his reader. "We're ready for the story about the jungle. Would I like a jungle, do you think?"

"Only if you didn't get eaten by a lion," Marcus said gleefully.

"Yes, Toby, you might very well like a jungle with all its exotic plants, animals and birds."

"What's *exotic* mean?"

Tate had just finished defining the word when a loud knock sounded. Tate set Toby aside and went to answer. A gust nearly tore the door from his hand, and when he looked out, there stood Joe Harper, a wild expression on his face. "Come in, man."

The two huddled in the entry, where Harper, spotting the boys looking up in curiosity, spoke quietly, his voice edged with dread. "Belle and Sophie haven't returned. The lightning is fierce and it seems to be snowing above the timberline. Will you come help look for them?"

Never had Tate felt such a powerful and instinctive need for action. Sophie? His Sophie? In danger… or worse?

"On top of everything else, one of those reporters was at the store this afternoon bragging about interviewing Sophie and Belle up on Flattop. What if there were more of those hooligans…?" The man couldn't put words to his fear.

"I'll meet you at the barn in five minutes and recruit a couple of the hands to join us."

"Hurry, please." Harper left the house, but when

Tate turned around, he was confronted by two ashen-faced boys.

"Is she all right?" Toby squeaked out.

"Miss Sophie?" Marcus managed.

Of course they had overheard. In his own rising panic Tate felt helpless to reassure them, but he must. "They are smart women. They will find a way to be safe." He held out his arms to embrace them. "Bertie will take good care of you, and now I must be off."

He had put on his coat, a poncho and a broad hat and was ready to join Harper at the barn when Marcus came up beside him and grasped his hand. "Bring Miss Sophie home, Papa, please."

Home? Yes, home. "I'll do my best, son."

Joined by John Tyler, Sam and Pancho, Tate and Joe did not spare the horses as they raced past Bear Lake and finally reached Sophie's Ranger and Belle's Doc. It was decided Sam would remain with the mounts while the other four continued the search. Although lightning still crackled across the sky, the freak snowstorm had quickly passed. There remained only an hour or so of daylight. The already penetrating cold would only worsen as night fell. Tate reined in his fear, summoning all his energy to lead the others at a grueling pace. By the time they reached the summit of Flattop, with no sign of the women, he knew they would have to proceed in the semidarkness. He had had the foresight to grab a couple of lanterns from the barn, which they paused long enough to light. The passage across the ridge was challenging even in the daylight, and their pace would be slowed by the precarious nature of the route. Every now and then one of the men would call out, "Belle! Sophie!" But the mountains yielded no reply.

As they slowly made their way along the ridge, Tate didn't want to think about the rocks below or the scree-covered slopes that could propel one down a mountainside with terrifying speed. One false step. That was all it would take. As they went higher, a dry snow dusted their path, adding to the necessity for caution when all Tate wanted to do was race forward. "Sophie!" he screamed into the growing darkness.

"Belle!" Joe echoed.

Nothing.

Tate hoped against hope that perhaps the women had found another route for their descent and might already have joined Sam and the horses. Wind gusts caused the lantern flames to flicker. Surely the women would not have continued in the face of the sudden storm. *Please, God, let them be safe.* Then he realized that it was indeed God who could deliver Sophie to him. As for the prayer he had so spontaneously uttered? It was his most effective tool…and his sole comfort. Up on this mountain, his human frailty had become all too clear to him. Yet one other force drove him relentlessly forward—his love for his precious Sophie.

"Do you see that?" Belle said, leaning forward beyond the rock shelf under which the women had sought shelter from the advancing storm.

"What?" Sophie sat under the rock overhang, her knees pulled up against her chest in the effort to keep warm.

"Lanterns, I think."

Sophie hastened to join her friend. Peering into the darkness, she stared in the direction Belle indicated. "The light comes and goes."

"Surely no one was so foolish as to come look for us. We are not idiots."

Sophie managed a rueful smile. "Only cold idiots."

"I know my brother. He was worried when we didn't return, even if he knows full well that I can take care of myself." She dug in her pocket and extracted a tin of matches. "Gather those pine needles and leaves where we've been sitting. If we spot those lights again, we can build a small fire, but we'll have to time it so whoever it is can see the flame."

Sophie bent to the task and soon had a decent pile of dry tinder and had even found a few twigs for kindling. She also had located a notebook in her pack and tore out the pages and added them to the stack.

"We'd have survived the night," Belle assured her. "Staying out during a lightning storm would have been not only risky, but idiotic."

From their vantage point, they watched the clouds disperse and a weak moon rise, shedding faint light on the rocks. They waited, all senses on alert. After long minutes, Belle grabbed Sophie's arm. "Did you hear that?"

"What?"

"Listen!"

Then, borne on the wind, came two mournful syllables. "So-phie!"

Belle once more looked out. "Someone's coming. I'm going to light the fire."

Sophie leaned over to blow gently on the tentative flame. After three matches, the fire took and both women gently fed it until they had achieved a healthy blaze.

Belle sat back on her heels. "Now all we can do is wait."

"There's one more thing." Sophie moved to the edge of the ledge and cupped her hands. "Tate!" She didn't stop to wonder why she knew it was he who had called out for her in the night. She just knew.

Within ten minutes, the search party had arrived. While Pancho held both lanterns high, Joe gathered his sister in his arms. "Don't ever scare me like that again!"

"We were fine, Joe. Really."

Sophie moved to Tate and slipped her gloved hand in his. "Thank you."

"The mountains are capricious," he said, his eyes dark coals warming her with their intensity. "They require respect." His stilted words didn't match his concerned expression.

"You're not saying what you're really thinking." She moved closer, feeling the comforting solidity of his shoulder.

He wrapped an arm around her and turned her to face him. Lantern light shadowed one side of his face, drawn with concern. "I have never been so afraid. I couldn't lose you."

She avoided dwelling on his words, which gave rise to such longing. "Belle and I are fairly self-reliant, but I regret we caused you distress."

He pulled her closer and tilted her chin so she couldn't avoid his eyes, watering either from the wind or from emotion, she couldn't tell which. In a choked voice, he spoke such welcome words she could scarcely keep her balance. "I prayed, Sophie. I prayed for you." Then he wrapped her in a bear hug. "And God is very good."

"Very good, indeed," she whispered against his chest.

Chapter Fourteen

At the end of the week, Sophie watched Marcus, his brow furrowed in concentration, adding Latin labels to a map of ancient Rome he'd drawn. Toby was worrying over multiplication problems. Grateful for the productive silence, she eased back in her chair, caught up in her own musing.

Shy was a word seldom used to describe her, yet she couldn't help blushing and becoming uncommonly quiet whenever Tate was nearby, which he now frequently was during the boys' study time. She would catch him looking at her over his newspaper, as if to assure himself she was still there. In the two days since what she knew he regarded as her mountain "rescue," she had tried to mask the self-consciousness she felt in his presence. It was as if they were involved in some intricate courtship dance in which neither was familiar with the steps. If she was honest, she had found her ordeal with the unpredictable mountain weather unsettling and in retrospect could admit she'd experienced relief when Tate and the others had appeared. But not merely relief. Nor gratitude. Something more. Indefinable but insistent. As if they had been destined to find one another.

She shook her head, disgusted with that line of thinking. Girlish whimsy! Anyway, time was becoming critical. She and Belle were joining Wild Bill and his party Thursday to mount the three-day Longs Peak attempt, weather permitting. Too much later than this early-September date, the threat of heavier snows would likely make the ascent impossible. Although she had as yet made no final decision concerning whether to remain in the mountains or return home for the winter, she knew if she elected to stay, provisions must be ordered. She had received a strongly worded letter from Caleb urging her not to risk a high country winter—and one from Rose, touching in her earnest hope that Sophie would return to her childhood home. But even if she returned to Kansas, Sophie couldn't impose upon family for room and board. She would have to find her own place. Perhaps the local school could use her services, but that prospect gave her little pleasure.

"I'm finished," Toby announced triumphantly. "Nine times seven is sixty-three, right?"

Sophie nodded.

"I'm pretty smart, you know," he said as if expecting applause.

"You are, indeed," Tate said from across the room. "Smart enough for a game of dominoes?"

Toby slid from his seat and went to fetch the domino tiles. After he and Tate had settled to the game, Marcus moved his chair closer to hers. "What about this winter, Miss Sophie?"

"What do you mean?"

"How will you make it from your cabin through the snow to teach us? I'm just getting the hang of Latin, and I need you." As if the idea had just occurred to him, he said, "Maybe you could live here for the winter."

Sophie's heart sank. She couldn't possibly consider being in the same house with Tate every day for months, all the time confused by the emotions he brought to the surface. "I have my own home," she said quietly.

"But it was empty before you came," the boy said with irrefutable logic. Then before she could stop him, he shouted across the room, "Papa, let's invite Miss Sophie to spend the winter with us so she won't have to be alone. That way we could continue our lessons with her."

Toby clapped his hands. "Yea! Miss Sophie could have the bedroom upstairs next to ours."

There was no deciphering the look on Tate's face—pleasure or distress?

Sophie stood and put her arm around Marcus. "This is a thoughtful invitation, Marcus, and I would enjoy spending more time with you, of course, but I have my own affairs to consider."

"We'll help you consider," Toby said. "I'm good at considering."

Tate rose to his feet. "Sophie, Marcus's idea is worth considering. We have the room."

Sophie mustered a smile. "Oh, so you're good at considering, too?"

He returned the smile. "Only when the outcome suits me. And this would."

"I'm sorry, Tate. I have to be responsible for myself."

"Have you determined, then, to leave the valley for the winter?"

"I'll deal with my decision after the summit attempt. For now, I'm focused on two things—your boys and Longs Peak."

He slumped. "Very well. But please think about Marcus's suggestion."

Eager to lighten the mood, Sophie smiled and said, "I suppose I could…*consider* it."

On Sunday Tate was surprised to find Belle and Sophie missing from the services his sons continued to persuade him to attend. Joe Harper explained that their Longs Peak guide had needed to go over their plans and was only available that morning. Uneasy about the direction of Sophie's winter plans and even more confused about what feelings, if any, Sophie might have for him, Tate was disappointed not to see her, no matter how awkward such a meeting might be. If she were any other tutor, it would make perfect sense that such a person board at the house. He harrumphed. She wasn't "any other tutor." She was a woman occupying more and more of his thoughts. Under no circumstances, even these, could he imagine facing her every morning over the polite distance of the breakfast table when what he really wanted was to take her in his arms. He'd been hopeful of her affections until she'd spoken of her fiancé. She had loved her Charlie with heart and soul. How could he hope to offer such a love? In fact, he'd begun to doubt he had ever truly loved Ramona or she him. If he moved Sophie in as the tutor, how could he keep his distance and conceal his feelings for her? Then there were the boys to consider. He winced. That word *consider* again. At the very beginning, he'd worried about their possible attachment to her. Better for all concerned to have a clean separation now than for the two of them to circle each other warily for weeks on end. An amicable parting of the ways would spare him and his sons further pain.

All the way home from the church services, while the boys chattered merrily, he reviewed the logic of his thinking. It all made perfect sense. A swift cut ensured rapid healing. Then as if a voice had thundered from the mountains, he faced the truth. Who did he think he was fooling? Logic had nothing to do with it. He didn't care what induced her to remain here or what the repercussions might be. No. He wanted Sophie to stay under whatever conditions. A winter without her would be intolerable. A week. A day…

"Papa, do you think we could be at the base of the trail on Saturday to cheer for Miss Sophie and Miss Belle after they come down from the top of Longs Peak?"

"What did you say?" Jarred from his thoughts, Tate thought he had surely misheard Marcus.

"Everybody was talking about it this morning," Toby added.

"About what?"

"The celebration," Marcus explained. "Lots of the church folk want to be there to greet them."

"And Mrs. Tyler 'spects some of those brazen snoopers." Toby paused. "What's *brazen* mean?"

Had he been so preocuupied all morning that he hadn't heard a word of this? Could he dare take the boys to such a gathering? What if something happened to Sophie on the mountain? They would be devastated. And yet if she and Belle were successful? It would be a feat Marcus and Toby would, indeed, want to witness and celebrate. "I'll see," he muttered, turning the buggy at the bridge.

"'I'll see.' That's all you have to say about the most exciting thing Miss Sophie has ever done?" Marcus stared straight ahead in defiance.

"Yeah, we know her better'n anyone," Toby said.

"And she's gonna be—" he paused for emphasis "—spectacular!"

Tate chewed his lip. He wanted Sophie to be spectacular. More than that, he wanted her to be safe. But what if...? He closed his eyes briefly against the reality of the risks she would be facing.

As soon as they got home and finished the midday meal, Tate buried himself in his office, searching for something—anything—to distract him from his mounting concern. Tiny Sophie, not that much bigger than Marcus. What chance did she have against the unforgiving peak? He turned to his ledger books, determined to lay aside his worry. Intent on the task of bringing his accounts up to date, he was disturbed by a knock on his door. Bertie didn't wait for his invitation to enter, but burst into the room. "Sir, I don't know how it happened, but Toby has gone missing!"

He leaped to his feet, barely fending off panic. "Missing? What are you saying?"

"I was picking berries in the back garden. Marcus was in his room reading and Toby told me he and Buster would play in front. When I went to check on him, I couldn't find him or the dog. I've looked everywhere."

Marcus sidled into the room, his eyes wide with concern. "Papa, I didn't see him."

"How long has he been gone?"

"I don't know, sir. Perhaps an hour."

Tate brushed past them, imagining his son being confronted by a mountain lion or slipping into the fast-moving river. "We've no time to lose. Bertie, alert the men and have them search behind the house. I'll start down the road. Marcus, you and Bertie keep looking in the house, in closets, cupboards, wherever you think your brother might hide."

His chest tight with fear, Tate threw a saddle on his horse and after satisfying himself that Toby was, indeed, not in the yard, galloped down the drive, pausing only at the bridge to assure himself Toby wasn't playing near the water. He reined in when he came to the road. Which way would the boy go? Of course, to Sophie's. Where else?

He had ridden only a quarter of a mile or so when he rounded a curve and spotted Toby, with Buster at his side, walking down the center of the road as if he hadn't a care in the world. Relief warred with his need to scold his son. He trotted closer, then dismounted, leading his horse toward the boy. The fears of the past few minutes had reminded him once again how precious his sons were to him. He knew he couldn't always protect them, but his instinct was to do just that. "Toby Lockwood," he called.

The boy whirled around. "Papa? What are you doing here?"

Tate bit his tongue. "Looking for you."

"I'm a big boy. Smart, too."

"Yes, but that doesn't give you license to wander off and worry Bertie and the rest of us. Did you tell anyone where you were going?"

He hung his head and traced a figure in the dirt with the toe of his shoe. "No."

"Didn't you think we'd worry when we couldn't find you?"

He shrugged.

Tate knelt in front of his son and took him by the shoulders. "You must never do this again. If you want to go someplace, one of us needs to come with you."

Toby looked up. "Will you come with me now? I need to go to Miss Sophie's."

"Why is that?"

"She wasn't at church this morning, so I have to tell her the end of the story. 'Bout Joseph. Guess what, you see Joseph becomes a really important man in Egypt and—"

"Not now, son." Tate paused to get himself under control. Then he arrived at the only decision that made any sense. "You can tell us all about it when we get to Miss Sophie's cabin."

After returning from Wild Bill's and a detailed orientation of their route on Longs Peak, Sophie turned Ranger loose in the corral and was leaving the barn when she spotted Tate riding toward her, Toby tucked against his chest and Buster trotting along beside them. She couldn't imagine what had happened. Marcus? But if something were wrong with him, Tate wouldn't have left home. As they neared, Sophie noticed Toby's flushed, excited face and broad grin. "Miss Sophie, Miss Sophie," he called out, "I got something to tell you."

Tate nodded at Sophie, looking apologetic, before dismounting and lifting Toby to the ground. "Is this a bad time?"

"No, I just returned myself. Please, come sit on the porch while I hang up my bonnet and get us all some water."

While Buster and Beauty ran around the yard, Tate settled in one of the rockers and Toby sat cross-legged on the floor, jiggling his knees in anticipation. Tate sighed. This is what comes of permitting your children to go to church, he thought. How could one Bible story have so fired his son's imagination? "I can't wait to tell her," Toby said. "It's a special story."

No sooner had Sophie distributed the tin cups and taken a seat in the other rocker than Toby launched in. "'Member Joseph was in the pit. Then he was saved and went to Egypt. But his brothers almost forgot all about him. And then…" He launched into the story, standing at times to act out parts.

Sophie smiled both because of the boy's enthusiasm and Tate's bemused expression. For a non-churchgoer, he must be wondering what he had spawned. Perhaps she should feel a hint of guilt, but she was too caught up in Toby's skillful retelling, culminating with Joseph's tearful reunion with his family. "See!" Toby exulted. "Everything came out fine. All because of God, right?"

If only it were that simple, Sophie reflected. Toby would learn soon enough that although God was always with him, life would still present disappointments, pain and grief. "What is the lesson of this story, Toby?"

"Even if your family does bad things, maybe you can forgive them someday?"

Sophie's heart contracted, wondering if Toby's remark was innocent or born out of his mother's departure. She glanced at Tate, whose jaw was working. He seemed unwilling or unable to meet her eyes. "That's a splendid conclusion. Forgiveness of others matters. Sometimes we even have to forgive ourselves."

"I 'spect I need to forgive myself." Toby leaned his chin on his fists. "I did a bad thing," he mumbled.

Before she could inquire further, Tate moved from his seat to join Toby on the floor. Gently he took the boy's hands in his. "Not so much a 'bad' thing, son, as something you did on impulse without considering how your action would affect others."

"I shoulda asked, right?"

"Yes."

"But you wouldn't have brought me here, would you?"

Sophie saw the struggle pass over Tate's face. "Possibly not."

"So I had to come by myself, but I should've told somebody. Marcus, maybe."

Sophie watched then as Tate gathered the boy into his arms. "I forgive you, son. And now that you understand that your action caused others concern, it's time to forgive yourself."

"And God'll forgive me, too?"

"Most assuredly," Sophie said. "Just like your own father, God is mighty partial to little children, especially ones named Toby."

"Really?" He took his papa's face in his hands. "See, I'm special."

"Indeed you are." The tremor in Tate's voice betrayed him. He stood the boy up. "Why don't you go play with Beauty and Buster while I talk with Miss Sophie?"

The boy started down the porch steps, then turned to Sophie. "And Joseph had a coat of many colors, too. I'd like one, I think." Then he ran to play with the dogs.

Tate released an audible sigh.

"What happened?" Sophie asked.

Tate resumed his seat in the rocker and told her about Toby's burning need to see her in order to finish the Joseph story. Then he rested his head on the back of the chair and closed his eyes momentarily. "I was panicked," he admitted. "What if something had happened to him?"

"What-ifs aren't nearly as productive as 'what is.' The fact is that your son is safe, he has told me the story and he knows you love him and forgive him. It was wise of you to bring him here and let the day play out for him." She hesitated, knowing how deeply she trusted what she was about to say. "Tate, you are a very fine father."

"I'm trying." He leaned forward, hands dangling between his knees, watching his son and the dogs. "You've been good for them, Sophie."

"I hope so." In this moment she wanted nothing more than to kneel before him, hold his hands and offer him reassurance. He had obviously been terror-stricken when he'd discovered Toby was missing. "But it will not do for them to become dependent on me." *Nor for me to need them so—all of them.*

"It may be too late for that." He gulped down his water, handed her the cup and rose to his feet. She stood, too, and for a long moment they looked at one another as if attempting to convey with a glance what neither was ready to say. "Will I see you again before your climb?"

"Most assuredly. Tomorrow and Wednesday I will come for lessons."

"Sophie, there's something I must say to you."

She waited, breathlessly.

"No matter whether you decide to come live with us this winter and continue teaching the boys, you have been a godsend." He chuckled wryly, apparently at his use of *God*. "See what you've done? I've even uttered a prayer or two lately."

"Don't thank me. Thank God."

"Marcus, Toby and I are planning to be at the trailhead when you return from your successful ascent of Longs." He tucked a stray curl behind her ear. "We're rooting for you, Sophie, and we always will."

With that he called to Toby, but before leaving the porch, he cupped her cheek in his warm hand. "Be safe."

He kissed the top of her head and added, "I will be praying for you."

Long after the two had ridden toward the ranch, Sophie stood on the porch, gazing into the distance. With those few words, Tate had just made her decision about where to winter that much more complicated.

As a final test, on Tuesday Belle and Sophie made one last conditioning hike, which included both a steep, rocky ascent and a precarious, narrow passage over a ridge. Along the trail they reviewed their necessary supplies and equipment in light of possible weather contingencies on Longs and agreed to wear britches under their shorter riding dresses to facilitate the rock climbing involved. "Just one more thing to annoy our detractors," Belle noted.

"Not to mention the gentlemen—and I use that term lightly—of the press."

"I can hardly bear their smug assumption that we will fail. Joe thinks they might even try to sabotage us. Especially if others in the hiking party bandy the dates around."

"It's not as if we're the first women to climb that peak."

"True, but there have been less than a handful," Belle pointed out, "and as Joe says, never a pair of attractive young females who have the potential to put men to shame."

"And the will," Sophie added.

Unexpectedly, Belle giggled. "Oh, to see the looks on their incredulous faces when we succeed."

Sophie smiled. "I have the banner ready."

"Despite those who are shocked by our effrontery in attempting to summit, we also have friends like Martha and Dolly Tyler who will be cheering us on. What about Tate and the boys?"

"They're excited for us, although I sense hesitation in Tate, primarily I think because of his concern for the boys in the event we encounter difficulty."

Belle sobered. "We can be under no illusions. This is a daunting and perhaps perilous endeavor upon which we're embarking. Now is the time for any second thoughts."

Sophie waited several minutes before replying, and in that time, she faced the factors arguing against her participation: the possibility of getting injured or even going to her death and the impact that would have on those she loved; the question of whether her own need to prove something was overpowering her reason; and whether in the deepest part of her being she somehow unaccountably hoped to find Charlie on Longs Peak.

"Sophie?"

The moment of truth had arrived. "I'm ready. No turning back."

"All right, then. We'll ride to Wild Bill's Thursday morning, and he'll guide us to the timberline where we'll camp overnight."

"And then on Friday?" Sophie could hardly contain her enthusiasm. "We'll show them all!"

Tate prowled around his office Wednesday like a caged tiger. Tomorrow Sophie and Belle would head up the mountain to the timberline camp. If he could stop time, he would. Terrifying eventualities plagued his thoughts—an icy trail, unstable footing, bone-chilling cold, howling winds and, worst of all, the threat of avalanche or rock slide. What if Sophie fell and sprained an ankle or broke a leg or wrist. Or, worse yet… He threw up his hands. He wasn't accustomed to lacking control.

Earlier this morning he'd tried to go sit close while she worked with the boys, but he couldn't stand being in such proximity, knowing it wasn't his place to beg her to reconsider the climb. Nor could he listen to the boys' excited questions concerning the day's lesson: the history of mountaineering. Why was she so determined to do this perilous thing?

He stopped at the window and glared at the mountains, silently cursing them. They had a hold on her that seemed to feed her and, at the same time, challenge her. And considering what he knew of Sophie, she would never back away from a challenge. But did she have any realistic idea what she was undertaking to do?

He pounded a fist into the wall. Of course she did, and his typically masculine, patronizing attitude was not helpful. Much as the prospect of the attempted ascent terrified him, he also knew she and Belle had prepared carefully and that Bill was a seasoned and conscientious guide. Her adventuresome spirit was an important part of what he loved about her. Her bravery coupled with her compassion was difficult to resist, and he no longer wanted to.

He turned away from the window and plucked his watch from his vest pocket. Nearly noon. No, she didn't need more cautionary words or judgment. She needed his heartfelt support, and he wanted to give it to her without reservation. He swiped a hand through his hair, squared his shoulders and left the room to find her.

"We'll be waiting for you at the bottom of the trail," Toby assured her as she put away the maps.

Marcus closed and shelved his book. "We are quite

proud of you, Miss Sophie. You are doing something remarkable."

"I'm gonna do it, too, when I'm older," Toby boasted.

Sophie gathered the boys to her. "Your encouragement means a great deal to me. I shall think of you as I climb, knowing that you are urging me on."

Toby interrupted. "And praying for you, too."

Sophie looked from one to the other, undone by the trust in their eyes. "Your prayers will be the best gift you can give me."

"I don't think Papa will mind. About the prayers," Toby said.

Marcus spoke quietly. "You know what, Miss Sophie? I think God has His hand on Papa."

Sophie swallowed, steeling herself not to cry. "We can certainly hope so. Your papa is very special."

Almost as if their thoughts had summoned him, Tate entered the room. "Am I interrupting?"

"No, Papa. We were just telling Miss Sophie how we'll be praying for her success."

Sophie glanced at Tate to see how he would react to Marcus's bold remark. With disapproval? Censure?

"I'm sure she will appreciate your efforts," was all he said.

"I am most appreciative of your support and will look forward to seeing you at the end."

"You will reach the summit, Miss Sophie. I just know it," Marcus said with conviction.

Toby nodded. "And none of those 'brazen snoopers' can stop you."

Tate moved closer, one hand resting on Toby's head. "We won't let any of those cads anywhere near Miss Sophie or Miss Belle. Now, then, go on and wash up for dinner."

The boys each hugged Sophie and wished her good luck and then left to do as their father had bid.

Sophie had already told Bertie she would not be eating with them in the interest of getting back to the cabin in time to pack up for the next day. This, then, was farewell, one fraught with an elusive significance. She stepped away from Tate and put the last pencils away. "I guess this is goodbye for now. The next time I see you I will have completed my goal, with God's help."

"If sheer determination is a factor, I have no doubt of your success."

"Thank you."

"May I walk you out?"

"I'd like that."

Outside the skies were a cloudless blue, and aspen trees speckled the green mountainsides with blazes of pure gold. Sophie took a deep breath of the refreshing mountain air, wondering for the first time if she wouldn't be wiser to enjoy Longs Peak from a safe distance. Then she mentally shook her head. No. It wouldn't be the same.

They were nearly to the spot where Ranger was tethered before Tate finally spoke. "Joe, the others and I will be doing all we can to keep those who wish you ill at bay. You and Belle deserve a fair shot at this feat."

"We appreciate your efforts." She wanted to say more, but the words stuck in her throat.

"There is something I need to tell you." He stopped walking and faced her, blocking her progress. "Sophie, you are aware at times that I have doubted you and questioned what I perceived as your rash behavior. Yet you have never done anything but be open and honest with me, and even cheerful in the light of my churlishness."

Sophie couldn't look away. He was obviously speaking with difficulty from his heart. He was a good man who had suffered much, but in him she saw such a capacity for love. She tried for a smile. "You are better and better with the boys."

"And with you?"

She laid a hand on his cheek. "Yes."

He took that hand in his and with his other arm, he pulled her close.

"Sophie, you are a rare and fascinating woman, and although you may sometimes lack good sense, you greet every day with joy. I'm trying to do that, even though my life hasn't always led me to that conclusion. Like your Charlie, I would like to be a man worthy of you." He released her and strolled on. "Maybe someday."

She was dumbfounded. What was he saying? *Like your Charlie?* Was that an obstacle between them? She knew it was for her, but for him, as well? She stared into the distance where Longs Peak dominated the horizon. Could she find answers there to the many questions that stood between her and her future? She hoped so.

She untied Ranger's reins and hesitated before mounting, searching Tate's face. How might her burning need to scale a mountain peak affect their relationship? And then to her immense relief, she received an answer.

He pulled her into a fierce embrace that seemed to go on forever before kissing her forehead and whispering, "Go with God, my dearest Sophie."

Before she could react, he wheeled and walked toward the house without a backward glance, leaving her with much to ponder.

Chapter Fifteen

Thursday morning before departing for Belle's, Sophie dampened the coals in the woodstove, glanced once more around the now familiar and beloved cabin and then stood quietly for a moment, her hand resting on her Bible. She remembered vividly the lines that had been the inspiration for her Colorado journey: "I will lift up mine eyes unto the hills, from whence cometh my help." These "hills" had not failed her. She had found peace in the solitude, friendships for the making and two young boys who had given her purpose. In a way, tomorrow's journey to the top of the world would be more one of homage than challenge. Uttering a soft prayer of thanksgiving, she shouldered her knapsack and left the cabin, knowing that regardless of what happened on Longs Peak, she would return a different person than she was today.

Beauty followed her to the Harpers', where she would remain until Sophie's return. Belle was ready when Sophie arrived, but pointed at the road beyond the barn where Joe was gesturing emphatically to two men, one of whom was Rupert Stowe, the pushy reporter. "They showed up about ten minutes ago, insisting on interviewing us. They've gotten wind of the timing of our Longs Peak adventure from some other hiker in our party."

"I suppose short of hog-tying them, all Joe can do is delay them."

"They won't get far before others come to help Joe fend them off. He and Tate have planned for this eventuality."

In the distance, Sophie spotted Jackson and John Tyler riding toward them. "Reinforcements are already on their way. Even if the newsmen follow us all the way to Bill's, I doubt they could keep up with us on the mountain."

"It might be fun to see them try," Belle hooted as she mounted her horse. "Shall we leave them with a word?"

Sophie grinned. "By all means."

The two rode up to Joe and the reporters, just as the Tylers joined the group. "Good morning, gentlemen," Belle said, edging her mount uncomfortably close to the interlopers, who were then forced to back up a step.

"Do you want to be the first with the big story?" Sophie asked, staring down at them.

"Look at you! You're a disgrace in those britches. You'll get your comeuppance. Wait and see," Stowe snarled.

"No, you wait and see," Belle said. "We're going to make history, and you can either celebrate us or paint yourselves as bigots."

"Unless of course you'd like to try coming with us," Sophie added with a mischievous grin.

Jackson intervened. "Never you mind, girls. These greenhorns don't know who they're dealing with here. Two mighty women who can run rings around them." He doffed his hat. "Good luck to you."

As the women trotted away, they could hear the argument erupting again as their defenders surrounded the two troublemakers.

"I could hardly eat this morning, I was so excited," Sophie admitted.

"But you did, of course?"

"Of course. Fuel for the journey." Sophie knew it was important to keep her emotions under control, but as she observed the passing scenery, dominated by the peak that drew her like a magnet, she was filled not only with purpose, but with an excitement unlike any she had ever known. She and Belle were really going to attempt this thing!

At midday they arrived at Wild Bill's cabin by the trailhead and joined the rest of the hikers attempting the ascent, which included two citified-looking men, a portly mining executive from Colorado Springs named Longwood Baker, a rancher from the eastern part of the state, the same obnoxious Englishman they'd met on the trail earlier in the summer and a handsome outdoorsy-looking man who had the courtesy to greet them warmly as opposed to the others, who made a show of ignoring them. Wild Bill gathered them all before they set off on horseback to reach the boulder field camp by nightfall. "Here're the rules. Do exactly what I say. Step where I tell you to step. If you tire and can't go on, speak up. Nothin' worse than folks underestimating this mountain. I don't wanna be dragging anybody up or down. You're all under your own steam, gentlemen." He paused, recognizing his oversight. "And ladies."

The rancher let his eyes roam over Belle and Sophie. "Not much worry about you two goin' beyond the boulder field."

"If there," the mining executive chortled.

"I say. Unprecedented, the nerve of these women," the Englishman snorted.

The outdoorsman spoke for the first time. "The proof will be in the pudding, gentlemen. I, for one, am willing to wait and see what these two fine women are capable of."

Sophie nodded in appreciation just as Bill gave the order to move out. She and Belle had known they would be joining others in their summit attempt and had fully expected the kind of scorn to which they were being subjected. It had been a pleasant surprise to learn that at least one of their fellow climbers had a streak of fairness. Belle and Sophie stayed near the end of the line as it wound its way upward through the forest and among the rocks looming on either side of the path Bill was blazing for them. Although the morning had been clear, clouds rolled in about three, followed by a brief downpour. The women had donned their rain ponchos in preparation, unlike some of the men who preferred to expose themselves to the elements. "I hope they're not always so stupid," Belle muttered. Other than Bill and possibly the man who had spoken up for them, Sophie had little confidence in their fellow mountaineers. Anyone could ride a horse to the timberline. Tomorrow would be a different challenge. She couldn't wait.

By the time Tate got to the Harpers', the immediate threat from the reporters had passed. Except for one thing. Joe handed Tate the latest Denver paper without comment. On the front page below the fold a headline read Female Folly to Hamper Longs Peak Party. Tate fumed as he read on.

The Misses Belle Harper and Sophie Montgomery in their misplaced zeal to undertake adventures suitable only to the stronger sex are jeopardizing the upcoming ascent of the famous Longs Peak. As if that were not sufficient scandal, their masculine attire is an affront to decency. Longwood Baker, wealthy Colorado miner, commented thusly: "We cannot afford to be slowed by these reckless females. It is irresponsible of our guide to have afforded them a place in our prestigious party composed of world-class mountaineers."

More quoted boasts followed, along with accounts of successful hikes up the mountain, including the fact that only three women had previously attempted to summit.

"Three successful women," Tate muttered as he read to the concluding sentence.

It is this reporter's duty to greet the party upon completion of their descent and report to you, gentle readers, details of the ways in which these improperly clad, ill-prepared females compromised this summit attempt.

Tate checked the byline. "Who is this Rupert Stowe?"

"One and the same rascal who, along with his fellow snoop, has been trying to interview Belle. They figured out when the girls were taking off. This morning they were waiting to ambush them with questions and, frankly, taunts. Luckily I got to them first. Then Jackson and John, who'd spied them on the road, arrived and together we were able to persuade the men to desist."

"So they didn't disturb Belle and Sophie?"

Joe's eyes glinted with amusement. "To the contrary, the gals disturbed them. Issued a challenge to join them on the trip up Longs."

Tate felt himself relax. "Let me guess. The reporters weren't *that* interested in firsthand news gathering."

"No, but they made a beeline for the telegraph office, no doubt to communicate their latest on-the-scene report."

"I don't think they're the last of the lot. On my ride over, I saw a party of five horsemen I didn't recognize heading off on the trail to Wild Bill's. There seems to be a great deal of interest in the ladies."

"I can only hope some in their hiking party are less mean-spirited."

"Truth to tell, Joe, other than Wild Bill, who seems to like the notoriety, they are going to have to rely on themselves. And I have the suspicion their fellow hikers are in for a huge surprise."

"We know these two. *Grit* is their middle name. I would never count them out."

"Nor would I. Still, I won't breathe easy until they return safe and sound."

"And triumphant," Joe said, sticking out his hand to shake Tate's. "You gonna be at the finish Saturday?"

"I wouldn't miss it. Nor would Marcus and Toby. They think their Miss Sophie can conquer the world."

Joe laid his other hand on Tate's shoulder. "And just maybe she's conquered you in the process."

Tate felt a blush creep up his neck. "Time will tell."

And so it would, he thought to himself as he rode home. If only he and Sophie could overcome their obstacles. He knew Sophie wrestled with her devotion to the memory of her Charlie and the possibility of her permanent return to Kansas, while he faced the difficulty of making himself vulnerable again and, beyond that, discovering if he was capable of loving another and being loved in return.

* * *

Just as the sun vanished behind the far mountains, Sophie, Belle and the others arrived at a clearing on the edge of the boulder field where the party would make camp that night. Of all the men, only the outdoorsy gentleman, who had introduced himself as Clark Elli-cott, offered to help them pitch their tent. They politely declined and proceeded to get theirs set up before many of the others had finished. In fact, the miner and the city gents were proceeding clumsily with muttered oaths. Bill built a small fire and soon had a pan of beans and a pot of coffee simmering. The rancher slipped a flask from his coat pocket and took a healthy swig. "Won't do to overindulge," Bill drily observed.

Belle and Sophie sat primly by, eating their supper and observing the others swapping stories and slapping each other on the back in shows of bravado. "Most of them are scared," Belle observed in a low voice.

"Especially Mr. Baker," Sophie whispered.

"I'm thinking that instead of our being a nuisance, some of them may well be."

"That one city fellow is already gasping like a beached trout." Sophie reconsidered her own confi-dence. "It won't do to become complacent just because we've trained and are acclimated to the altitude."

"It's going to be hard, Sophie. Very hard."

"But exciting!"

Belle smiled in agreement.

Bill stood by the campfire. "This is not a night for revelry. You will rouse before dawn, eat and be ready to set forth at first light."

Before retiring for the night, Sophie paused briefly to study the sky ablaze with starlight. It was as if heaven could be hers if only she could reach out and touch one of those stars. She hugged herself against the alpine chill. *Charlie. You seem so close, yet so far away. But always in my heart.*

Once inside the tent, she rolled up in a blanket, uncomfortably aware of the rocky ground on which she lay. Thus cocooned, she closed her eyes in what was a futile attempt to sleep. What was it that compelled her to try to summit? Undertaking the cause of emancipation for women? Her own stubborn determination to do what others claimed she could not? To experience the majestic scenery? All of those and none of them. In her heart, she knew why. Foolish as it might sound, she believed that once atop Longs Peak, she might be free of the burdens that had so long defined her.

She must have eventually dozed off, because the next thing she knew, she was being shaken awake. "It's time," Belle said in an awestruck tone.

Sophie sat up and echoed her friend. It was indeed time. Although she felt the acceleration of her heartbeat, she also experienced a calm sense of purpose. "Today is our day."

Friday. The day. From his first glimpse of the sun, Tate had been fraught with nervous energy, unable to concentrate. Marcus and Toby had besieged him at breakfast. "Do you think they've started hiking?"

"How long will it take them to reach the summit?" Their questions only served to echo his own desire to follow the progress of the hiking party. Yet all they could do was wait until tomorrow when the group would descend from the timberline camp where they'd camp tonight after the summit attempt. He lingered at the table after the boys had gone outside with Buster and Minnie. When Bertie came to clear the dishes, she gazed at him with motherly concern. "She'll be fine, sir. You'll see."

Not only Joe, but now Bertie. Was his affection for Sophie that obvious? "I know, but still, it's an arduous trek."

"She's up to the task. I'm very proud of her."

"As am I," he said. At first Sophie's advanced ideas about the role of women had shocked him. After all, he was the man who thought he had married the ideal wife—a socially adept hostess with charmingly conventional views who adoringly respected his authority. What did he get? Ramona. Sophie, on the other hand, was a tomboyish independent thinker with wit and intellect the equal of any man. She was by no means a woman to be tamed. He grinned at the improbability of that ever happening.

He left the table and walked to the library alcove, now bereft of the liveliness of Sophie's presence. He *was* proud of her. She had the imagination, confidence and determination to undertake the most difficult of physical challenges. Beyond that, however, as evidenced by her care of his sons, she had a boundless capacity for love and compassion. He hoped that in the days following the Longs Peak climb he could find the courage to express his admiration of her. *Admiration?* That was hardly the word. He simply couldn't imagine going through life without her.

Sophie was grateful for her sturdy, comfortable boots. It was painstaking work traversing the uneven boulder field covered with rocks of all sizes, as if a giant had randomly strewn them. She had to watch the placement of each foot, lest she turn an ankle or catch her toe in a crevice and trip. At times she had to skirt larger boulders or climb through them on all fours. At first glance the route to the Keyhole rock formation marking the beginning of the summit trail had seemed quite manageable. Now Sophie acknowledged the difficulty of estimating distance in such a vast, monochromatic environment. She could hear the gasps and grunts of her fellow hikers and the steady wheeze of Mr. Baker, who trailed her by twenty feet. The rancher seemed fixated on following Bill as closely as possible. As for the others, they streamed out across the field, progressing at a steady pace. The day was clear, and the early-morning sun warmed the back of Sophie's neck. She pulled the brim of her hat lower and marched on. Belle, though not lagging, brought up the rear, more as a means of urging Mr. Baker along, although Sophie knew he would never claim to need such help.

Marmots scuttled through the rocks and overhead birds soared on the slight breeze. When Sophie stopped to look back at their camp, she was surprised how tiny the tents appeared to be. She noted that the summit, which had once looked so attainable, was much higher and farther away than she had figured. When they stopped at the Keyhole for a rest and water break, Belle sidled up to her. "I'm not sure Mr. Baker is going to make it. Look at his boots."

Sophie winced in sympathy. They were brand-new, and the pompous man had made the mistake of removing one and peeling off his heavy socks. The blister bubbling up on his heel caused her to cringe. He would be lucky to get the boot back on, much less undertake the most difficult part of the hike. Meanwhile, Bill hunkered in quiet conversation with the more slightly built of the two city gentlemen, whose face was the color of pea soup. Bill put a hand on the man's head and pushed it between the fellow's knees. Then he stood and called out to the group. "This is it. If you are having any difficulty at all, I cannot permit you to endanger or delay others on our summit attempt. The air is thinner, the wind fiercer and the climbing far steeper from this point on. Mr. McConnell here—" he nodded toward the city man "—is suffering from altitude sickness and has elected not to proceed. However, I am unwilling to leave him alone. Anyone else ready to stay behind?"

No one answered. Sophie sneaked a peak at Baker, who continued staring at his foot as if it had betrayed him.

"Baker?" Bill's voice was more command than question.

"I will not remain. It's the place of one or both of these women to give up at this point. They have no business being here anyway."

Sophie put a hand on Belle's arm to forestall an injudicious remark.

Clark Ellicott stepped nearer Baker. "They would not be here if our guide did not consider them prepared for what lies ahead. You, sir, are the one who failed to foresee the discomfort of new boots. I propose you put your boot back on and walk a few steps."

Belle nudged Sophie, both of them knowing what would happen.

Somehow the man forced his foot into the boot, but not without much unsuitable language. When he stood up and put weight on his foot, he howled.

Bill walked over, plucked a tin of ointment out of his pocket and handed it to Baker. "You are not going anywhere. Not while I'm your guide. Take this ointment, apply it to your foot and, as soon as McConnell recovers, make your way back to camp. We should join you mid- to late-afternoon." Then without a backward glance, Bill motioned for the others to follow him. "Carefully," he ordered as he led them forward.

The trail to the summit followed the west side of the mountain. The way was narrow and below them opened up a wide, deep gorge. In the distance, closer mountains crowded on the horizon. A gusty wind blew beyond the Keyhole. Sophie paused to swallow the bile that had risen in her throat. A misstep could prove deadly, as one might bounce over rocks and slide on scree clear to the yawning chasm floor. Then her training kicked in. *Don't look down. Follow the leader. Take it one step at a time.* "You're doing great." From his position directly behind her, Ellicott encouraged her. "Let your pace become rhythmic. And don't forget to breathe."

Good advice, because Sophie had noticed greater difficulty in pulling air into her lungs in the thin air. "Have you done much mountaineering?" she asked to keep her mind off the perilous trail.

"Mainly in the Alps and the Adirondacks," he answered.

"Where are you from?"

"New York. And you?"

Where *was* she from? Kansas? Colorado? "I'm in transition," she finally responded.

They trudged on a few more feet. "Mountains have a way of clarifying things," he said as if that was all one needed to know.

Preoccupied by the conversation, Sophie had failed to notice they were now going downhill, rather than uphill. "What in the world?" she muttered.

Ellicott must've heard her, because he said, "We have to go down before we can go up."

She knew he meant those words literally, yet they

took on greater significance when applied to her life. She looked ahead and saw that what he said was true. Bill halted the group at the point where their descent ended. "Before you lies some tricky climbing. Do not attempt anything foolish. Ask for help if you need it. Rests should be short. Do not sit down. Save your energy by gently pacing yourself."

Belle came alongside Sophie and tilted her hat back to have a better view of the upcoming climb. "We've done some climbing like this. Just not as long or as steep. Success is going to depend on our perseverance."

"We haven't come this far to turn back."

"Especially not when I heard that rancher fellow and McConnell's friend guffawing and laying odds against our chances."

Sophie glanced at the individuals in the party. "Our Englishman seems to be having difficulty despite his fancy gear. Every time he comes near me, he shakes his head and mutters, 'Bother,' as if we are the reason he's struggling to keep up."

Bill gave the order to begin the ascent, a winding path around the southwest side of the peak. "See you on top," Belle said, before moving off.

"Good luck to you both," Ellicott called as Sophie fell in behind Belle. She had known she would have to push past her discomfort. Her calves and thighs were burning and her breath sounded ragged. At this high altitude, the sun bore down, reddening her face, despite her wide-brimmed hat. One step, two steps...ten steps. She trudged mechanically, following wherever Belle trod. Visible ahead of them now was the summit. So close and yet such a rigorous climb lay between here and success. At that point Sophie blocked all other thoughts from her mind. Seventy-five steps...

one-hundred twenty steps… The two-syllable rhythm she'd adopted seemed to be propelling her toward the overarching sky. *Char-lie, Char-lie, Char-lie.*

Tate knew he couldn't spot the hiking party from his vantage point, but that didn't prevent him from looking through the telescope at intervals. He had to get out of the house before nerves did him in. He went looking for the boys and their dogs and found them outside, marching around the lawn as if they were hiking. Toby held a long stick in his hand as a make-believe alpenstock. "How about a real hike?"

Toby grinned broadly. "In the mountains like Miss Sophie?"

"No, more like in the hills behind the ranch, where we can get a better view of Longs Peak."

"But not of the mountaineers," Marcus pointed out. "But okay. It's kind of boring around here. We're excited for tomorrow when we can go to the trail." Tate knew that if he himself was apprehensive about Sophie, his sons would be equally concerned until they saw her again, safe and in one piece.

"Do you think she's decided?" Toby inquired as they neared the top of the hill.

"To stay with us for the winter," Marcus elaborated. "She's a really good teacher. She listens. And makes lessons fun."

"Yeah, I can remember what I learn really good."

If only she would stay, Tate thought to himself. The boys needed her. Yet there still remained the obstacles of propriety and his own tenuous self-control where Sophie was concerned. If money were all it would take… Yet he knew her salary weighed lightly in her decision compared to the tug of her Kansas home.

The three found a large rock. They clambered to the top and sat staring at the majesty of Longs Peak. Tate handed them each a square of the corn bread Bertie had sent with them. Then out of the blue, Marcus began a conversation that stunned Tate. "Papa, Miss Sophie didn't have a mother."

Toby interrupted, "She died a long time ago."

Marcus continued, "We don't really have a mother, either."

Tate dug his fingernails into the lichen atop the boulder, dreading what was coming.

Marcus looked up at the sky, then into the valley, as if he wanted his eyes to fall anywhere but on his father. "I gotta ask," he said finally.

Tate held his breath.

"Why did our mother leave us? Did Toby or I do something bad? We must've, because most mothers don't run away—"

Tate laid a steadying hand on the boy's leg in the attempt to stem the flood of emotions threatening to pour from his normally stoic son. "It was nothing you did, nothing at all."

"But she didn't like us or she'd have stayed and been our mother."

"Instead she left us," Toby said forlornly. "She didn't love us. I don't remember her ever tucking us in bed like Miss Sophie did."

Tate gathered each of them closer, and when he spoke, he willed away the tremor in his voice. "Your mother left us for a number of reasons, mainly because of decisions I had made that she found impossible to live with. I am the one who came west to try to make a fortune. She didn't ask for that. She would've preferred to stay in the East and live a comfortable life. She could not share my enthusiasm for Colorado and wanted us to leave. My business was too involved and successful by then for me to do that. When you and she came to join me in Central City, she didn't want to be there. Sometimes when people are very unhappy, they find it more and more difficult to cope with responsibilities."

"Like us," Marcus said flatly.

"Yes, like us," Tate agreed. "Your mother has a delicate temperament and is easily made nervous, even to the point of illness."

"I kinda think she didn't touch me much, and she yelled a lot," Toby said. "I thought all ladies were like that until Miss Sophie. She even gives me hugs."

"Your mother needed to return to the East, boys, and I couldn't."

"So you had to keep us."

"It wasn't like that at all, Marcus. I *got* to keep you. No gold or silver strike comes close to being as important to me as you are." Tate took a deep breath. "I love you, and all I've ever wanted is what's best for you."

Toby snuggled closer. "Miss Sophie. That's what's best for me."

"I know, son. She is special."

"That's why she has to stay this winter," Marcus pleaded.

"If that were within my power, boys, I would make it happen."

"You can do anything," Toby assured him.

Anything but make Sophie love me. I am no Charlie.

Marcus turned to him, excited. "I know what will make her stay. It's simple. You can do it. Marry her, Papa."

Toby clapped his hands. "Bully for you, Marcus."

"Whoa." Tate held up his hands in mock surrender. "Let's get the lady off the mountain. Then we'll see."

"That's what you always say. 'We'll see.'"

"Marcus, some things are beyond my control."

Marcus stared at him, his mouth quirking in a mischievous grin. "All right, then. We'll see. And sometimes 'we'll see' means 'yes.'"

On the hike back to the house, Tate's emotions vacillated between distress that his sons had thought they were to blame for Ramona's abandonment and elation that the boys would welcome Sophie into their family. Passing the barn, Sam stuck his head out. "Two gentlemen to see you, sir. Major Hurlburt and a younger man." He nodded toward the house.

Tate dismissed the boys to play stick ball, while he hurried inside. Robert, here? And another? Sure enough, when he entered the living room, Robert and a handsome, fit, younger man rose to their feet. "Robert, welcome. I didn't expect you. Is anything amiss?"

Robert strode across the room and shook Tate's hand warmly. "Not at all. We have come to witness the triumph of Sophie's mountaineering feat." He turned to the other man, whose warm hazel eyes were fixed on Tate. "Son, I would like you to make the acquaintance of Caleb Montgomery. He's come all the way from Kansas to cheer for his sister."

Sophie's brother smiled. "And to take her home. Despite her assurances to the contrary, I do not think she could endure a long winter by herself in this environment. She loves it here, of course, but I'm here to talk some sense into her."

Tate felt the floor tilt beneath his feet. Of course. It made perfect sense. Her family loved her. They would not want her to suffer hardship. His mind raced with objections. He would not have long to make his case to Sophie, if there was even a case to be made now. Gathering his wits, Tate finally offered Montgomery a welcome and bid Bertie bring some refreshments.

He learned that Sophie had written the Hurlburts with the date of the summit attempt. At Caleb's request, Robert had telegraphed him. Caleb explained that the family, worried both about Sophie's groundbreaking hike and her winter plans, had designated him to convey the family's love and concern. The two men had ridden over from Dunraven's hotel, where they were staying. After fixing on an hour to come by the next day for Tate to lead them to the base of the trail, they left. Tate slumped into a chair. Montgomery had seemed so at ease, even pleased to meet him and discuss his plans for Sophie. Tate wondered if they suspected the toll that extending hospitality had taken on him when all he wanted to do was cry out, "No!" What chance would he have to influence Sophie's decision in light of the arguments of her loving family?

Chapter Sixteen

Despite the sun, the higher they climbed, the colder it got. Sophie had worn gloves initially, but now scrabbled bare-handed, seeking purchase in the barren rock ahead of her. Her fingernails tore in the effort and a steady wind buffeted her, yet each yard of progress was a small victory spurring her on. The party was more strung out as they confronted the steeper trail just below the summit. Whether it was the effect of the previous evening's strong drink or not, the rancher had dropped out halfway up the final ascent and had agreed to wait at that point for those closing in on the summit. Yet his condition didn't stop him from taunting the two women when they stepped around him. His ill temper only fueled Sophie's determination. She looked up and spotted Belle ahead of her, nearly spread-eagled in the attempt to inch up a large boulder. Sophie closed her eyes briefly, summoning every ounce of will. Her chest heaved with exertion, and her mouth filled with cotton. Yet she couldn't, *wouldn't*, give up. *Char-lie. Char-lie.* She tried to focus on his laughing eyes and merry disposition, but it was as if the more altitude she gained, the more elusive her memory of him became. *This is for you,* she wanted to say to him. With that thought, she barely had time to duck as a loose rock from above cascaded past her, echoing on its way to the bottom. She corrected herself. Although this climb would honor Charlie, it wasn't for him she'd undertaken the hike. It was for herself. She had been lost and needed to find her way. Muscles coiled and aching, she continued to climb. Then, as if she'd summoned them, came the words from the Bible verse on Lily's sampler: "…and He shall direct thy paths." She acknowledged she was at a crossroads in her life and any decision could be made only with God's help.

After that, there was no time for daydreaming, only the relentless pressure to find the strength to put one foot ahead of the other. She could see the summit, yet even so, she had to pause to let a spell of dizziness pass. *Hang on, hang on,* she told herself over and over. Her ears filled with a muted roar, and she feared her chest would burst with the effort of drawing even a shallow breath.

"You're almost there," Ellicott shouted down to her.

She dug deep into the last reserves of her will, planted her left foot, hauled herself up with her right hand and found herself on a narrow path where she could stand, her legs trembling beneath her. In the corner of her vision she saw such an awe-inspiring glimpse of the panorama awaiting her at the summit that she once again felt faint… *And He shall direct thy paths.* With a surge of energy, she climbed the last obstacle and reached the top of the world. At once she was enveloped in Belle's ecstatic embrace, both of them laughing and crying at the same time. "You did it, ladies," Ellicott observed with a broad grin.

"We did it!" they cried, pummeling each other on the back.

Sophie withdrew a small American flag from her knapsack. "I told you I'd wave a banner if we made it." Holding the emblem high above her head, she let the wind whip it horizontal.

Belle applauded before taking the stick from Sophie's hand and running in a large circle, exulting all the way.

Bill approached them. "I gotta tell you, I had my doubts, but you gals have made a believer of me. Congratulations."

McConnell's friend nodded congratulations while the gasping Englishman shook his head in bafflement before collapsing onto a nearby rock.

Looking around, Sophie observed that only five of the eight who had started out with Bill had completed the climb. She began exploring the flat surface of the summit, larger than she had supposed. In every direction was a breathtaking vista. Mountain upon mountain rolling to the north, south and west. To the east, a long view of the smaller front range and finally a glimpse of the prairie. And the vastness, the indescribable sense of space. She could hardly make sense of the distances visible to the eye at every turn. An elation unlike any she had ever known filled her heart, and she couldn't help hugging herself at the wonder of it all, thanking God for this privileged view of His creation.

Then Clark Ellicott's simple words came back to her: *We have to go down before we can go up.* She had been down. She had lost two of the dearest, finest men in the world, Pa and Charlie. She had made a friend of sorrow. In the same way that her vision had been blocked in the lowland of grief and confusion, now the spectacle of these magnificent heights spoke of a broader view, of new beginnings, of possibilities beyond her limited understanding. Colorado…how could she leave? Pa had understood. *Be happy there,* he had whispered with his dying breath.

Overhead, clouds were forming and far to the west, she noticed the first streaks of lightning. She began to sense static electricity in the air. "Time to move out," Bill bellowed.

Taking one last, lingering look at the scene before her, Sophie fell in with Ellicott and Belle as they made their way to the summit's edge for the descent. "You intrepid ladies will go down in history," the man said. "Two of you at a time climbing Longs Peak with nary a complaint."

"Thank you," Belle said, "but I hardly know about 'history.'"

"I do," Ellicott replied, looking mischievously from one to the other. "Some of my colleagues have not only predicted your failure, but have made narrow-minded fools of themselves in the process. I, however, will tell quite a different story."

Sophie raised an eyebrow. "Colleagues?"

The man tipped his hat. "Clark Ellicott, associate editor of the *New York Herald.*"

Sophie and Belle stared at him, then began laughing. He joined in. "Yes, indeed, quite a different story."

Saturday morning, Robert and Caleb arrived bright and early at Tate's. Since it was several miles to the trailhead, Tate had Toby ride with him, while Marcus mounted a gentle mare. Along the way, Caleb spoke of Sophie in loving terms, even telling how it had been she who persuaded him to travel all the way to Saint Louis to pursue and court his Lily. Marcus raised some questions about the man's army experience, and although he answered pleasantly, if briefly, Tate could tell this was not a subject he preferred to discuss. Hard to say what he might have been through. In spite of himself, Tate took a liking to the man. If he could find fault, he could indulge his resentment of Caleb's mission to take Sophie back to Kansas. If her brother Seth and sisters-in-law were as fine a company as Caleb, though, Tate could understand why Sophie was considering returning there. Upright and straightforward, her brother was proving to be a thoroughly decent fellow. He had profusely thanked Tate for being such a good neighbor to Sophie and for offering her the tutoring position. He was a natural with the boys, treating them with the respect and affection innate in folks who enjoy children.

"Do you think Miss Sophie made it?" Toby had asked that question at least three times.

Each time, Marcus had replied with disdain, "Why wouldn't she?"

Montgomery rode closer. "It is quite dangerous, I assume."

Tate nodded. "There was no dissuading her."

Montgomery smiled. "That's our Sophie."

Our Sophie. It had a nice ring to it.

When the group dismounted for rest and lunch, Tate drew Caleb to the side. "I know you have come to persuade Sophie to return to Kansas with you, and I imagine you share my concern about her remaining in her cabin during our harsh winter. However, Marcus, Toby and I have asked her to consider staying with us during those months to continue her work with the boys. She is an exceptional teacher."

Caleb looked him straight in the eye as if taking his measure. "Yes, she is exceptional, and I would not have her character compromised in any way. People talk, as you know."

Discomfited, Tate nodded. "Although I have a house-keeper, I suppose gossip might follow. However, as I'm sure you're aware as a parent yourself, where the welfare of my sons is concerned, I will spare nothing. They are understandably quite attached to Sophie."

"And what about you? Are you 'quite attached' to my sister?" He made Tate wait. "It is my duty to protect her."

Tate summoned words difficult to utter. "Sophie has told me about her Charlie. It is clear she loved him deeply. Despite my growing affection for your remarkable sister, I have done my best to keep my distance, respecting her devotion and grief where another is concerned. If circumstances were different, if I felt she were inclined to me, then…" His voice faded away.

Montgomery clapped him on the back. "Thank you. I think I understand the situation now."

But did he? That was the question Tate mulled over as they neared Wild Bill's place. From a distance he could pick out the Harpers and Tylers, as well as some other neighbors. The grounds were teeming with onlookers, including some citified-looking enough to be newspapermen. The carnival-like atmosphere was boisterous with gibes being exchanged between those rooting for Belle and Sophie and their loudmouthed detractors. Toby turned around to face Tate. "Why are those men saying bad things about Miss Sophie?"

"Because they do not think women should climb mountains or that they can be successful in doing so."

Toby appeared to be thinking over the comment. Finally he said, "That's silly. Miss Sophie can do anything."

 ⁻ With that comment, Tate's stomach tightened. Could she do anything? Could she not only scale a formidable peak, but agree to stay with him in Colorado? Much as he liked and admired Caleb Montgomery, he would not let Sophie go without a fight.

Just then Marcus, who had already tethered his horse, ran up to him and Toby. "Somebody saw them, Papa. Far away on a ridge. But coming. Coming!"

Tate watched Robert Hurlburt reach out to grab Caleb's hand. "Courage, lad. If I know Sophie, she's leading the pack."

At the boulder field after a good night's rest, the party prepared for the ride back to Bill's base camp. Sophie did her best to tame her runaway curls and finally gave up, mashing them with her sorry-looking hat. She had done her best to wash some of the dust off her face and had covered her raw hands with gloves. She grinned. Hardly a fashion plate. In the interests of propriety and in anticipation of the judgment of those waiting to greet them, both she and Belle had donned knee-length skirts to cover their hiking bloomers. When they had returned exultant to their tents last night, they were met with McConnell's abashed congratulations and Baker's insincere and terse "Unbelievable." Apparently unused to defeat, the rancher said nothing and sulked until bedtime. She supposed she and Belle would have to endure the same mixed judgment from others when their feat became public knowledge. As she mounted Ranger, she allowed herself a rueful grin. Men!

As they left the boulder field, Sophie turned for one last look at the grandeur of Longs Peak before the view was swallowed by trees. It would forever remain for her a symbol of the power and presence of God. It was there she had finally understood that life goes on, *must* go on, despite sorrow and setbacks. *Thank You, Lord, for directing my path.*

As eager as she was to reach the end of the journey, she reminded herself to savor every turn in the trail and the delights it offered her. She, Belle and Ellicott brought up the rear, each lost in thought as if loath to conclude such an adventure. Ellicott was the first to speak. "Your menfolk must be very proud of you."

Belle laughed. "My brother will be."

"And my employer," Sophie added.

"You mean to tell me neither of you is spoken for?"

"There aren't a great number of candidates up here," Belle reminded him.

"Even so…" He rode on for a time. "It will take some fine men who appreciate strong women to match the two of you. If they see in you what I do, they will be extremely fortunate."

"Thank you," Sophie said simply. "Without you, this trek would have been much more difficult."

"Yes," Belle added. "We appreciate your open-mindedness."

As eager as they were to reach the bottom, Bill halted them for an early lunch of biscuits and tinned ham. The women refreshed their canteens from a lively stream and sat with their backs against a boulder. "There's a bittersweet quality to what we just did, isn't there?" Sophie remarked.

"You mean because we succeeded and have no further goal?"

"It was such fun to look forward to this. And now…?"

Belle sat up straighter and looked at Sophie. "And now? We're going to begin planning for Pike's Peak."

If she lived to be a hundred, Sophie would never be able to explain how Belle's words set her body tingling with excitement. *Exactly. That is exactly what we'll do.*

When they were half a mile from Wild Bill's and the trailhead, Sophie tensed with apprehension. How would others, especially the naysayers, react to her and Belle's success? And how was she to deal with the decision facing her about remaining in Colorado to tutor the Lockwood boys or returning to her Flint Hills family? During this trip she had realized what she must do, but it would not be easy and might hurt some she cared about deeply. Before she let herself dwell on what might happen in the upcoming days, she reminded herself to enjoy the moment and take satisfaction from the obstacles she and Belle had overcome.

Then, rounding a bend, Sophie became aware of shouts and cheers echoing from the valley floor just below. She had assumed there would be a few folks waiting to greet them, but this sounded like a crowd.

Ellicott pointed ahead. "Get ready, ladies. You are about to be the center of attention."

Sure enough, as the train of horses made its way across the pasture to Bill's, cheers and catcalls resounded. Reaching the hitching post, Sophie slid from Ranger's back and turned to face the spectators. The first person she saw was Grizzly, nodding happily, his face wreathed in a smile. The second was Toby, who ran toward her, shouting, "Did you do it, Miss Sophie? Did you do it?"

She held out her arms. "Yes!" she called at the top of her voice just as the boy vaulted into her embrace. "Yes, Toby, we did, indeed, stand atop Longs Peak."

"I knew you could do it," he affirmed, hugging her around the neck.

When she looked up, Tate and Marcus were waiting, grinning from ear to ear. "You can do anything," Marcus said.

Tate stood behind Marcus, his eyes warm with pleasure. "I'm proud of you, Sophie. You are unstoppable."

Despite the fact that her feet ached and every muscle screamed, she felt buoyant. "Thank you."

Then Tate lowered his head and stepped aside. Sophie's jaw gaped. It couldn't be. "Caleb?" She set Toby on the ground and ran the few steps to her brother, who picked her up and whirled her around and around before returning her to her feet and studying her face.

"Don't ever scare me like that again, sister, but I am so proud of your achievement. You've never taken no for an answer."

Sophie held on to his shoulders. "I owe all my daring to you and Seth. Thanks for always letting me try things."

Keeping his arm around her, he indicated Robert Hurlburt, who stood nearby.

Sophie turned. "Robert? How good of you to be here. Did you bring Caleb up from Denver?"

"Yes. I am pleased to offer Effie's and my congratulations."

A perplexing thought occurred to Sophie and she pivoted back to Caleb. "I'm delighted you're here, but this is roundup time in Kansas. Why did you come?"

"To celebrate with you, of course." His expression sobered. "And to take you home with me."

"But—"

"Don't be your typical stubborn self, Sophie. Estes Park is lovely in the summer. But it is no place for you in the winter. Seth, Rose, Lily and I fear for your safety. Most important, we miss you and want you to come home now."

"Now?"

"With me."

Now? Everything was happening too fast. Sophie looked about in confusion. Where was Tate? Where were Toby and Marcus? Much as she appreciated her family's concern, this decision was not up to them. It was hers to make, with God's help. And then she spotted the Lockwoods, hand in hand, walking rapidly toward their horses. Before she could call out to them, a horde of newspapermen surrounded her.

"Miss Montgomery, an interview please!"

"Surely you thought about turning back?" She recognized Rupert Stowe's snivel before others shouted him down.

"Let me photograph you."

"Can you prove you made the summit?"

She thought she would go mad in the cacophony of shrill, demanding voices. She covered her ears. "Not now!" she finally said forcefully. Caleb took her by the arm, and as Robert led the charge, they made their way to a picnic table laden with dishes where Martha and Dolly were presiding. The two women rushed to embrace her, while their menfolk shielded her temporarily from the reporters.

"Well done, Sophie," Martha declared. "You two have advanced the cause of women tenfold." Over Martha's shoulder, Sophie saw Belle holding court with a group of reporters. Just as well. She herself was not in the mood right now.

As the celebration continued and after she had spoken briefly to the newspapermen, Sophie finally had a moment to reflect. She should feel fulfilled, exultant, yet something was missing. In her heart, she knew what, or rather who—Tate and the boys.

"Tired?" Caleb asked as the throng began dispersing.

"I am."

"Would you join Robert and me at our hotel to spend the night in luxury? My treat."

The thought of a hot bath, a down mattress and rich furnishings nearly sent her to her knees. "Not today, thanks. I need to go home."

"Home?"

"To my cabin. Perhaps before you leave, you can come see my place."

"Before *I* leave? What about you?"

"I can't make any promises, Caleb. Not yet. There is something I have to do first."

He pulled her close and tucked a curl behind her ear. "We never could tame you, Seth and I. We love you, Sophie, and want your happiness, but your safety is paramount. Take some time to consider what we are asking. Robert and I will be here until Tuesday morning."

"Thank you for understanding."

Caleb led her to Ranger and helped her into the saddle. He took off his hat and studied her, before adding one final comment. "Tate Lockwood is a good man, sister."

Weariness overwhelmed her as she rode to the Harpers', where she fetched Beauty and started on toward her cabin. Despite her aching body, her mind was fastened on her plans for the next few hours. She *was* unstoppable. She *didn't* take no for an answer, and she would *not* be tamed. If she could perform the astonishing feat of conquering a peak higher than fourteen thousand feet, nothing was going to prevent her from making her own decisions. The mountains had taught her about the vast opportunities that lay beyond her limited vision if only she had the courage to seize them.

Tate had tossed and turned throughout the night and awoke as if drugged, with the blankets tangled around him. He hoisted himself to the side of the bed and held his head in his hands. The boys had not understood why he'd hustled them away from yesterday's celebration, why they hadn't rejoined Sophie or why he'd been silent all the way home. "Why can't you be happy for her?" Marcus had challenged him with his usual piercing insight. Tate raked a hand through his hair. He'd seen the look on her face when she spotted her brother and he'd envied their spontaneous affection. With a sinking heart, he'd known his and the boys' futures were in jeopardy.

He stood and moved to get dressed. Caleb was right, of course. Sophie could not remain in that ramshackle cabin during a high country winter. Tate had offered her a place here, but even as he'd done so, he'd known there were drawbacks to that plan, especially for her. Yet he'd promised himself he'd fight for her. That meant only one thing—an offer of marriage. Marriage. An institution that had failed him once. He had to be absolutely certain he could offer Sophie the independence, companionship and love she needed from a mate. As for him? He'd been lonely many times in his life. Sophie had brought light and joy. He prayed he could trust in her enough to overcome his past and embrace the future.

He had one last opportunity. Sophie had stopped by on her way home yesterday afternoon to give Toby the flag she had waved atop Longs Peak and to ask Tate to join her this morning at Bear Lake for a hike, just the two of them. After breakfast, he set forth anxious for what the day would bring. He feared she was trying to find a gentle way to say goodbye, far from where the boys might create a scene. Given the fact of her joyous reunion with Caleb and the powerful statement his presence made, Tate allowed himself little hope. Was the God he now talked to on occasion a God of surprises? He devoutly hoped so.

Sophie tied Ranger to an aspen tree and walked to the shore of the small lake, sparkling blue and silver in the morning sun. Above loomed Flattop and its sister peaks. Across the way spruce trees lined the shore and a deer and fawn lapped at the water. Pristine. Still, except for the murmur of the aspen leaves. In her hand she held a slim volume. She knew what she must do. "Thy will be done," she whispered prayerfully as she turned toward the approaching horse.

Tate waved, dismounted and joined her. "Good morning."

She slipped the book into her pocket and smiled in greeting. "Shall we walk?"

He offered his arm, and they started slowly around the lake, neither of them speaking. Finally he said, "Are you sure you're ready for another hike so soon?"

"We're not going far," she answered.

Without another word, she led him to a spot up the trail beyond the lake where a small glade opened up. Nearby she could hear the trickle of a mountain spring. A small bench-like stone invited them to sit.

Tate broke the silence. "It's rather like a cathedral here."

"So it is." Sophie reached in her pocket, drew out the book, opened it to a marked page and began to read.

"Once again
Do I behold these steep and lofty cliffs,
That on a wild secluded scene impress
Thoughts of more deep seclusion; and connect
The landscape with the quiet of the sky."

Tate smiled in recognition. "The Wordsworth."

Sophie glanced around, taking in the scene. "Fitting, don't you think?" She pointed to the words he'd inscribed: "May the memory of the beauty and wonder of nature bless you." He studied them for a long minute. She swept her arm around the glen. "Is that what you really want? For me to enjoy all of this...in memory?"

"No. I want you here, but only if you want to be. You have family in Kansas, you have the memory of Charlie—"

When she took both of his hands in hers, the book slipped to the ground. "I left Charlie at the top of Longs Peak."

"What do you mean?"

She could sense the tension in his body and longed to resolve what lay between them. Yet could she be sure of him? "Charlie was very dear to me. He taught me a great deal about love and commitment. I will always treasure his role in my life and miss him. But, Tate, Charlie is gone. I am here." She cleared her throat, hoping to clarify. "As improbable as it sounds, I experienced a kind of epiphany on the summit." His fingers tightened on hers. "Up there, one can see for miles and miles. The views in every direction are limitless, and the sky seems both close enough to touch yet millions of miles away. I realized I had to let Charlie go. At one time, I felt him here in the rocks he so loved. But feel."

She guided his hand to the stone upon which they sat. "This is hard, cold. But you? You're warm."

She heard him draw a quick breath before he asked, "Does this mean you'll winter with us and teach the boys?"

She knew it was now or never, and she was not about to shirk from the unknown. "This is not just about the boys." She stood up and pulled him to his feet, all the time fixing her eyes on his. "It has everything to do with you. Your strength and love have become the cornerstone of my life. I don't want to live with memory. I want to live with you."

"Sophie?" He took hold of her shoulders and pulled her close. "Sophie, you mean you're not leaving?"

She pursed her lips impishly. "Well, sir, that rather depends upon you."

He looked so flummoxed she nearly laughed, but then he wrapped her in his arms and held her for a very long time. When he finally pulled away, she dabbed at his cheeks, wet with tears. "My darling Sophie, without knowing it, I have waited for you my entire life. I love you so."

"Oh, dearest. I love you, too. I was so afraid you wouldn't—"

"*You* were afraid? I didn't think I had a chance once Caleb arrived." His relieved laughter was music to her ears.

"I have to warn you, though, I'm looking for another adventure."

"Oh, no, not another mountain?"

"Well, that, too, but that isn't what I have in mind."

"What, then?"

"This is most unconventional, but then I've been accused of that before. So—" she ran a hand through his unruly hair "—Tate Lockwood, would you marry me?"

He blushed. "How clumsy of me. I was so caught up in the happiness of the moment, I failed my courting duty. Would I marry you? Of course. The bigger question is whether you will marry me."

"I told you I wanted another adventure. Living with you, Marcus and Toby qualifies as the most magnificent of adventures. Frankly, Tate, I cannot wait to be your bride."

Later as they ambled arm in arm toward their horses, Tate asked, "What about your family? Caleb?"

Sophie grinned. "You know what? Once Caleb met you, something he said made me think he's already figured it all out. My happiness is all that has ever mattered to him and my family."

"I will do everything in my power to justify their faith in me."

When they reached their horses, Sophie looked into the loving eyes of her husband-to-be and said, "Shall we go tell the boys?"

"They'll be overjoyed. As you know, Toby thinks Miss Sophie can do anything."

"Even get their father to marry me."

"Even that," he said, laughing down at her. "Because—" he turned to the mountains, cupped his hands and shouted "—I love you!"

Luv-yoo, luv-yoo, luv-yoo, the mountains replied. Sophie shivered. God's help *had* come from those very hills of which the Bible spoke. She turned to Tate and snuggled against his broad chest. "Take me home," she whispered.

Epilogue

Sophie watched from the window as Tate, followed by the two red-faced boys, dragged the tall spruce through the snow toward the house. In addition to the Biblical Christmas story, Marcus and Toby had been studying Christmas traditions around the world and had requested a tree like those used in Germany and England. Tate had built a stand for it, and this evening they would place it in the living room and decorate it with colored paper cutouts and strands of popcorn. A fire blazed in the hearth. The smell of a roasting hen wafted through the air. The scene seemed ideal, like something out of a book. Except for... Sophie clutched two unopened letters in her hand, which Sam had brought home from the Harpers' post office—one addressed to Tate and the other, to the boys. Letters that threatened to jeopardize the happiness they had all enjoyed since she and Tate exchanged vows three months ago in a ceremony that had been quickly arranged so Caleb could give her away.

Tate and the boys came tromping into the house, laughing and talking noisily about the fact they had found the finest tree in all the forest. The rambunctious puppies added to the din. Sophie thrust the letters in her pocket and summoned a smile. "So you were successful?"

Marcus regaled her with an account of their search as he shed his coat, hat and boots. "This tree was just waiting for us," he concluded.

"Wanna see?" Toby asked, grabbing her hand and leading her to the door. "It's really big."

Sophie made suitable sounds of approval. Tate put his arm around her waist. "A new tradition for our first of many Christmases together."

The boys raced past them toward their rooms. "Lovely," she murmured in an attempt to match his enthusiasm.

Something in her tone must've alerted him, for he turned her toward him and studied her face. "Sophie, dear, whatever is the matter?"

She never wanted to answer him, never wanted the perfection of her precious family to be compromised. "Let's go to your office."

Once there, she shrugged her shoulders in defeat. "Here," she said, handing him the envelopes bearing a Philadelphia return address below the name *Ramona Lockwood.*

"What?" Tate's face drained of color as he sat down. "Why her? Why now?"

Sophie took a seat beside him. "I don't know."

"There's only one way to find out," he said decisively. He slit the letter addressed to him and read silently.

Sophie could hardly draw a breath. What if Ramona was making a claim for the boys? Finally Tate set the letter aside and reached out a hand and clutched hers. "She does not want Marcus and Toby. In fact, she wishes legally to relinquish all claims."

Sophie felt the tension leave her body. "I was so

afraid." She swiped at a tear moistening her cheek. "What does she want, then?"

"She's written Marcus and Toby to explain why she cannot assume any role in their lives and to ask their forgiveness." He held up the remaining letter. "She would like me to share this with them."

"I should be rejoicing, but that sounds sad."

"More than likely, not sad at all. She is marrying an English aristocrat and moving permanently to London. No doubt a dream fulfilled for her," he added.

They sat, hands entwined, for several minutes. Sophie knew Tate was asking the same question she was: *How would this communication affect the boys?*

Finally, after scanning the boys' letter, he stood. "I see no point in prolonging the inevitable, and they need to hear her message. In the long run, this may be a positive development for Marcus and Toby and for all of us as a family. I will fetch them and meet you in the living room."

Sophie walked slowly down the hall, wondering yet again how any mother could have abandoned her children. How sad that Ramona had never come to know Toby's charm or Marcus's intellect.

Marcus caught up with her. "Papa says we have something to discuss."

"Yes."

"As a family, he said. I like being a family, don't you?"

"Very much."

Tate entered the room with Toby, and they all took seats around the fire, Marcus impassive and Toby fidgeting with his shirt buttons. Tate caught Sophie's eye, cleared his throat and began to speak. "Boys, we have something to share with you from today's mail. I have had a letter from your mother—"

Toby interrupted, "But, Papa, Sophie's right here. Why would she write us?"

Marcus kicked his brother gently. "No, Toby. Not Sophie. Our mother from before."

Sophie clutched her skirt and prayed for a swift conclusion to the conversation.

"Marcus is correct," Tate said. "This is a letter from your birth mother."

"I don't like her," Toby muttered.

"Son, we cannot always know what makes people do what they do. I think you will understand more fully when you read what she has written to you."

"She can say what she wants," Marcus argued, "but that won't change what happened or how I feel."

Sophie intervened, "Boys, it is natural that you would harbor hurt and resentment. But Jesus teaches us to forgive. It is not an easy lesson, but one that frees us to love even more fully. You both have so much love to give, as I've discovered from the generous way you have accepted me into your family. Why don't you read your letter in the spirit of forgiveness?"

Tate raised his fingers to his lips and sent her a kiss.

"Very well," Marcus said, removing the letter from the envelope. "I will read it aloud."

He began in a cold, steely tone.

"Marcus and Toby, you were always fine little chaps, so I am supposing you are turning into equally fine young men. I pray you do not assume any blame for my decision to leave you and your father. Any fault was mine. I am of a fragile disposition and was accustomed to genteel ways and had always been cosseted by my family. Living in Colorado was a shock in every way. I could not summon love, but rather lost myself in resentment and pain. Ultimately, I feared for my sanity.

I am not proud of my actions or inactions and ask your forgiveness. There is no need to answer this letter. I send it only to clear my conscience and assure you that you played no part in my decision to leave. I am remarrying and will be making my home in England. You will not hear from me again."

Marcus threw down the letter. "Just as I suspected. She never loved us. There's not one word about love here."

The anguish on Tate's face wrenched Sophie's heart. "Some people are incapable of the kind of love we need," she hastened to assure Marcus. "Instead of anger, I pray that you will see that your mother is a tortured soul. She has reached out with the only explanation she is capable of giving. For my part, though, she is to be thanked for the wonderful young men she has left for your father and me to rear—two loving sons I am blessed to call my own."

Toby had been sitting cross-legged, his brow furrowed, listening intently. "I'm glad I don't remember much about her." He shrugged helplessly. "I prob'ly shouldn't say this, but that is a sad letter. And, Marcus, what if she was still here instead of Sophie?"

"I don't want to think about that." Marcus glanced over at Sophie. "If Jesus could forgive her, I 'spect we should try."

"That is exactly what we will do," Tate said. "Perhaps we could start by praying for her each day. I suspect she is in need of prayer."

Sophie smiled at her husband. "That is precisely what God would have us do."

Marcus looked thoughtful. "Maybe this letter really does help because I won't have to worry or wonder any longer. Besides, now Toby and I have Sophie, and we know she cares about us."

"I most certainly do."

Toby stood up and draped an arm around Sophie's shoulders. "I'm not calling her Sophie anymore, 'cuz she's the mother who takes care of us and plays with us and teaches us things—our *real* mother. My mama." The boy leaned down and gave her an awkward hug.

Tate crossed the room and pulled her to her feet, gathering her into his arms. Amid her joyful tears, she could feel the boys clutching her around her waist. "Mama," Marcus said. "We love you."

"And I love you," she managed between sobs of joy.

Tate's lips brushed her cheek. "You know something, Mama Sophie? As Toby always reminds us, you can do anything!"

Raising her head, she sought her husband's eyes. "Correction. *Together* we can do anything."

* * * * *

COMING NEXT MONTH FROM
Love Inspired® Historical

Available June 2, 2015

WAGON TRAIN PROPOSAL
Journey West
by Renee Ryan

When Tristan McCullough's intended wagon train bride chooses someone else, Rachel Hewitt accepts a position as his children's caretaker—not as his wife. She'll only marry for love...yet perhaps the McCulloughs are the family she's always wanted.

HER CONVENIENT COWBOY
Wyoming Legacy
by Lacy Williams

When cowboy Davy White discovers a widowed soon-to-be-mother in his cabin, he immediately offers her shelter from the blizzard. As their friendship grows, so does Rose Evans's belief that Davy is her wish come true for a family by Christmas.

THE TEXAN'S TWIN BLESSINGS
by Rhonda Gibson

Emily Jane Rodgers dreams of opening her own bakery, not falling in love. Then she meets William Barns and his adorable twin nieces, and soon the ready-made family is chipping away at Emily Jane's guarded heart and changing her mind about marriage and happily-ever-afters!

FAMILY OF HER DREAMS
by Keli Gwyn

As a railroad stationmaster and recent widower, Spencer Abbott needs help raising his young children. He's surprised when Tess Grimsby fits so well with his family—maybe she's meant to be more than a nanny to his children...

LIHCNM0515

REQUEST YOUR FREE BOOKS!

2 FREE INSPIRATIONAL NOVELS
PLUS 2 *FREE* MYSTERY GIFTS

Love Inspired® HISTORICAL

YES! Please send me 2 FREE Love Inspired® Historical novels and my 2 FREE mystery gifts (gifts are worth about $10). After receiving them, if I don't wish to receive any more books, I can return the shipping statement marked "cancel." If I don't cancel, I will receive 4 brand-new novels every month and be billed just $4.99 per book in the U.S. or $5.49 per book in Canada. That's a saving of at least 17% off the cover price. It's quite a bargain! Shipping and handling is just 50¢ per book in the U.S. and 75¢ per book in Canada.* I understand that accepting the 2 free books and gifts places me under no obligation to buy anything. I can always return a shipment and cancel at any time. Even if I never buy another book, the two free books and gifts are mine to keep forever.

102/302 IDN GH6Z

Name	(PLEASE PRINT)	
Address		Apt. #
City	State/Prov.	Zip/Postal Code

Signature (if under 18, a parent or guardian must sign)

Mail to the **Reader Service:**
IN U.S.A.: P.O. Box 1867, Buffalo, NY 14240-1867
IN CANADA: P.O. Box 609, Fort Erie, Ontario L2A 5X3

Want to try two free books from another series?
Call 1-800-873-8635 or visit www.ReaderService.com.

* Terms and prices subject to change without notice. Prices do not include applicable taxes. Sales tax applicable in N.Y. Canadian residents will be charged applicable taxes. Offer not valid in Quebec. This offer is limited to one order per household. Not valid for current subscribers to Love Inspired Historical books. All orders subject to credit approval. Credit or debit balances in a customer's account(s) may be offset by any other outstanding balance owed by or to the customer. Please allow 4 to 6 weeks for delivery. Offer available while quantities last.

Your Privacy—The Reader Service is committed to protecting your privacy. Our Privacy Policy is available online at www.ReaderService.com or upon request from the Reader Service.

We make a portion of our mailing list available to reputable third parties that offer products we believe may interest you. If you prefer that we not exchange your name with third parties, or if you wish to clarify or modify your communication preferences, please visit us at www.ReaderService.com/consumerschoice or write to us at Reader Service Preference Service, P.O. Box 9062, Buffalo, NY 14240-9062. Include your complete name and address.

LIHI5

Rachel Hewitt survived the journey to Oregon, but arriving in her new home brings new challenges—like three adorable girls who need a nanny, and their sheriff father, who needs a second chance at love...

Read on for a sneak preview of Renee Ryan's
WAGON TRAIN PROPOSAL,
the heartwarming conclusion of the series
JOURNEY WEST.

"Are you my new mommy?"

Rachel blinked in stunned silence at the child staring back at her. She saw a lot of herself in the precocious six-year-old. In the determined angle of her tiny shoulders. In the bold tilt of her head. In the desperate hope simmering in her big, sorrowful blue eyes.

For a dangerous moment, Rachel had a powerful urge to tug the little girl into her arms and give her the answer she so clearly wanted.

Careful, she warned herself. *Think before you speak.*

"Well?" Hands still perched on her hips, Daisy's small mouth turned down at the corners. "Are you my new mommy or not?"

"I'm sorry, Daisy, no. I'm not your new mommy. However, I am your new neighbor, and I'll certainly see you often, perhaps even daily."

Tristan cut in then, touching his daughter's shoulder to gain her attention. "Daisy, my darling girl, we've talked about this before. You cannot go around asking every woman you meet if she's your mommy."

"But, Da—" the little girl's lower lip jutted out "—you said you were bringing us back a new mommy when you got home."

"No, baby." He pulled his hand away from her shoulder then shoved it into his pocket. "I said I *might* bring you home a new mommy."

When tears formed in the little girl's eyes, Rachel found herself interceding. "I may not be your new mommy," she began, taming a stray wisp of the child's hair behind her ear, "but I can be your very good friend."

The little girl's eyes lit up and she plopped into Rachel's lap. No longer able to resist, Rachel wrapped her arms around the child and hugged her close. Lily attempted to join her sister on Rachel's lap. When Daisy refused to budge, the little girl settled for pulling on Rachel's sleeve. "You don't want to be our new mommy?"

The poor child sounded so despondent Rachel's heart twisted. "Oh, Lily, it's not a matter of want. You see, I'm already committed to—"

She cut off her own words, realizing she had no other commitments now that her brother was married. He didn't need her to run his household. *No one* needed her. Except, maybe, this tiny family.

Don't miss
WAGON TRAIN PROPOSAL
by Renee Ryan,
available June 2015 wherever
Love Inspired® Historical books and ebooks are sold.

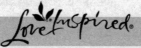
Can a widow and widower ever leave their grief in the past and forge a new future—and a family—together?

Read on for a sneak preview of
THE AMISH WIDOW'S SECRET.

"Wait, before you go. I have an important question to ask you."

Sarah nodded her head and sat back down.

"I stayed up until late last night, thinking about your situation and mine. I prayed, and *Gott* kept pushing this thought at me." He took a deep breath. "I wonder, would you consider becoming my *frau*?"

Sarah held up her hand, as if to stop his words. "I…"

"Before you speak, let me explain." Mose took another deep breath. "I know you still love Joseph, just as I still love my Greta. But I have *kinder* who need a mother to guide and love them. Now that Joseph's gone and the farm's being sold, you need a place to call home, people who care about you, a family. We can join forces and help each other." He saw a panicked expression forming in her eyes. "It would only be a marriage of convenience. The girls need a loving mother and you've already proven you can be that. What do you say, Sarah Nolt? Will you be my wife?"

Sarah sat silent, her face turned away. She looked into Mose's eyes. "You'd do this for me? But…you don't know me."

"I'd do this for us," Mose corrected, and smiled.

LIEXP0515

The tips of Sarah's fingers nervously pleated and un-pleated a scrap of her skirt. "But we hardly know each other. What would people think? They will say I took advantage of your good nature."

Mose smiled. "So, let them talk. They'd be wrong and we'd know it. I want this marriage for both of us, for the *kinder*. We can't let others decide what is best for our lives. I believe this marriage is *Gott*'s plan for us."

Sarah's face cleared and she seemed to come to a decision. She smoothed out the fabric of her skirt and tidied her hair, then finally took Mose's outstretched hand with a smile. "You're right. This is our life. I accept your proposal, Mose Fisher. I will be your *frau* and your *kinder*'s mother."

Don't miss
THE AMISH WIDOW'S SECRET
by Cheryl Williford,
available June 2015 wherever
Love Inspired® books and ebooks are sold.

LIEXP0515